"Anne Rutherford brings the world of Restoration England to vivid life, from the teeming streets to the halls of the royal palace. Her heroine, Suzanne Thornton, has always done what she must to survive in a cruel world where women count for little, and now she must solve a murder to save the one person in the world she truly loves."

—Victoria Thompson, national bestselling author of
Murder in Murray Hill

"I read this book in one sitting, captivated by Rutherford's vivid depiction of actors and aristocrats, political intrigue, and her strong, resourceful heroine. The world of Restoration London and its theaters leaps off the page in this impressive novel."

—Carol K. Carr, national bestselling author of
India Black and the Gentleman Thief

PRAISE FOR ANNE RUTHERFORD
WRITING AS JULIANNE LEE

A Question of Guilt

"An interesting historical fiction novel . . . An intriguing saga."
—*Genre Book Review*

"Lee's excellently researched novel is written in a fluid, engaging style and is full of intrigue, cover-ups, and plots. Her investigation of this historical mystery provides a vivid theory of what might have happened between Mary Stuart and Henry Darnley and will keep readers turning the pages." —*Historical Novels Review*

WITHDRAWN
continued

"Julianne Lee's *A Question of Guilt* is a sprawling tale of treason, justice, and the secrets people keep. It is very much rooted in historical facts and . . . the writing style is flawless."

—*Romance Reader at Heart*

Her Mother's Daughter

"An epic tale of passion, intrigue, tragedy, betrayal, and treachery all combined into a story too powerful for history to contain. With creative weaving, Julianne Lee has combined true characters with possible dialogue and intent that ring true to the story and time period. For any fan of historical entertainment, *Her Mother's Daughter* is a definite must-read book."

—*Night Owl Reviews*

"For the many readers who like to focus on the Tudor era, this is a read that must be added to your library, both for its original storytelling and the unique approach the author utilizes to tell this compelling story of Mary Tudor." —*Burton Book Review*

"*Her Mother's Daughter* seamlessly displays the often overlooked woman behind Queen 'Bloody' Mary. Julianne Lee handles a typically despised character so beautifully that the reader develops unexpected sympathy for a queen who clawed her way out of the depths of disrespect only to find more loneliness and desperation . . . Lee's engaging novel submerges the reader into local and worldwide political intrigue to fully depict the world in which Mary lived . . . [A] wonderfully written book." —*Romance Junkies*

"Lee presents an unbiased portrait of Mary Tudor, and for readers eager to find out what happened following the death of Henry VIII, this novel is highly satisfying." —*RT Book Reviews*

The
Twelfth Night
Murder

ANNE RUTHERFORD

BERKLEY PRIME CRIME, NEW YORK

THE BERKLEY PUBLISHING GROUP
Published by the Penguin Group
Penguin Group (USA) LLC
375 Hudson Street, New York, New York 10014

USA • Canada • UK • Ireland • Australia • New Zealand • India • South Africa • China

penguin.com

A Penguin Random House Company

Berkley Prime Crime Books are published by The Berkley Publishing Group.
BERKLEY® PRIME CRIME and the PRIME CRIME logo are trademarks of Penguin Group (USA) LLC.

Library of Congress Cataloging-in-Publication Data

Rutherford, Anne, 1956–
The Twelfth Night murder / Anne Rutherford.—Berkley trade paperback edition.
pages cm—(A Restoration mystery; 3)
ISBN 978-0-425-25561-2 (paperback)
1. Theater—England—London—Fiction. 2. Female impersonators—Violence against—Fiction. 3. Murder—Investigation—Fiction. 4. London (England)—History—17th century—Fiction. 5. Great Britain—History—Restoration, 1660–1688—Fiction. I. Title.
PS3618.U778T84 2014
813'.6—dc23
2014017920

PUBLISHING HISTORY
Berkley Prime Crime trade paperback edition / September 2014

PRINTED IN THE UNITED STATES OF AMERICA

10 9 8 7 6 5 4 3 2 1

Cover illustration by Griesbach/Martucci.
Cover design by Jason Gill.
Interior text design by Tiffany Estreicher.

For my editor, Ginjer Buchanan,
who over the decades has changed my life
in ways I can't begin to explain.

Author's Note

The Twelfth Night Murder is the fifteenth historical novel I've written for publication. Ordinarily I would never take liberties with history, since I have immense respect for the truth. However, in this series I found it inconvenient that Shakespeare's Globe Theatre was torn down by Cromwell's anti-cultural administration a number of years before I needed it. I am as annoyed by that as the people of London at the time must have been. But unlike them I am working inside a fictional world of my own design. By definition, many of the things in this book are untrue. Among those things is the presence of Shakespeare's Globe Theatre. I needed a theatre, and it was just as well to have a fictional one. Such a small thing, and I'm sure I've made actual errors of greater consequence than this. So please forgive me my deliberate anachronism, and any other minor flaws I may have perpetrated more accidentally.

Over the years I've thanked folks who have helped me in

my research and my efforts in publication. Today I would like to give a nod to my readers, who are the reason I continue to write. You've been such an appreciative audience, and I've been so neglectful in acknowledging you. Thank you all for your attention. I hope you will enjoy this, the third in the Restoration Mysteries.

For news of future books in this series, sign up for the free *History Geek* newsletter at julianneardianlee.com /historygeek/newslettersignup.html.

Anne Rutherford
julianneardianlee.com/anne/annerutherford.html

Chapter One

In the dressing room after the day's performance at the Globe Theatre, Suzanne Thornton sat before the paint table, and sagged happily, exhausted but exhilarated. A dozen or so candles lit the room with a lively, warm flicker. The Players around her chattered and laughed, in high spirits after a show that had been well received by their audience. In spite of the January cold, with the promise of snow in the air—or perhaps because of it—The New Globe Players' presentation of Shakespeare's *Twelfth Night* brought much applause and laughter of the kind that made the performers want to join in. Sometimes it was difficult to keep a straight face in the comedies, and that was Suzanne's great weakness onstage, for in the past she had never had much to smile about and these days she was sorely tempted to laugh whenever she could.

Nevertheless, it was a joy to have returned to the stage. After a lifetime of struggling to escape the predatory notice of those more powerful than herself, and at her age when there were few opportunities to attract benevolent attention from anyone, appreciative audiences were a delight. Life was finally looking up.

She picked up the troupe's newly purchased mirror from the table and propped it against a ceramic mug filled with paintbrushes standing on end. The mirror was small, but was all she could afford for The New Globe Players just then, and far nicer than the large, ragged shard they'd all been using up to last week. At the moment, Matthew had the old mirror, a big piece of broken, silvered glass, with patches of the silvering missing from the back and its sharp edges filed down and covered in melted wax. It sat propped against a small wooden box of lead powder, all of which smelled sharply of sheep fat and oil, with an underlying earthiness of talc. To Suzanne it was a smell uniquely theatrical. It smelled of home.

Matthew sat opposite Suzanne, removing white lead paint from his face with linseed oil and speaking to Liza, the girl who was their Viola these days, in cheerful, self-congratulatory terms. Besides playing the central character in *Twelfth Night*, Liza was the girl at the center of Matthew's affections, and just then he sounded a bit condescending in his assessment of her performance that afternoon. He seemed disparaging of women acting on the stage, telling her she had done well that day, for a woman.

"Nonsense," Suzanne said in a light, *don't be silly* tone as she wiped oil over the blacking around her eyes until she looked much as she often had in her youth after having been beaten by her father. "She was absolutely perfect. No man could have played that role better than our woman."

From across the room, Louis chimed in. "Kynaston could have. He's far prettier than Liza, and his voice carries into the rafters. The man's a genius."

Suzanne shook her head. "He's a sodomite, and should have been born a woman."

"He's not prettier," said Liza in a defensive, slightly horrified voice. "He's a skinny, soft boy whose balls never dropped, and the only reason anybody thinks he can play women is that they've never seen a real one onstage before."

"He's an artist," Louis continued. "I saw him once. In *The Maid's Tragedy*, last year." His voice took on a note of admiration Suzanne thought a little strange. She'd often heard people talk of Ned Kynaston that way. She'd also seen him on the stage, and knew he possessed a beauty so androgynous that it seemed the whole of London wanted to bed him, men and women. She herself confessed to a slight attraction, though her preference was very much for hard-edged, mature masculinity and not so very much for Kynaston's bee-stung lips and doe eyes. He really did seem an innocent, prepubescent boy, though he was in his early twenties and by all accounts was not so very particular where he slept.

She said, "The fellow is exceedingly fair, and decidedly undecided in his sex. But that doesn't make him a woman, or even a facsimile to portray us on the stage. At best he paints a picture of us in broad strokes so that the male audience can comprehend in unsubtle ways. In short, young fellows, he simplifies so those such as you might comprehend womanhood on an elementary level, which is, after all, your capacity."

Louis and Matthew fell silent and gazed at her for a moment, Louis with a puzzled crease between his eyes and

Matthew's eyes narrowed in search of a suitably witty retort. He didn't find one. Liza snickered to herself with a breathy, *hee-hee* sound.

Matthew opened his mouth to respond, but was interrupted when one of their young boy actors, who went by Christian, blew into the room at top speed, skidded to a stop just inside the door, and said in a near-shout, "Mistress Thornton!" He swayed where he stood at the end of his slide. "You've a visitor!"

There were always visitors after a show. Everyone in the audience who thought they might have a chance at going backstage to socialize with the actors came after the show or before it. Horatio, who directed the plays and often acted in them, was ever struggling to keep the green room and dressing room from filling wall to wall with those who wished to be actors but hadn't the talent or discipline for it. Some sought sexual liaison with the performers, and others simply wished to bask in reflected glory and tell of it later to their friends. Since the Globe Theatre was not the most fashionable playhouse in London, the quality of their visitors was never high, and Horatio's effort was mostly aimed at keeping out those who would steal costumes and properties. She asked, "Who is it?"

He shook his head. "Dunno, mistress. She's a queer old woman, I vow. Dressed a bit strange, like she was fresh from the countryside but . . . I dunno. Strange."

Suzanne was tired. It was time for supper, and she could smell it being prepared by her maid downstairs. Having spent the entire afternoon entertaining people, she was ready to have the evening to herself. "Tell her I've gone home. Since I live on the premises, that won't be a lie."

"Very well, mistress." With that, Christian bolted from

the room as speedily as he'd arrived, leaving Louis to close the door behind him. The boy returned in but a few moments, before Suzanne could wipe the remaining paint from her face.

"Mistress Thornton, begging your pardon and sorry to disturb you again, but the woman outside is insisting she be permitted to see you."

Suzanne turned from her mirror, resigned to deal with this. "What, exactly, does this woman want?"

"She says she would warn you."

Warn? As much as Suzanne knew this must be a ploy of some sort, her curiosity was now piqued. Ignoring a warning was one thing, but to never even hear it was tempting fate a bit too much. She said, "Very well. Show her in."

Christian ran out again at full speed, dodging others standing in the room awaiting a turn at the table.

Suzanne hurried to get as much paint from her face as she could, and had begun wiping the oil with a dry cloth when Christian returned with an old woman in tow.

The crone was old indeed, and dressed very strangely. She wore no bodice, but only a skirt and a long maroon scarf tied at her midriff that restrained her blouse. Another scarf, an orange one that bore a ragged fringe, lay draped about her hips. From its knot at her side hung a purse of bright, shiny red silk. The skirt was a lively orange and red print, faded now but clearly it had once been bright and eye-catching. Her blouse was relatively new and of a deep turquoise color that argued bitterly with the rest of the costume. Beneath the baggy and loosely woven cotton, her large breasts swayed and sloshed without restraint. Its sleeves gathered at the wrist then splayed in copious blue lace to beyond her finger-tips. Her hands were quite lost in it until she flipped it back to reveal them and the enormous jeweled rings she wore on gnarled fingers. Her hands were great clusters of knobby knuckles and semiprecious stones, connected by fingers little more substantial than her bones. Yet another scarf, this one of bright green, adorned her head, secured at the nape of her neck with a simple brooch of plain copper. Long, wavy gray hair spilled from under the scarf, nearly to her waist. Amid the festive explosion of color she wore a wide smile and revealed a surprising number of teeth for one so obviously aged.

"Hello," she said, her words oddly clipped and her smile a bit stiff. "'Tis a good thing to meet you today, mistress. I've got an earful for ye." She nodded as if to affirm her words, then turned her attention on Matthew at the table and gave him a hard stare.

Matthew seemed unsure what she wanted from him, but then realized it was his seat she expected. Without argument, he vacated the chair and took his mirror and rag with him to stand aside, where he resumed wiping oil from his face. The woman sat, and returned her attention to Suzanne.

"My name is Esmeralda La Tournelle. I am the astrologer to King Charles and many of his court."

Suzanne recognized the name. La Tournelle had a long reputation in London for her odd predictions that often were realized. Many Londoners, especially those of the Puritan and Presbyterian bent, decried her as a devil woman, but Suzanne couldn't dismiss her or her craft entirely. She knew from experience there was something to observing the movements of planets in God's orderly creation. She nodded to the old woman. "A pleasure to meet you, Mistress La Tournelle." It was indeed a pleasure, for the woman's fame was far greater than her own, and a presence of power followed her like a cloud of energy, a nearly visible thickening of the air around her so that one couldn't help staring at her. She seemed to fill the room all by herself, leaving little space for anyone else. All eyes were on her, and all conversation in the room ceased.

"Call me Esmeralda. I'm mistress of naught other than my fate. I've come to do you a good turn." Now her graciousness filled the room and everyone in it was put at ease.

Suzanne smiled, but was buying little of it yet. "And what will this good turn cost me?"

The woman's eyes darkened and she lost her smile. Her back straightened and she raised her chin. "I charge them as come to me, and them who has more money than they truly need. You ain't among them. Not yet, in any case. I've come to warn you of an event that will possibly change your life."

"I expect there will be a great many events in my future that will change my life. It is the nature of the world, and of life as God has given it to us."

The woman shook her head. "This is a crossroads that you must avoid, and you will come to it soon."

"Why must I avoid it?" Suzanne glanced at the others in the room, inviting them in on her jest. "My life isn't so perfect that I wouldn't want a change."

A low chuckle riffled through the room.

"Hear me, Mistress Thornton." A severity hardened the lines in La Tournelle's very lined face. Her pale blue eyes appeared icy, and a shiver skittered down Suzanne's spine.

All of a sudden the woman's presence made Suzanne uncomfortable, the way bad news made one wish to return to the moment before. She wished she hadn't allowed Christian to bring this strange, old woman into the room. Suzanne would have liked to have her removed, but her bourgeois upbringing wouldn't permit her that sort of gracelessness. Her manners may have been ordinary, and over the years many had worn off or had been beaten from her, but there were some things one just did not do. Particularly since life was improving and she hoped it would continue to do so. She smiled at her uninvited guest and said, "I'm listening."

The old woman leaned close as if imparting a secret, though everyone in the room was listening and most were leaning in, the better to hear every word. She said, loudly enough for all to hear, "Beware the river tonight for it will bring you death."

"The river?" The wide, filthy Thames was not far from the theatre, and when the wind was from the north one could smell it and the things floating on it. "How will it do that?" Suzanne had no plans for boating or bathing that night, but her favorite public house was in a short alley just off Bank Side. She would more than likely come very near the water sometime that evening. "I should stay away?"

La Tournelle gestured overhead with one gnarled hand and waving fingers, staring upward as if gazing at a night sky. "The stars have revealed to me that your life will be changed soon, by water, and death stalks you."

"As it does us all."

"It will figure significantly during the coming weeks. You will be consumed by it, and it may consume you."

Suzanne opened her mouth to point out the oxymoronic nature of her comment, but changed her mind as she saw the different meanings of "consume." But La Tournelle still made little sense. "Do you mean I'll drown?"

The old woman shrugged. "That is one possibility, if the sign is to be taken literally."

"And if not literally?"

"The water will figure mightily in your life."

"Any water? Not necessarily the Thames?"

"Do you know any seamen?"

There was the pirate who had attacked her a couple of months ago, but she shook her head. That man was in prison, awaiting hanging or pardon according to the king's pleasure. She didn't know any seamen, and had never seen the ocean. Nor even the English Channel, for that. She'd lived in London her entire life and for lack of means had never strayed far.

"Then I suggest it would be the Thames."

"And I'm to stay away?"

"Aye."

"For how long?"

The old woman looked off to the side for a moment, thinking, calculating, then replied, "I think three weeks. Four at the most."

To stay away from the Goat and Boar for an entire month would be torture. Impossible for her. "I don't think I can do that. Are you saying that if I walk down Bank Side, no matter how sure-footed, I'll fall off the bank and drown?"

"Someone will drown. It may be you, it may not. Or it may not be drowning at all. But you will be affected by it one way or another, and severely."

Others in the room laughed, a tense, uncomfortable chuckle. Suzanne sat back in her chair and clasped her hands. Her knuckles went white, though she struggled to appear as if she didn't believe any of this. "How do you know this?"

"The stars never lie. They are as God made them, and they show us the entirety of existence, for all creation is interlinked and purposeful. God knows every sparrow that falls, because He created not only the sparrow, but that which destroys it."

"You think the stars cause things to happen?"

A slightly amused look crossed the woman's face. She sat back in her chair and folded her hands in her lap. "Of course not. The positions of the planets relative to each other and the stars in the sky do not influence. Only God can do that. The stars merely speak to us, and tell us of what will be."

"So you believe in God?"

"I could hardly advise the king, did I not. His majesty could never be known to consult a heretic, could he?"

Suzanne allowed as that was true. She said, "I've consulted with astrologers before, but I must tell you I've never done well by it. I find that when I follow the recommendations of someone who has read my horoscope, the results are never what I expect."

"Then it is your expectations that are faulty. Those who aim to make themselves richer or more powerful by reading the heavens are doomed to failure. One can never bend creation to one's own wishes. One can only take heed of what must be and act accordingly."

"So I should keep away from the Goat and Boar for a few weeks?"

"You should beware of the water, whatever water there might be, and if water flows near the public house then you would do well to avoid the place."

"Why me? Of all the people in London who might need this warning, what has brought you to me?"

"Mistress Thornton, God has sent me to you." She said it with a note of exasperation that she must repeat herself.

"God? You've spoken to Him, then?" Suzanne hoped this wasn't going to disintegrate into the rant of a madwoman. She'd been willing to consider keeping away from the river for a while, but if this woman revealed herself to be insane then Suzanne would have to go to Bank Side only for the sake of demonstrating to the rest of the troupe that she hadn't been taken in by madness.

"Not to hear His voice, at all, mistress. I mean, I've had some dreams. I've awakened in the night with a strong, ugly feeling regarding you. I was moved to come speak to you. Warn you."

"Ugly feelings regarding me are not all that uncommon, I vow. How do you even know who I am?"

"Oh, all of London knows who you are, Mistress Thornton. You've quite a name this past year or so."

Suzanne's head tilted a bit, and she crossed her arms. "Indeed? And God has been telling tales about me?"

"Aye. He's sent me a strong message, that you will be influenced by water, and soon."

"I'll drown."

"I never said 'drown.' I said your life will be changed."

"So I'll still be alive?"

"Possibly. Possibly not. And whether you die or not, it may not be the water will be the direct cause."

"So . . . let me sort through this. In the next few weeks I may or may not die, and if I do it may or may not be of drowning."

"The only thing certain is that your life will change, and 'twill be caused by water."

"But we don't know what water it will be. Probably the Thames, but not necessarily."

The old woman nodded and smiled. "Now you see."

Suzanne saw nothing, and only her belief in the basic principles of astrology kept her curious about what this all meant. She stood, indicating that her guest should ready herself to leave, and said, "Well, I thank you for your advice,

Mistress La Tournelle. I shall take your premonition under advisement."

The old woman hesitated, and a sour look crossed her face in realization that she was being dismissed without consideration. She stood, gave a quick nod, and said, "Then I hope you'll beware, for I am a Christian woman and I never like to see anyone suffer."

"I appreciate that. Our boy will show you out, and I thank you for coming."

"Oh, I was already in the theatre, mistress. I came to see the play this afternoon. Excellent play, I'll add. You all should be pleased." She nodded and waved to the other players in the room, who acknowledged the praise with smiles, nods, and murmurs of thanks. Then the old woman followed Christian from the room and they watched her go.

They waited while she removed from earshot, her footsteps fading down the stage left stairwell and out the rear to the house.

When they were all certain she'd gone, Matthew stared after her and said, "Well, there's a woman with a belfry chock full of bats."

A nervous laugh riffled about the room, and Suzanne had to chuckle as well. "Water, she says. And with the Thames only a stone's throw away from this theatre."

"Perhaps she means rainfall?"

Louis added, "Maybe you'll have a rain barrel fall on you?" Everyone laughed at that, and he added, "Don't you be climbing atop any cisterns, then, eh?" That brought more laughter, and Suzanne joined in. She resumed the removal of her makeup, and stared into her mirror, thinking hard.

Chapter Two

Having cleaned up and retreated to her quarters downstairs, Suzanne considered her options for the evening. Most nights she would head to the Goat and Boar for some supper, some ale, and some good company. For more than twenty years Southwark, and particularly Bank Side, had been her home, and she knew nearly everyone within a half mile of the Globe. Even more, during her years as a whore in Maddie's brothel on Bank Side she'd serviced a great many of her neighbors. Though wealthy and adventurous clientele from across the river had been a significant part of her trade, her bread and butter had always been the neighborhood itself, where her regular customers had lived, worked, and taken their recreation in the brothels and animal-fighting arenas.

She'd accepted her lot without shame, for prostitution had been all that was open to her, and the money had kept herself and her son alive. She felt that if God had wanted her to do something else, He would have presented her with an opportunity to do something else. Pregnancy had kept her from marrying, and she couldn't imagine life without Piers. He would be twenty this year, and he'd grown to be a good, honest man. Whatever she'd done to that end was worth whatever cost to her reputation or her soul.

In any case, she still enjoyed the platonic company of many of the men she'd known then, and some of them worked with her in the theatre. Were she to heed the recommendation of Mistress La Tournelle, it would be a long, lonely several weeks away from her dearest friends. She didn't relish hiding in her room.

She opened the armoire in the small bedroom she occupied, in her apartments tucked in a corner of the Globe's basement floor. Whitewashed stone walls brightened the odd corners and nooks of it. The floor was mostly even, though it had a slight slant at one end, where it took a step up to a tiny alcove where stood her writing desk and a wooden chair with a tall back and heavy arms. The armoire wobbled somewhat on the uneven stone, but was steady enough when she jammed a bit of wood beneath one of its feet. The thing was a rather old piece of furniture, and smelled musty, but she'd had it since the year she'd started up with her former patron nearly eleven years ago and it was holding up nicely. It looked somewhat German, painted with vines and flowers along its frame and sides. Having had little of worth in her life, she was now rather attached to it. It represented a significant improvement in her life recently.

The same was true about many things she'd acquired, and also about some of the people in her life, some old friends and some newly met. As she gazed at the clothing in her armoire, most of it bought very recently, she considered who she would miss, were she to stay away from the Goat and Boar as recommended. Big Willie Waterman, of course. He was a musician who worked often with her Players and sometimes played small roles, but he was most fun when holding forth in conversation or fiddling freely on his instrument at the public house. Then there was Warren, Willie's flautist friend, whom Suzanne knew less well. The two played often together, and if Willie was hired for a play, Warren usually was as well. Willie, Warren, the Goat and Boar proprietor Young Dent, and the performers in The New Globe Players filled her evenings with good company. She was closest to Matthew, Louis, and Liza, and of course Horatio, who directed the Players and whose love of Shakespeare was everpresent. He was like an uncle to her and represented the only family she had ever trusted. Even Daniel had never been the rock Horatio was to her.

Oh yes, Daniel as ever. Daniel Stockton, third Earl of Throckmorton. He was Piers's father and the man Suzanne had once loved so much she threw her life away on him at seventeen. With him the question was never whether she would miss him, but would he miss her? Would he even notice her absence? And could she afford to care anymore whether he did? Because now there was also Diarmid Ramsay, the wild Highland Scot who was even less trustworthy, and one was never sure how he made his living. Sometimes he played roles at the Globe, but not often enough to account for his lack of other employment or property. He was known to do some buying and selling, but without patent to speak of, and one was never clear about where the goods had originated. The only certainty about Ramsay was that he was by far the best source for Scottish whisky in all of London. Oh, but he was ever so much more fun!

What would happen, then, were she to hide herself in the theatre and away from the river? She had to smile at the thought. Daniel and Ramsay would be very unhappy fellows.

She looked over at her desk, where sat the volume of Aristotle Daniel had given her. It had taken her weeks to plow through it once, and now she was working her way through again to understand it better. Tutelage had been scarce in her youth, and her reading skills were not strong, but her desire to read and understand great works burned nearly as hotly as her instincts in raising her son. She could stay at home tonight and let her maid serve her something to eat, and spend the evening absorbed in ancient Greek philosophy.

There was wine here; she didn't need to go to the public house for it. There was always wine now, and of higher quality than she'd known even while under the wing of her patron, William. He had been a Puritan riddled with shame for his sin of fornication, and pretended to make up for it by keeping her home free of anything he considered luxury. Her clothing had been black, her food plain, and her wine cheap. There would have been none at all, had she not insisted he allow it. Now, since his death and since Daniel had provided her with the financial means to create The New Globe Players, she wore brightly colored silks and soft linens. Even a little jewelry, though she still could only afford plain silver without stones.

She turned back to the armoire and considered dressing to go out. Then she turned to her desk where Aristotle awaited. Then back to the armoire.

Should she avoid the Thames? What might she miss if she stayed in? Should she resume her reading tonight and possibly be a better person for having studied? Daniel had said she would enjoy Aristotle, and he'd been right. Nearly every page contained something she'd heard said but had never before known who'd first said it. Now her reading was a bit like putting together a puzzle, where the pieces became a whole that made sense. She liked puzzles. Solving them made her feel intelligent, as her father had always given her to believe she was not.

The actor, Ramsay, wanted to marry her, where Daniel did not. Could not, for he was married to someone else. Daniel's commitment to his son and herself had never been strong enough for him to even acknowledge Piers. His wife didn't know about him, and Daniel liked it that way.

Ramsay, however, had made his desire for commitment clear. Had he been a steadier sort, she might have married him by now. But he was not, and his comings and goings were irregular in the extreme. Since he was not in any of the plays currently being staged or rehearsed, she'd not seen him all week, and that didn't reflect well on his dependability.

However, she missed them both and wanted to spend the evening among friends. Again she looked to the armoire, and this time her hand of its own volition reached for a delicately and expensively embroidered shirt and silk breeches. A man's costume that pleased her for its comfort and practicality, with just enough of the feminine about it to avoid confusion.

Sometimes she wore dresses when in public, for a different sort of practicality. Though Londoners took pride in being surprised by nothing since the return of the king from the eternally blasé Continent, dressing in unquestionably feminine attire cut down on social friction when she was among strangers. Wearing a dress while out among people who didn't know her saved on having to explain herself. However, during evenings at the Goat and Boar, and at the Globe while not onstage, she enjoyed the comfort and the attention she received dressed in doublet, breeches, tights, and flowing linen shirt.

And Daniel's Cavalier's hat. Recently, in a playful moment on New Year's Day, she'd appropriated a hat belonging to Daniel. As the Earl of Throckmorton and one of the King's Cavaliers, he'd returned from exile with the king nearly two years ago and had worn this hat in the triumphal parade through London. Wide of brim and flat topped, it bore a feather so long it now tickled the backs of her legs when it swayed with her movements. One of the many things she liked about this costume was that in men's clothing she was able to dress herself and not have to call for Sheila's help.

Ready for the Goat and Boar, she called for Sheila to have her fur-collared cloak and matching leather gloves for her, and then was on her way to the public house and maybe some fun among her favorite people. Never mind the old woman's premonition. There was no telling what that was about in any case, and she tried to forget it.

The Goat and Boar lay in an alley off Bank Side, from which there was no access or egress but from that street. There was no entrance to the public house except by walking along the embankment just west of the bridge. Tonight Suzanne, in spite of herself, walked as close to the buildings away from the bank wall as she could. Braving the Bank Side was tempting fate, but not too much. Probably. She stared over at the water's edge, and slowed.

It was just a river. Even were she to fall in, she wouldn't necessarily drown. She knew how to swim, having learned as a child in a pond on her uncle's farm. Tonight she wasn't even wearing skirts that might pull her under. If she fell in, it would be a simple matter to swim to a quay, or even float downstream to one, and climb out. The river was filthy, not deadly.

She stopped walking, and stared some more. Why should she fear something told to her by someone she didn't know and hadn't asked? The woman knew the king, but she shouldn't be taken as a prophet of any kind. After all, Daniel also knew the king and she certainly never took his word as gospel. Not anymore, in any case. It was silly to avoid the river when it couldn't hurt her. She took some steps toward it.

As she crossed the street, evening traffic passed around her, this way and that. Street vendors cried their wares to her, but she ignored them. A carriage approached and its driver shouted at her to clear the way, so she hurried a few steps closer to the brink. Clopping horses and rattling wheels passed harmlessly behind her, and she gazed some more at the river.

Braziers here and there flickered up and down along the stone riverbank. There weren't many boats on the water this time of day and this time of year, but a few showed torchlight and bobbed like water candles in the current. The dank smell didn't seem so bad to her; she was used to it. Here in Southwark, all her life the water of the Thames had helped weave the fabric of her days and nights. Her early childhood had been spent in this very street, living and working in the brothel. Maddie was dead now, and her house had been made tenements still occupied by whores and thieves who now paid rent instead of working for it. Her days there had been nearly half a lifetime ago, but since then she'd never strayed far, and the smell of the river still spoke to her of home.

"Whatever has got you so enraptured?"

Suzanne jumped. Daniel's voice spoke so close to her ear it seemed to come from inside her head. He laughed and she turned to slap his arm. Up the street she saw his carriage standing near a brazier, and realized it was the one that had nearly run her down.

"I didn't mean to startle you. You were staring so intently at the river, I thought you might have seen something particularly interesting you could share with me." His smile was wide and handsome, with teeth only slightly discolored by age. He was nearly forty, slightly older than herself, and few men his age could boast a full complement. She saw him as the youth who had once been her lover, who still touched a small, dim place in her heart.

Those days when she'd been a young, stupid girl had been the time of magic, when anything she wanted had seemed possible and nothing mattered more than their love. Even then he'd been married, for a man of his station must marry for political and financial advantage and she'd offered neither. But that had never been large in her thoughts. She'd given him everything, and he'd squandered it. This bank had been their meeting place.

"I was only taking in the beauty of the river."

That brought a short bark of a laugh. "If you say so, though I can't imagine anyone thinking that stinking runnel a thing of beauty."

Suzanne only shrugged and declined to argue. She thought the river at night was a lovely sight, so deep in the darkness, and torchlit barges moving silently along it. She didn't care what he thought. "Come," she said, and took his arm though it hadn't been offered. "Let us go to the Goat and Boar. I'm thirsty for a glass of wine."

"An expensive one, I'll wager."

"Of course. Anything less would not be worth the swallowing, much like most men I've known."

Daniel let out a long guffaw.

The Goat and Boar was lively that night. When Suzanne and Daniel arrived they were hard-pressed to find a seat in the throng. An extra table had been brought to seat patrons, and even so, every chair in the room was occupied. Several men stood by the hearth where a mutton joint that dropped fragrant grease into the fire was nearing edibility. They were holding cups and tankards as they argued amiably about bears and bulls that fought dogs in the arenas near the bridge. Some tarts loitered here and there, young girls Suzanne didn't know. The faces of the whores changed far more often than those of the men in this place, and keeping up with the comings and goings of the girls on Bank Side was near impossible.

Suzanne looked around to see if any of her Players were there, and her heart lifted to find an entire table of them. The small one at the back was surrounded by actors and musicians from the Globe. Matthew, Liza, Louis, Big Willie, whose physique belied his name, and Horatio, whose wig just would not stay straight on his entirely bald head. It canted to one side, though he was forever straightening it with an absent shove.

And Ramsay. Diarmid was there, wearing his bright red kilt and a clean, white linen shirt with the drawstring at its neck untied and hanging loose over his chest. His Highland bonnet of blue wool sat on the table before him, next to his cup of whisky. At the moment he was laughing at something someone had just said, but when he looked up and saw Suzanne on Daniel's arm his smile died.

Then he resurrected it, for Ramsay was not one to let himself appear defeated. Or even damaged. He leapt to his feet and gestured to his chair that Suzanne should sit instead of himself. Suzanne sat, gladly, for she didn't care to stand and had not come with Daniel. She didn't mind letting Ramsay play the gentleman in front of the actual gentleman.

Now Ramsay and Daniel stood, Ramsay with his whisky and Daniel looking around for somewhere to sit. Louis, knowing his place as the least man present, hopped to his feet so the earl could take his chair. But Daniel, though he gazed at it for a moment to consider sitting, smiled and shook his head. His glance at Ramsay told Suzanne that though his rank entitled him to the chair, he would stand as long as Ramsay did. Daniel was a veteran of the civil war, and he liked to remind everyone that Ramsay was nothing but a soft actor. He gestured to Young Dent, the proprietor, for a whisky for himself and wine in a clean glass for Suzanne. *Expensive* wine.

Matthew said, loudly over the roar of voices in the close room, "I'm surprised, Suzanne, to see you so near the river tonight."

She laughed. "It takes more than dark mutterings from an old witch to keep me away from the Goat and Boar."

"What dark mutterings do you mean, Suze?" Ramsay asked. His far northern brogue had smoothed out some during his months in London, but his speech was still quite crisp with rolling Rs and slender vowels.

She waved away the subject as if it were nothing, though she didn't really feel it was. "Oh, just an old woman who told me to stay away from the water for some weeks."

"Said she was going to drown, she did," said Louis.

"Did not. She only said my life would change and death was involved."

"Sounds a great deal like drowning to me."

She shrugged and laughed. "In any case, I can hardly stay away from the Thames for so long. Most weeks I cross it more

than once. I'd hate to be utterly trapped in Southwark." She
tossed an insouciant grin to Ramsay and Daniel, and found
them staring hard at each other, their postures with chests
out and chins up, like roosters in a fighting ring. A smile
twitched at the corners of her mouth. Men had fought over
her before, but only when very drunk, and the contest had
always been over the money she cost rather than her affections. To see Daniel and Ramsay like this was not just a
surprise, but a pleasant one.

One of the tarts moving through the room in search of a
patron for the evening sidled up to Daniel, clearly the more
affluent of the men at that table. The girl was uncommon-
pretty. Her cheeks glowed with natural, ruddy health
beneath porcelain skin. Her lips were full and soft, and when
she smiled they showed dimples at the corners that seemed
in turn to light up her eyes. Her high spirits and quick laugh
made her eminently likeable, and Suzanne found her fascinating. There was something about this girl that simply lit
up the room with joie de vivre. Suzanne couldn't help smiling with her.

She pressed her bosom to Daniel, batted her eyes, and
vowed she was so thirsty she could just blow away on the
slightest breeze. The way her mouth caressed the word
"blow" with O-shaped lips, it was plain what she would give
in return for a drink.

Daniel replied, "Nonsense. You're as full of piss and vin-
egar as any girl I've ever seen." Suzanne knew he would buy
the girl an ale, but he'd give her a hard time about it first.
He might even expect her to take him upstairs immediately
and save the drinking for after, but she thought probably not
tonight. He wouldn't care to leave herself and Ramsay in the
same room.

The tart's bosom wasn't as ample, and therefore not as revealed, as those of other girls in the room, but her lips were very soft and plump. They were painted a bold crimson that stood out in her very pale face like a winter rose on snow. When she smiled her teeth were large and quite white. Surely she must have been younger than she at first appeared. Tall for her age, and therefore no more than twelve or thirteen. Hardly old enough to have a bosom at all, never mind an ample one. During Suzanne's day as a tart, she'd seen so many young girls such as this, she came to realize that at seventeen she'd entered the profession very late. She'd been nearly a hag when she'd started at Maddie's, where other girls had arrived so young many couldn't remember any other life.

The girl wore a wig of nearly white blonde, and a dress of blue satin adorned with a profusion of cream-colored lace at wrist and breast, where it somewhat mitigated her lack of mature curves. Her waist was miniscule, so narrow Suzanne might have spanned it with her own rather small hands. Daniel's one hand rested at the small of her back, and was barely hidden by it. The girl held a fan she waved before her face in tiny, precise movements while she eyed Daniel like a large cat sizing a doe for a kill, with an energy and mischief that mesmerized. Suzanne watched with an amused smile, as if enjoying a well-acted play.

Then she realized what she was seeing was a true act. More than the usual feigned interest of a prostitute for a client, Suzanne sensed this was a put-on from the very bottom of it. The veins on the girl's hands stood out in bulging blue ridges. When her fan dropped a little too low, in her throat could be seen a distinct Adam's apple. A small one, to be sure, but it was there. She began to notice other things. The girl's posture was just a tiny bit *too* feminine. Like a caricature of a female rather than a girl who has been one her entire life. The voice was too soft. Too . . . practiced. Suzanne realized what she was looking at was a boy in a dress. A boy just beginning his entry to manhood.

A smile of mischief spread across her face as she watched Daniel flirt with the boy. Did he know, or would he soon learn a handful of what awaited beneath those skirts was more than he'd bargained for? Suzanne in the past had sometimes passed herself off as a boy, for men of that persuasion rarely cared for the boy bits and she could often service such a client without even disrobing much. She knew there was a demand for boys in dresses, but she'd never come across one. The laws against sodomy being what they were, those who practiced it kept to themselves for the most part. So far as she knew, this was the first male tart she'd ever seen.

Daniel's expression never betrayed a knowledge he was about to go upstairs with a boy. Furthermore, as his conversation with the young sodomite progressed, it became plain Daniel did intend to take him upstairs. His hand went into the slit at the side of the boy's dress, as the boy pretended coyness and stepped away from the earl. He snapped his fan closed and wagged it side-to-side in a *no-no* gesture. Daniel laughed as if the boy were joking, and pulled him by the waist to press himself against his belly. Suzanne watched closely to see whether Daniel would sense something beneath the copious skirts, but he seemed not to notice anything amiss. His grin was wide as the boy smiled behind his fan and looked up at him with dewy eyes and dimpled cheeks. Daniel looked as if he might steal a kiss.

It was definitely time to put a stop to this lest he embarrass himself. "Daniel!" she cried, and put a hand on his arm.

"Daniel, you must taste this wine! 'Tis the finest Young Dent has ever served here!"

Daniel was awfully taken with the boy in his arms, if not smitten. It took another pull at his arm to get him to even look at her. She grabbed his collar and yanked him hard enough to bend him at the waist so she could speak directly into his ear. "Daniel! Stop that now!"

He laughed, ready to ignore her as if she were only jealous of the prostitute, and that surely was the reason for this display. But she held tight to his collar and continued, "That is a boy you're about to bed!"

He laughed again, certain she must be having him on.

"Heed me, Throckmorton! Look at him!" She shook his arm in an attempt to bring him to his senses.

Daniel saw her eyes, and the smile left his face. A frown put a crease between his eyes, puzzled, and he looked at the boy. For his part, the boy maintained his femininity though he knew he'd been revealed. He graced Daniel with the softest, most adoring eyes and pursed lips Suzanne had ever seen, even in a skilled prostitute.

But Daniel finally saw through the ruse. He straightened and reddened. Then he looked around to see who else had seen, and found the entire table of Players watching, some grinning and others unsure where to look from embarrassment. There was no saving the moment. So, with all the social grace bred into him by generations of noble ancestry, he took the boy's free hand and quite formally bent and kissed the back of it in the Continental manner. Then he straightened and said in the warmest tones he could manage at the moment, "I must apologize, mistress. I fear I've just remembered a commitment I've made elsewhere. I hope you will forgive me, for I must cut short our conversation."

The boy said, "Another time, then?"

There was a snort of laughter from someone at the table. Suzanne looked to see who it was, but couldn't tell by their faces. They all listened intently for Daniel's response.

He replied, "I doubt our paths will cross again."

The boy's eyes betrayed disappointment, but he curtsied with utter grace and said, "As you wish. I should have liked to make your acquaintance, but one must accept what one cannot change."

"Indeed."

There was another snort, and this time Suzanne caught Louis laughing into his cup. She threw him a sharp look, and he looked away, struggling not to giggle.

The boy tart tapped the end of his fan against Daniel's chin, then ran it down his chest as he turned away from his would-be client and the rest of the table, immediately off on his quest for someone with interest as well as money. He disappeared into the press in an instant, and Suzanne looked to Daniel for his reaction.

The red cloud of embarrassment hovered over him as if he were smoking that tobacco plant from the New World. Suzanne could almost see it rising from the top of his head, in waves of heat.

Ramsay said, "That boy is one of the most beautiful women I've seen in my entire time here in London. 'Tis a pity he lacks the one grace I find indispensible."

"Quim?" asked Louis.

"Bosom. I like a nice cushion for my face." He gestured to his chin with a mannered flourish of his fingers in wicked satire of the upper classes, and his accent was for the moment straight from Puritan Parliament. The table roared with laughter.

"Polite little fellow," remarked Matthew. "He didn't even seem studied."

Suzanne agreed. There was a difference between those who studied manners and those who had been born to them, and that boy had appeared utterly natural.

Daniel finally was able to speak. "He might have been a bit more honest about his . . . equipage. That would have been more polite, I think." Then he turned to Suzanne. "And you might have told me."

"I did. As soon as I realized it myself. He was extremely good, wasn't he? I've never seen better, on or off the stage."

Ramsay turned to look after the boy, though he'd quite disappeared into the crowd. "I wonder if he even has his *equipage*, as you say. I saw no hint of a beard. Could be a castrato?"

"No beard yet. If he was over thirteen, I'll eat my hat."

"My hat, you mean."

She laid a hand against the Cavalier's hat on her head. "I suppose you must have eaten the bird already. All that is left is this feather." She flicked the long feather so it flipped up and down like a horse's tail.

That brought another roar of laughter about the table, and the ugly mood was entirely lifted. Daniel could now shrug off his embarrassment, and conversation turned to that evening's performance. The boy tart was tucked away in everyone's minds, to be brought out again for a good laugh on another day.

Suzanne had no idea at that moment that nobody would ever again laugh about that boy.

Chapter Three

The next morning Suzanne attended rehearsal for *Julius Caesar*, playing the role of Calpurnia, Caesar's wife. It was a small role, and suited her for that, for it meant little work. She'd recently played Lady Macbeth and was ready for a rest. Besides, she'd resigned herself to smaller roles these days. The few large roles for women were usually for younger women, and there were still many men to take the meatier roles for older women. Today she wasn't needed in any of the scenes being rehearsed, but sat in a lower gallery to observe the development of the rest of the play. She felt it always went better for the play as a whole if the entire cast paid as much attention as possible to the other scenes if they could. A play was never rehearsed as a whole until its opening, and so the actors were kept busy throughout the morning working on this scene or that, but Suzanne encouraged those who had less to do onstage to pay attention to scenes that didn't involve them. It made for a more cohesive performance when it all was finally strung together as a whole. Sometimes the difference was negligible, but most times it was significant.

Though this play was currently onstage with the Duke's Men on the other side of the river, and The New Globe Players' patent required they not stage any Shakespeare within two weeks of either of the royal troupes, their experience this past year was that the safest play to rehearse was one that was currently on one of the royal stages. By the time The New Globe Players would be ready to put it on themselves, the other troupe will have finished with it, their audience will have been saturated, and the royal troupe would be unlikely to suddenly decide to perform it again at a whim, thereby cutting short a run by The New Globe Players. Too many times the royal troupes had thwarted them by choosing the very play The New Globe Players were readying for the stage at that moment. Following the two royal troupes was always the safest strategy, and since their Southwark audience was a different set of folk entirely, it never mattered to their coffers that the play in question had already played out the nicer neighborhoods.

On the surface of it The New Globe Players appeared at a terrible disadvantage to other theatre troupes, but the truth was quite the opposite. By the timing of Suzanne's request for a patent, and by the fact that her theatre was best suited for an audience disparate from the more fashionable ones who frequented the royal playhouses, with their new-style farces from France and the invention of the thing they called a "proscenium arch," which framed each scene like a picture and allowed for more complex set pieces, her Players were privileged among the commons troupes about town in that they were permitted to perform Shakespeare at all. Lesser troupes than they were limited only to ancient mummeries and the commedia dell'arte plays that predated even Elizabeth. The Globe, built by Shakespeare decades ago, was now the only London theatre dedicated to Shakespeare's work in its purest form, without editing or extempore additions of any kind. The stage, of Elizabethan design, was unsuited to those newer plays being written since the king's return from France.

That Suzanne's Players weren't permitted to stage those plays mattered little to her troupe, for by their location and by their admission prices, the Globe attracted the lower classes who generally preferred the plays staged in the old style. That and the larger capacity than the other houses, due to the galleries having benches rather than chairs, put The New Globe Players in a rather tidy niche all their own. Suzanne had learned long ago that the trick to successful sub-rosa existence was to always be just barely below the notice of those who might cause her trouble. The Globe happened to be on the right side of the river for that.

Horatio, who had long ago named himself after Hamlet's friend and had never revealed his real name to anyone, rather enjoyed his role of Protector of the Text and didn't mind at all the constraints put on the troupe regarding altering it. He worshipped the work of the bard, and would never change a word. He often exhorted the actors under his direction to do their clowning around and rude invention during rehearsal, for it would not be tolerated during performance before an audience, by the audience, the king, or himself. Were he to allow any noticeable change, and were such behavior to be told around at Whitehall, the Players could lose their patent. Because the king was known to drop in on them incognito, discovery was a real possibility.

Today Horatio watched patiently as Louis, playing Marc

Antony, delivered the central speech of his role with the pommel of his stage dagger pressed to his breeches like a large, silly erection. He strolled about the stage, waggling it and his hips eloquently each time he uttered the words, *"Brutus says he was ambitious."* His deadpan was perfect, and not a twitch of a smile. He finished to enthusiastic applause, and brought the scene to a stop as he accepted the acclaim of his fellows with deep bows and flourishes.

Horatio waited for the hilarity to die, then said, "Very well, Louis. Now let's try it a little less à la commedia. This is, after all, a tragedy."

"It surely is a tragedy."

A few of the troupe chuckled, but Horatio frowned his lack of amusement. "If the quality of today's rehearsal isn't to your liking, Louis, then perhaps you should look to your own performance." Sober silence fell over the actors on the stage. Horatio let it sink in for a long, disgusted moment, then said, "Once again, Louis. *'Friends, Romans,'* et cetera, and so on." He waved a hand to gesture that the work should continue.

As Louis began again, the large audience entrance door at the front of the theatre opened just enough to allow someone inside. Suzanne looked to find Constable Samuel Pepper shoving the thing closed after him. It was heavy, and so he couldn't get it entirely shut by himself. After a couple of attempts, putting his shoulder to it, he gave up and left it ajar. Suzanne left the rehearsal and went to see what it was he wanted. A visit from the constable was never pleasant and never good news. She approached him with a great deal of trepidation in her heart. She met him near the door, out of earshot of the rest of the Players.

"Good morning, Constable." She greeted him with far

more warmth than she felt, and a smile she hoped at least appeared sincere.

Samuel Pepper was a lazy man, who carried far more weight on his short frame than would have been practical for someone much taller. His walk was a rolling trundle, and even a short stroll for him required enough effort to make him red in the face. He didn't sweat so much today as he usually did, for the sun hung behind a thick overcast and the temperature had sunk low in this midwinter season. The heavy, dark wool cloak bundled about him had wicked dampness from the street when it brushed the ground, so an inch or two of wet rimmed its hem. The collar was far too wide, even for a man as wide as himself. All in all, the garment was plainly too large for him. His black hat pointed sharply to the sky, which betrayed it as from Cromwell's time. Even Puritans didn't wear pointed hats anymore. It therefore bore no feather, but neither did it have a buckle. Not even a small one. It struck her as rather feminine, the sort of hat one might find on an old woman. Today his breathing wheezed with congestion, and Suzanne feared to come too close lest he be catching in the winter cold. Breathing ailments held a particular horror for singers and actors, who, even if they survived the illness, could not work without a voice while recovering.

"Good morning, Mistress Thornton," Pepper greeted with a smile that struck her as even more forced than usual. He was certainly not happy to be there and more than likely wished to be back at his office, imbibing the French brandy he kept there for his morning company. Probably he would have liked the brandy to dull the illness she now saw in his eyes and heard in his voice. Whatever had brought him there that morning surely must be important, for him to have given up his brandy on such a day.

"What can I do for you, Constable? I hope you're feeling well enough to be out and about in this cold."

He coughed to demonstrate just how sick he really was, and said, "I come to ask a favor."

A favor? And he was admitting it? His errand must be even more serious than she'd thought. But a weight lifted from her heart, for she realized he must not be there to arrest anyone. He was the one who needed something from her this time, and that put her at an advantage. "What might I do for you?" She cared very little about helping Pepper, but it was always good to be on the right side of the law in a neighborhood where on any given day most folks were guilty of one minor thing or another. More than once she'd had to talk him out of taking away someone she cared about, and had not always succeeded.

"I . . ." He paused for a long, painful coughing fit. Suzanne stepped back as he bent and hawked phlegm onto the stones at her feet. Then he straightened, dabbed his wet lips with a handkerchief, and continued, "Mistress Thornton, I am here about your boy."

"Piers?" Panic rose in her chest and she placed a palm over her heart as if to hold it in place. "What has happened to my son?" Piers lived in some rooms in the neighborhood, but she hadn't seen him since yesterday and so couldn't be certain he was all right.

Pepper's eyes narrowed in puzzlement for a moment, then it cleared as he remembered Piers. "No, my dear woman. Nothing like that. Not your son, but your other boy. This lad is one of your Players."

"Christian?" Other boys came and went in the troupe, as

they were needed for small and female roles, but since most theatre troupes were beginning to cast real women to play the roles of women, the demand for adolescent boys was declining. The Players had only Christian living on the premises who could be termed a "boy." He was ten last October. She turned toward the stage to look, and there he was, looking at her to see what she wanted. She asked Pepper, "What do you want with Christian?"

Pepper squinted at the boy on the stage, puzzled once more. "That is your boy actor?"

"It is."

"He's the only one in your group?"

"Currently, yes." She gestured to Christian that he should never mind, and should return to the rehearsal. The boy complied, and once again attended to Horatio.

Pepper thought for a moment, then said, "It appears I've made a mistake. It also appears I do need your help even more than I'd thought." He seemed deeply disconcerted by this unexpected development, whatever it was.

"Perhaps if you told me the story from the beginning."

He nodded, and frowned as he thought for another moment. Then he began, "There was found this morning a body floating in the river."

Suzanne's interest piqued, and so did her sense of alarm. "In the river, you say?"

The constable nodded. "Indeed. Not far from here."

"Who is it?"

"I couldn't say. Though I thought I knew." He glanced over at Christian again. "I find I was mistaken." Pepper returned his attention fully to Suzanne and continued, "He was found caught among some flotsam near one of the water-wheels in an arch at the south end of the bridge." He gestured in the general direction of the bridge, which was the only route across the Thames in the city except by ferry.

"Did he fall from the mill above?" This certainly wasn't the first body ever to be pulled from the river near that bridge. People jumped, were pushed, or fell accidentally with appalling regularity. The hundreds of shops and households ranged along the sides of the road crossing the bridge all had windows looking out over the river, and the bridge was one of the most crowded streets in London. The waterwheel that turned the mill at the south end of the bridge had claimed many victims over the years.

Pepper shrugged. "Hard to tell, I vow. Not from the street, I think, the way the structures are situated on that side of it. A fall from a window, perhaps, but by the way he was stuck in the current against the pier I should have thought he'd come from farther upstream."

"Bank Side, then?"

A doubtful nod, and a shrug in reply. Pepper appeared at a loss, but Suzanne had a sense she wasn't being told everything. She asked, "What brings you to me today?"

"As I said, I thought he was one of your actors."

"What made you think that?"

"He looks a mite like your boy, Christian." He nodded in the direction of the stage. "I remember interviewing him last summer."

"But even though your dead body is not our Christian, and you plainly don't know its identity, you still think I can help you with this investigation. What makes me so likely?"

"He must be an actor."

"You don't know his name, or anything else about him. You now know he's not our boy; how can you still think he's an actor?"

"It's true. Apparently I've never seen him before, and there is no telling what his name is, nor from whence he came. But his attire told me he must be an actor in a play somewhere, and your theatre is the closest playhouse to where the body was found."

Impatience rose, and Suzanne wished the constable would simply spit it all out for her. "What attire? Why must you be so circumspect?"

The constable blinked some, and for the first time since she'd known him he seemed unsure of his words. "Well, Mistress Thornton, my sensibilities were quite shaken when I saw what I never expected to see in my lifetime. I cannot compass the meaning of it, and can only hope he belongs to another troupe of actors. For either he's an actor, or else he's a . . . well . . ."

She sighed. "A sodomite? Is he wearing a woman's frock, then?"

Pepper nodded.

Suzanne gazed at him for a moment, wondering how a man executing his office could be so tender about that subject. Unseemly as it was, it couldn't possibly be something he'd never encountered before. Pepper was lazy and avoided work, but Suzanne had always assumed he was capable of accomplishing that work. Now she doubted it. Finally she said, "Well, Constable, I assure you there are hundreds of men in London who enjoy wearing dresses, and a surprising few of them are actors. Particularly our Christian, who would not be found dead in one, literally or otherwise, except onstage where it is understood he is playing a role that does not necessarily reflect his own personality. So I assure you your corpse is not one of ours. We are missing nobody today. Is that information all you came for?"

Pepper drew a deep, thoughtful breath as he struggled with the decision of what to say next. He said, "I wonder, Mistress Thornton, whether you would care to come look at this corpse?"

"Look at it? What for?"

"You see, the poor fellow did not drown, nor was he killed by the waterwheel. He was stabbed in the throat."

"Murdered?"

Pepper nodded. "I'll need far more information than I have available to me in order to find his killer."

Suzanne weighed her next words more carefully than usual, for the first ones that came to mind were quite sharp and therefore ill-advised. She said, "Not to put too fine a point on it, Constable, but you must admit that a desire to learn the truth has never caused you so very much trouble in the past."

"True, Mistress Thornton. Ordinarily this corpse would have been buried without much to-do and forgotten, but I'm afraid your late successes in discovering the perpetrators of such murders have created an expectation in the crown that is more than I can live up to."

A smile tickled the corners of Suzanne's mouth, for she knew well the cases he meant. "Indeed? The murders I've solved for you have got the king thinking you can solve them yourself?"

He nodded. "I'm afraid I've been told that I'm to find this boy's murderer, since I appear to be the only man in all of London so very talented at this sort of deduction."

Suzanne's smile grew to a full-fledged grin. "Well, Constable, I imagine that puts you at a singular disadvantage regarding your office."

"The magistrate has full confidence in me. It is a two-edged sword."

"Misplaced as that confidence is."

That stung Pepper, and he blinked. "I do my best."

He didn't, but Suzanne wasn't going to argue that point. "The question is, will you succeed?"

"I have full confidence in you."

"I haven't agreed to help. What do you offer in the way of compensation?"

"The knowledge that justice is done?" His tone was hopeful, and betrayed his understanding that she knew justice was a fantasy and she would want more for her trouble.

"There is no such thing as justice this side of heaven."

Pepper nodded the truth of that, and his voice took on the strident tone of one playing a trump card. "Then perhaps you would consider that I have the power to keep the assorted thieves and cutthroats attached to your troupe safe from arrest?"

Alarm skittered up her back. This was skating into a risky subject. She was ever forced to not look very closely at the character of the actors in her troupe, and tended to look the other way on most things so long as nobody stole or fought while on the premises. "You would commit malfeasance?" They both knew he did so every day, but this argument was all she had at her disposal.

He shrugged. "To a point. There may be some instances where circumstances could be interpreted in your favor." Suzanne waited for the rest of his explanation, and then the other shoe dropped. "But remember, by the same token they might otherwise be taken as not in your favor."

"That sounds very much like a threat." Trepidation weakened her voice, and she coughed to clear her throat.

"Not at all. 'Tis nothing more than an arrangement of mutual respect and support. One hand washes the other, you understand. I would be predisposed to be lenient with those associated with someone I respect."

"And need."

"Also that." There was no shame in him. This was a simple agreement and nothing more.

She considered his words, and understood that were she to refuse the alliance there would certainly follow a flurry of retaliatory arrests and other sorts of harassment to demonstrate his power. Pepper could bring her enterprise to a complete halt if he wished, and as self-centered as he was, he would surely make certain she would have to close her doors just to show her he could. Further, he could accomplish it in short enough time that Daniel would be powerless to thwart him. She said, "Very well. I promise nothing, but show me the corpse. Where is it?"

Pepper's relief was palpable, and a wide, small-toothed smile spread across his face. "Excellent! Come with me!" He waved her along to accompany him, and turned toward the front entrance, which still stood ajar.

"This way, Constable." Suzanne gestured toward the rear of the theatre. "You might be aware there's a back entrance to this building. You don't need to shove that enormous entrance door back and forth by yourself."

Pepper looked at the huge audience entrance. "I see." Suzanne gestured for him to follow her, and they went out the back.

The walk wasn't far, from the Globe to the Tooley Stairs just downstream from the bridge. Suzanne had supposed he would take her to a medical or funereal establishment, but it turned out Pepper had not moved the body at all. At the bottom of the stairs near the water's edge lay a mound of muddy blue fabric and stained white lace, surrounded by a cluster of onlookers. Halfway down the stairs Suzanne faltered and came to a halt as she realized what she saw. "Oh," she said.

Pepper stopped a couple of steps farther on, and turned to look up at her. To speak he had to raise his voice over the roar of current rushing through the stone piers that held up the bridge, its roadway, and the tall buildings lining either side of it. "What is it, Mistress Thornton? Do you know him?"

She shook her head and slowly resumed the trek down the steps. Pepper preceded her, glancing back at each step to watch her face. "No, but I saw him last night. He was selling himself at the Goat and Boar."

Pepper reached the bottom of the steps. He paled at her words. "Selling himself? As a girl? Openly?"

She nodded as she carefully circled the waterlogged corpse. It wouldn't do to slip off the side and fall into the rushing water below. The words of the astrologer yesterday echoed in the back of her mind as she spoke to Pepper. "As openly as any girl. He was quite a convincing one, and fooled nearly everyone. It was almost impossible to tell he was a boy."

The corpse lay in an undignified heap, knees splayed and one arm laid over his face as if he were ashamed to be seen. The blonde wig had gone missing, revealing a tangled mass of shoulder-length, nearly black hair. The dress had been rent down the front, and his shift as well, exposing his utterly flat boy's breast. The bones beneath his skin stood out, with so little flesh he seemed nearly skeleton-like. A long, black slit marred his white, almost bluish throat, and other, smaller stab wounds dotted his chest. Many more wounds than it would have taken to kill him. "This is how he was deposited after being pulled from the water?"

"Not intentionally, you understand," said Pepper. "The

corpse is still stiff." He shoved one bent knee with his shoe to demonstrate. The entire body shifted as if carved from a single block of wood. "This is how he lay in the water. Facing downward."

The boy's face wasn't nearly so beautiful this morning as it had been the night before, all the life in it having fled. His rosy cheeks and lips, painted on, were still red, but they were now damaged and indistinct with smudged and smeared color. Eye blacking ran down his face like gray harlequin tears. His pale, nearly translucent skin had a porcelain quality, like a perfectly wrought statue of such fine skill this boy's face might grace the gallery of even the king. A portrait of grief.

The face was no longer graced by the joyful animation she'd seen the night before. The dimples were gone forever. At the Goat and Boar, this boy had possessed a lively expression and an easy smile. He'd been enjoying himself, happy to be in conversation with Daniel, and eager to give him a good time. Perhaps even to have had a good time himself. But now the boy's face was reduced to only its features. Pleasing enough in themselves taken individually, but tragically lacking any spark of life or happiness. The painted red lips no longer pursed, but were slack and slightly agape. The dull and sunken eyes saw nothing, filled with river water that resembled tears about to fall. He looked as if he might draw a breath and emit a sob.

Then she saw there was something in his mouth. Something white showed between his front teeth. She stepped closer to look, but there was no telling what was inside there.

"Constable," she said, and pointed. "Be so good as to remove whatever is in his mouth."

Pepper took a step backward, as if resisting a shove toward a distasteful task. "I beg your pardon?"

"There's something in the boy's mouth. Take it out so we can tell what it is."

"Touch him, you mean?" Pepper's hand retreated into his cloak, lest it somehow be forced to do Suzanne's bidding.

Suzanne wasn't about to touch the body herself. Though she didn't particularly fear her own death, she was terrified of the ghosts of those who had gone before her. Touching a dead body was sure to bring bad luck at least, if not a true haunting of a disturbed spirit. And she knew this boy's spirit was a strong one. "Of course, touch him. Take that white object from his mouth. Surely you don't expect me to do it."

A woman standing nearby heaved a great, impatient sigh, reached over, and dug her fingers between the boy's teeth. She yanked out something soft and white that had some blue bits and black spots of blood. When she saw what it was, even she dropped the thing and stepped back, wiping her hand on her skirt.

The object now lying on the boy's chest was a severed willie.

Chapter Four

"Oh!" Suzanne turned away, as did nearly everyone watching. She pressed a palm to her mouth, and gasped for breath as tears of shock and grief stung her eyes. "Oh, that poor boy!"

When she could look again, she saw how small it was. Shriveled and bluish white, there wasn't very much to it at all. It hardly even looked like what it was, but nothing more than a pale, purplish knob on a bit of wrinkled skin.

"Do you suppose it's his?" asked Pepper. He reached down and with two dainty fingers lifted the hem of the blue dress. Suzanne looked just long enough to glimpse the red-black patch between the boy's legs where the appendage should have been. She turned away, and Pepper dropped the skirt.

Those watching were silent for a long moment, shocked. Suzanne drew deep breaths to hold down her gorge. Then she straightened and smoothed her cloak to regain her dignity, and put her mind back on the proper course to learn this boy's killer. She asked Pepper, "Where, exactly, was he found?"

"Does it matter?"

"I don't know yet whether it matters, and can't assess the importance of it until I know. Where was he?"

Pepper pointed upstream to the waterwheel slowly turning in the current by the southern bank. This one turned a stone in a mill directly above. The wheel at the northern bank drove a water pump.

Suzanne looked at where the water rushed between the stone piers set in the river on starlings, shoved the wheel, then eddied and surged onward toward the open river. The space was close enough to catch many bits of flotsam in the water. Most of it stayed for a while, then eventually was dislodged or rotted away and carried off down the river to the sea. Branches from well upriver were caught and clung to each other, and in turn caught other items such as discarded rags, broken furniture, and anything else that would float. She said, "The boy was lodged amongst all that rubbish along the bank?"

Pepper nodded.

Suzanne looked down at the body again, then her gaze took in the gawkers standing around. "Who discovered him?"

The onlookers glanced around at each other, and a woman stepped forward. "'Twas myself, my lady." She curtsied, and that felt strange to Suzanne. Most people could tell her rank, and she was certainly no lady.

But she maintained her dignity and said, "My name is Mistress Thornton. What is yours?"

The woman was now able to look her in the face and said, "My name be Weaver, mistress." She was rail thin and ragged enough for a street dweller. Though her face and hands had been washed recently, the dirt began at her wrists and disappeared into the sleeves of her filthy dress. At one time this dress had been a fine gown, but by the cut of it Suzanne could tell that had been decades before. Now the thing was reduced to a threadbare and baggy drape that had faded to a dull pinkish from what might have once been rich crimson. Raw, hemless edges at neck and wrists suggested lace had been removed from the dress and sold. Probably long before it came into the Weaver woman's hands.

She said, "I were down here a-washin', and I seen this here boy all shoved up under the bridge. They's lots of things that gets hung up down here, and at first I thought it were only a dress someone had lost or thrown in. That's an awfully pretty dress, sez me, and I thought I could get it and keep it or sell it. But when I seen its owner was still a-wearin' it, I hurried straightaway to find the authorities." She nodded in the direction of the constable.

Suzanne nodded. "Who brought the boy from the water?"

Two men behind the constable raised their hands. One of them, with an oar in his hand, said, "When this woman came screaming bloody murder up to the church, St. Olave over here"—he nodded toward the spot just downstream from the stairs, where the tops of graveyard monuments could be seen in the churchyard—"we got our boat and went for a look-see. He were dead, all right. Couldn't hardly get him over the side, as stiff as he were. His legs was all awkward-like, and that dress all filled with water. We nearly tipped over the boat and drowned ourselves in the current."

"When you pulled him from the water, did you tear the front of his dress? Be honest. I don't care whether you did; I only need to know what happened to the boy."

The boatman shook his head. "No, the dress was like that when we turned him over." He hurried to add, as if he thought he would be accused of the murder, "And the cut in his throat as well. That were there before we got here."

Suzanne nodded. "I am sure you didn't cut a dead boy's throat."

The boatman and his partner seemed relieved to be off that particular hook.

Mistress Weaver said, "Do you think he'll be needing that there dress anymore?"

Suzanne was inclined to tell her she was out of luck, and saw Pepper was about to say something ugly to that effect, so she said quickly to cut him short, "Wait a week, then come to the constable's office and perhaps the dress can be yours. A reward for your diligence in summoning the constable so quickly."

The boatman said, "And how about us, for pulling the body out of the water as we did?"

Disgust rose. Suzanne replied, "You've a use for a torn dress? Or the shift? Perhaps we should save the willie for you?"

He fell silent, embarrassed.

Pepper said, "I thank you for your assistance, good man. You've done your duty as a Christian toward this unfortunate child."

The boatmen both nodded, but nevertheless were plainly disappointed.

Suzanne addressed the others standing around. "Did anyone here see anything else? Did anyone see the boy when he was alive?" She knew there was a public room full of men and whores who had seen him alive the night before, including herself. She was going to have to get names from Young

Dent and search down anyone who might know something. The crowd here on the quay knew nothing, and shook their heads. These were all more or less honest day dwellers, who rose with the sun and did their sleeping at night. It was the night folk who might have witnessed this murder, and they were the ones who would be the most reluctant to provide information even if they had it.

She gazed at the bridge starlings once more, and the water rushing between them, and in her mind's eye saw how the body had floated between them on the current. Perhaps it had gone beneath the waterwheel to be shot out the other side and caught in an eddy by the bank. The body might have fallen from the bridge. She looked upriver, at the stone banks of Bank Side that disappeared around a bend to the west. The body could have come from anywhere along there, or could have entered the water from any of the four stairs between it and the bridge. The victim may even have been killed on the other side of the river, a bank dotted with wharves, but she felt it unlikely. Had he entered the water from the north bank, the current would most likely have also deposited him on that side. Since the boy had been seen in Southwark that night, she felt strongly he must have entered the water there. That, at least, defined the area she was most likely to find witnesses. She would be able to concentrate her questioning on this section of Southwark, and wouldn't have to go far afield unless she found nothing here.

"Well, Constable," she said, "I suppose we need to find a wagon in which to transport this poor fellow."

Pepper looked at the stairs leading upward to the alley that came to the river from Tooley Street, and sighed.

Later that day, once a wagon had been found to move the murdered boy and the body carried up the stairs by the boatmen, Suzanne and Constable Pepper were able to make a leisurely examination in the back room of a hospital. There several oaken tables stood about, bearing two other unfortunates who had died in the area that day. Each was covered with a stained and worn linen bedsheet, and they made Suzanne take frequent glances from the corner of one eye, lest one of them move. The littlest one, who was either a dwarf or a child, looked as if it must be breathing. How could a child not be breathing? It was too terrible to contemplate, so her eyes insisted they saw the tiny chest rise and fall.

A box filled with assorted medical tools sat on the table where the murdered boy lay. Pepper investigated the contents, and began laying out little knives, a thing that looked like a pair of tongs, a small hammer, an extremely sharp chisel . . . and some other things she couldn't even guess at.

The heavy, carved door at one end of the room stuttered open in its ill-fitting frame and in came Marcus White, the coroner. The man was tall, skeletally thin, and he walked with a long, lurching stride that quickly ate the space between the door and the table where Pepper and Suzanne stood. He dressed more richly than was appropriate for his station, and he barely glanced at the two living persons in the room. His attention was riveted on the boy, whose legs still splayed indecently and whose arm lay over his forehead. Out of the water and nearly dried, he almost appeared as if he were even at that moment under attack, and struggling to save himself.

White took one of the victim's knees in hand and tried to straighten it, but the corpse was still as stiff as when it had been found. He grunted, then tried an arm with the same results. He said, with utter certainty, "He's not been dead more than half a day or so."

Suzanne said, "I saw him alive yesterday evening."

White looked at her as if just discovering she was in the room. "Do tell. You knew him?"

"I only saw him last night. It was before midnight, but he was stiff like this when he was found this morning."

"Then certainly he was murdered near midnight or within one or two hours of it, which is what I said." His voice carried an edge of insult, as if she'd questioned his expertise.

She opened her mouth to explain she'd only meant to affirm what he'd said, but thought better of saying anything more on it. Instead she said, "Was the dress torn before or after the stabbing?"

The coroner gazed at the dress front, and picked at it to assess the stains on it. He lifted and arranged the blue fabric and its lace, and laid it against the boy's pale chest. "The stabbing came after the tearing, I think. There are knife marks in the dress, but none of them align with these wounds when the dress is put back together. See?" He lifted the torn bodice to show that the holes were not over the wounds. "The dress front was hanging over here instead." He demonstrated how the fabric was dangling to the side, and the two holes matched perfectly with the one stab wound low in the chest. "The cloth was folded back onto itself, when this wound was made."

Suzanne now imagined a struggle in which the dress was torn then a knife came into use. The sequence didn't make much sense, so she knew she was missing something. She would have to think hard on it.

White took hold of the front of the dress and yanked to tear it off, but Suzanne held out a hand to stop him. "Wait. Can we keep this as whole as possible?"

The coroner gave her a puzzled look. She noted he was

not generous with words, and answered his unasked question. "Not for me. It's been years since I would be seen wearing a torn dress taken from a dead boy. However, you're going to throw it away, aren't you? It's of no use to you. I've promised it to someone."

"Ah." He nodded, and began pulling the dress from the corpse without tearing it. The procedure took a bit longer, particularly with the joints still stiff, but when the garment was off Suzanne gathered it into a bundle and set it aside for the Weaver woman.

The boy, seen naked, seemed even younger than she'd thought at first. The male bits still attached were very small and entirely hairless. The chest was also hairless, but the most telling was that he had no hair under his arms. "Not yet at sexual maturity," said White, as if musing to himself.

"Not ever," murmured Suzanne.

The coroner picked up the tiny knob of flesh that had been in the child's mouth, and peered closely at it. Then he set it next to the spot from whence it had come, making certain the thing belonged there. It fit. Then he looked at it again.

"Cut, not bitten. Sharp knife."

Suzanne shuddered at the thought of biting such a thing entirely off. There had been times in her dark past when she'd wanted to do that to a client who had hurt or angered her, but she'd never done it and couldn't imagine doing it to a boy this age. She said, "Can you tell whether he was already dead when it happened?"

The coroner threw her an appalled look, horrified she could think of such a thing. She said, "If I'm to reconstruct what happened in order to learn who did this, I must know everything that happened and in what order. Then I might know why it was done, which will give me a better chance at knowing who did it."

White leaned over the body to peer at the wounded crotch and said, "He was dead. No stray cuts that would have been inevitable in a struggle."

"Could he have been tied up?"

White looked the body over, then replied, "No. There are no marks from a rope of any kind." He walked around the table to have a look at the boy's hands, which were still frozen at head height. "No cuts here. The removal of his appendage was neat and tidy, and accomplished with a leisure of time. Surely he must have been dead, or at least insensate."

The relief at that news surprised Suzanne. It seemed she was becoming too involved in this and taking it too personally. She shook herself out a bit and took another deep breath. "He wasn't drowned."

"Plainly. I don't even need to look inside his chest to know that."

She noted, "He had no linens beneath the dress."

White shrugged. "Not terribly rare. A goodly number of corpses come to me half clad. Sometimes the drawers are stolen by the discoverer of the body, sometimes by the murderer, sometimes they were never there to begin with. Particularly women come without them, for when they're murdered they're nearly always violated first. Or later, and not necessarily by the killer."

Suzanne blanched, but pressed on. "And you can tell the difference between violation before or after?" She told herself she shouldn't be surprised. She'd heard often enough about men poking holes in pumpkins and melons; she knew a dead body was not safe around many a man who thought nobody would find out.

"Usually. Hard to say, but there's a different sort of damage as happens when a body is still alive and can . . . well, bleed."

Suzanne nodded. A hollowness in her belly and a lightness in her head made her wish for someplace to sit, but there was none. She continued in spite of it. "Can you tell whether this boy was violated in that way?"

Both White and Pepper stared blankly and blinked at her for a moment. Pepper said, "You can't possibly be serious."

"The boy was selling himself. He may very well have been raped by the man who killed him. Someone who simply didn't wish to pay him for his services."

"If he was selling himself as you say, then rape would be impossible. A tart cannot be raped, and that applies to a male harlot. Especially it should apply to a male selling himself as a girl."

Suzanne couldn't miss the unmistakable implication that wanting to be female was a disgusting thing. Rage warmed her cheeks, and she struggled to hold her temper. "Can we look regardless?"

"You wish to violate him again?"

"I wish to learn the truth. Whatever we find may turn out to be significant within the context of whatever else we may find. I must know everything knowable. If you please, turn him over and have a look."

"I've been the coroner here in Southwark for a very long time—"

"Please look."

White emitted a snort of impatience, then proceeded with the examination. It took little effort to turn the small corpse on its front, which raised the boy's behind off the table in its slightly bent and stiff configuration. He pressed aside the buttocks to peer between them, which took some effort with the muscles so stiff. He grunted at what he saw.

"I see nothing. No suggestion of any recent activity here."

"How recent do you mean?"

He shrugged. "Honestly, I wouldn't know. This isn't the sort of examination that is the usual for me. However, I see no residue, and no bleeding. I suppose he may have been used that way in the past, but I feel certain not last night."

Suzanne knew it was entirely possible—perhaps even likely—the boy had only ever used his mouth to service clients, and that told her something about why he had not been open to Daniel about his true sex. "Thank you, Marcus. Now we know something about the killer we wouldn't have known had you not looked."

"What do we know now?"

"Why, that the killer was not necessarily a sodomite, of course."

By the time Suzanne returned to the theatre, she'd missed all of the rehearsal of *Julius Caesar*. In the dressing room as she painted herself for her role as Olivia in *Twelfth Night*, the sense of pressure and lack of preparation to go onstage made her think hard about what she was attempting in helping Constable Pepper, and whether she could accomplish it. It annoyed her that he expected her to do his work for him, and the more she thought about it, the more annoyed she became. She was afraid that if he kept this up she wouldn't be able to continue performing, in order to make Pepper happy and keep him from harassing the Players.

The performance that night confirmed her fear. All through it she found herself distracted, not concentrating on her lines and her character. Her very mouth didn't seem to want to form even the simplest words, and she fumbled so many of her lines she could hear tension in Liza's voice as the young girl struggled to cope. Liza herself had a perfect memory and never had to put forth any effort to remember lines, and thought everyone should be able to do it. She was unable to understand those who weren't similarly talented. Every aspect of her character was printed indelibly on her mind, and her every performance was utterly smooth and flawless. But she had a temper, and as they all came offstage at the end of that night's performance, it was plain Liza would have had many sharp things to say if Suzanne had not been, in effect, the owner of the troupe and her de facto employer. Liza quickly cleaned her face and left the building with her mouth a hard line. Suzanne watched her go, and fell into deep thought about what she must do.

That evening at the Goat and Boar the crowd was a bit less than it had been the night before. Tonight the only patrons were the one table surrounded by Globe actors, and so they had the entire public room to themselves. Even the tarts had taken the night off and none were in evidence. Suzanne ate a supper of mutton and Irish bread that was not nearly as good as what Sheila would have served at home, but the company here was far more mixed and lively than it could have been in her private apartments. Here in such a public place she enjoyed the presence of Daniel, Ramsay, and her son at once, something that rarely happened in the basement of the Globe, and when it did the room always became entirely too small for comfort.

Suzanne sat back while chewing on a chunk of meat and sipping on a clean glass of Young Dent's most expensive French wine. It happened that today's costliest wine was worth the price. She said, "I must tell Horatio tomorrow we'll need to recast all my roles for at least three weeks. Particularly Olivia and Calpurnia. I'm going to be quite preoccupied with this favor I'm doing for Constable Pepper."

"What favor?" asked Ramsay.

"I've been requested to solve the murder of that boy tart who was in here last night."

Ramsay sat up, surprised. "That boy was murdered?"

Piers said, "What boy?"

Ramsay replied, "There was a wee lad in here last night, looking to sell himself. He thought the earl might have a taste for his wares and would trade some silver for them."

Daniel's expression was sour. "He looked enough like a *wee* girl I might very well have. I still have my doubts he was a boy."

"He was. I saw his willie," said Suzanne.

"You looked?"

"I could hardly miss it. It was severed and stuffed in his own mouth."

A moment of dark, shocked silence fell over the table. Then Ramsay said, "He was exceeding-comely."

Everyone nodded, but nobody spoke further on it.

Suzanne retreated to the issue she'd raised originally. "I won't be able to solve this case for the constable and continue in the plays. Even were I able to spend the time, there is that my mind simply cannot compass both tasks at once."

Daniel said, "Be kind to yourself. Perhaps it would be best to not take on too much."

Ramsay said, "Och, you're bright enough to do both. Don't let anyone suggest you're not capable." He tossed a frown in Daniel's direction, and was ignored.

Suzanne shrugged. "It's not a question of intelligence. It's that I find myself thinking of one when I should be thinking of the other."

Daniel sipped his whisky, then said, "I can't imagine why you feel obligated to that lazy lump of lard and need to solve his cases for him." His look was still sour, and his voice took on an edge of true disgust at the constable.

Piers's eyes narrowed and he supported the sentiment. "I agree. If you leave off one task, it should be the investigation. Let the honorable Constable Pepper do his own bloody work."

"I daresay he's not up to the task himself. If I don't do it, nobody will. Or even can."

"How is it your responsibility to solve the murder of a boy nobody even knows?" Daniel's attitude toward the child who had deceived him seemed a little harsh, and that made Suzanne all the more eager to take on the investigation.

Ramsay remarked, "Surely somebody knew him."

Suzanne said in response to Daniel, "'Tisn't a responsibility. But Pepper has made it clear he would treat all the members of our troupe with utmost respect, should our paths cross for any reason in future."

"He should do that in any case, given my own interest in the Globe, and the king's interest in theatre in general." Daniel had provided the cash needed to buy and restore the neglected building last year. "Pepper should treat you all as if I were standing at your backs."

"Truly, Daniel, we shouldn't overestimate the new status of our actors, even though the king enjoys the plays and the company of the most beautiful of the actresses. Most people don't hold us in high regard. Besides, you know in any situation there are gray areas. There are so many ways to dissemble or deliberately misunderstand. He could do quite a lot of evil, had he a mind to, and by the time you had some-thing to say about it the damage would be done. Better to do this thing and avoid trouble at the outset. Besides, I want to do it. I feel rather sorry for the poor boy; he was such a pretty child, and so full of life. Now all that's gone, and a beautiful soul has been taken from the earth."

"You don't know anything about his soul."

"He made me smile. Even for those few moments he stood by this table, he brightened the room." She graced Daniel with such a sunny smile it warmed herself, and added, "So I believe we will recast my roles so I can focus my energies on finding his killer."

ALTHOUGH more and more women were taking roles onstage these days, and some women had been doing so incognito for years, it was still technically illegal for women to act on the stage. The law yet insisted that women not be allowed to perform in public, and an experienced actress was hard to find, so Horatio hired a man to fill Suzanne's shoes for the time being. Daniel insisted the king would soon decree women should be allowed onstage, but Charles hadn't yet done so and Suzanne preferred to be circumspect about the two women in the troupe who pretended to be men playing women. It often struck Suzanne that in *Twelfth Night* Liza essentially was a woman pretending to be a man playing a woman pretending to be a man. It made her dizzy enough to laugh.

In any case, though actresses had a natural advantage in portraying women, truly skilled ones were rare for lack of experience. There weren't enough women on the stage in London to fill all the female roles in all the playhouses, and so there were still men who played women. Besides, The New Globe Players needed someone who could step into some roles without rehearsal to speak of.

The one hired the next day to replace Suzanne was a veteran actor who never played men, and who had worked for The New Globe Players before, most notably as the nurse in *Romeo and Juliet* last fall. Even offstage, dressed as a man, he had an unmistakably effeminate air about him. Suzanne wouldn't have called him actually "feminine," for there was far too much about him that, had he been a woman, would have marked him as "too masculine." His jaw was square and his lips not particularly generous, but the way he stood and moved, the lightness of his voice, his mannerisms and gestures were all an exaggerated parody of the feminine. A little too much of what was meant, and that worked for the stage but not terribly well for society.

His name was Walter, but he went by Little Wally and insisted everyone call him that, or simply "Wal." Everyone in the troupe thought it great fun they now had Big Willie and Little Wally, and to further the irony, Little Wally was the larger. Not by much, but he was an inch or two taller than the tiny, wiry musician.

Watching Wally paint his face for his role as Olivia before the performance of *Twelfth Night* that very night, Suzanne saw he was prim and precise as a French princess, outlining his eyes and making the most of his lips with long practice and an eye for emphasizing his best features and minimizing his lesser ones. He mitigated the squareness of his jaw by using less of the white powder at the sides of his face and rubbing an ever so subtle dab of white paint at the tips of his nose and chin. The effect narrowed his face just slightly, and distracted the eye from the masculine corners of his face.

A tiny bit of rouge above his eyes and some overpainting of his too-thin mouth also helped draw attention from the jaw.

He noticed her watching and gave her a demure smile, then returned to his task. She'd seen men like this before, of course, but they were rare and those who weren't actors never flaunted it. Nobody wanted to be arrested for sodomy, and so most who were naturally effeminate did their best to hide their true natures, whether or not they were actually sods. Wally didn't seem to care what the world thought of him, and so always presented himself as effeminately as he pleased. Suzanne had no idea whether Wally preferred women or men, and knew better than to ask even did she care.

Chapter Five

The hiring of Wally left Suzanne free to set forth on her search of the truth about the unknown boy in the dress. First she went to talk to Young Dent at the Goat and Boar about the night they'd seen the boy there. Unfortunately the proprietor had no memory of any boy in a fine blue dress. He'd been so busy serving his clientele he couldn't remember any of their faces. Neither did he remember ever seeing anyone fitting the description of the boy before that night. He was most apologetic, but simply couldn't remember him.

Next Suzanne made a visit to the astrologer who had warned her away from the river the night of the murder.

The woman had a shop across the river, very near the Royal Exchange. The Exchange was one of Suzanne's favorite places, filled with shops and places to eat and drink, and swarming with people who interested and amused her. The rooms maintained by Mistress La Tournelle were tucked in the corner of a building on the other side of Thread Needle

Street, with an entrance below street level that was hard to find.

The structure was of stone, and to get to the shop one descended half a flight of stairs and followed a short corridor beneath an arch, then around a corner between this building and the next, which was more like a tunnel with the upper floors overhanging. There a door of heavy oak was set into the stone wall, and painted on it in crimson and black was a circle surrounded by astrological sigils. The signs were quite intricately drawn, with significant skill and great detail, somewhat resembling the Celtic knots of the north, but with the grace of a centuries-old illuminated manuscript. They seemed to dance around the circle, entrancing the eye and keeping her for the moment from knocking.

She returned to herself and knocked, and a distant voice from well within bade her enter. She lifted the iron door latch and went inside.

The shop was close and very warm, well lit by a swarm of candles set in assorted sticks and dishes, as well as a good-sized brazier that stood on a large, wooden table. Behind the table piled with glass jars, wooden boxes, and books stacked on one another with pages open or marked with pieces of ribbon or paper stood Mistress La Tournelle. The scarf on her head was no longer present, which left her hair a wild mane of wiry gray, but otherwise she was dressed in the same outfit she'd worn three days before. She greeted Suzanne with a sincere smile and set aside the book she had in her hands.

"Greetings, Mistress Thornton! So good to see you! Come!" She gestured to a chair near the end of the table where the brazier stood. "Come, sit. Let me bring you something to drink. Some wine? Chocolate, perhaps?"

Suzanne adored chocolate drink. It was an expensive

habit, but one she didn't care to break. She noted Mistress La Tournelle's generosity in offering it. "Thank you, I'd like some."

La Tournelle went to the next room for it, talking as she went. "I knew you would come to see me."

Of course she did. She was an astrologer; it was her business to know these things.

The woman continued, "I hope you've avoided the river these past few days."

"As a matter of fact, I did not."

La Tournelle poked her face from the kitchen to read Suzanne's expression, but learned nothing. "You didn't? What happened, then?"

"Your prediction came true. There was a death, and my life has been changed."

The old woman considered that a moment, then returned to the task of setting a pot of chocolate on the hearth to heat. Then she stepped into the doorway again and said, "You're still alive." She sounded surprised.

"I am, indeed. However, someone else is not. A boy was found dead, floating in the river not far from Bank Side, and I have been recruited to investigate the murder. As a result, I've been forced to leave my work as an actress for a time and am now working for the benefit of Constable Pepper of Southwark."

La Tournelle appeared relieved. "Oh, good," she breathed. "Nothing terrible has happened, then."

"I'm certain the dead boy would disagree with that assessment."

The old woman waved away the notion. "To you, I mean. Whenever I report something regarding someone who has not asked, I always have a dreadful feeling I may have caused whatever event follows that person. Some do accuse me of influencing their lives, and I would deny it, but even so I often have doubts in my heart." She pressed her palms to her chest.

Suzanne leaned forward in her chair and said, "Well, mistress, I might point out that I would rather be playing my roles onstage than to be poking around London after a man who would stab a boy, cut off his willie, and stuff it in his mouth."

"The boy didn't drown?" La Tournelle seemed disappointed, and the horror of what Suzanne had just said seemed not to make a mark on her thoughts. She began to wonder whether the woman's empathy were genuine, or manufactured.

"He was murdered, then thrown into the river. They found him at the bank just downstream of the bridge, caught among some flotsam. It was a terrible thing."

"Oh yes. Terrible." The old woman was suddenly reminded that her prediction had been about a soul who had once been living and now was not. She ducked back into the kitchen, and after some clinking of stoneware and clanking of pot, returned with a rough-hewn clay cup emitting steam from the top. "There you are," she said, and shoved aside a stack of books to make room, then set the cup on the table where Suzanne could reach it.

Suzanne picked up the cup to sip from it, and the chocolate was delicious. "This is delightful, Mistress La Tournelle."

"Oh, call me Esmeralda."

"I come as a client."

"Even so."

"Very well, Esmeralda, and you shall call me Suzanne." She raised her cup to the old woman and continued, "You do your own cooking?"

"I prefer it." She settled into a chair nearby. "I'm rather

good at it, and would be hard put to afford to hire someone more skilled than myself."

"Well, I think you tell the truth, judging from this fine chocolate." And also judging from these small, cramped quarters, which spoke to her financial state. She seemed to have a firm and proper idea of priorities regarding money.

Esmeralda nodded her thanks, then folded her hands in her lap and buckled down to business now that pleasantries had been accomplished. "So, Suzanne, what brings you to me as a client today?"

"You've intrigued me by the strange accuracy of your prediction the other day."

"Not so strange, by my lights. And not so terribly accurate in my experience, I'm afraid. I would have sworn the death would have been yours."

Suzanne was a bit nonplussed by the woman's bluntness, but only blinked once and continued. "Nevertheless, it seems to me your story was more about the poor victim than myself."

"We aren't none of us alone on this earth." She raised her hands and gazed upward, to indicate all the earth and the heavens as well. "All is entwined, everything connected to everything and everyone. That is why we can know of things that haven't yet happened, for all was set in the beginning, when there was only the Word." She returned her hands to her lap and graced Suzanne with a beatific smile that seemed utterly genuine. Esmeralda was the most peaceful soul Suzanne could remember ever meeting. She reflected that she might be as serene, had she been able to see the future and lived a life with no ugly surprises.

"I hope you're right, and that in you I might have a thread to lead me to the boy's killer."

The woman's eyes widened, and her eyebrows raised. "You think I know who the murderer is?"

Suzanne shook her head. "No, but you plainly have an insight into this event I do not. I think if we follow it, we might find ourselves heading the right direction."

"We? I must advise you, Suzanne, I have no stake in others' lives. I only see what I see and that is all."

Again Suzanne was struck by lack of empathy, but it occurred to her that Esmeralda's heart was hardened by too much exposure to others' fortunes and misfortunes. She thought it must be terribly wearing to deliver news that could be good or bad, over which she had no control. Too much empathy would certainly make for a sad life. She said brightly, "Then let us learn what there is to learn and see where it takes me. What do you charge for your service?"

Esmeralda nodded, down to business again. "Very well. I'll need half a crown for my fee, if you please." She watched as Suzanne drew the silver coin from the pocket under her dress. The coin disappeared immediately into the old woman's pocket, then she said, "Tell me your birthday, then. And time of birth, if you know it."

"I do, but what importance is it?"

"Oh, my dear!" The old woman rocked back and waved a hand that Suzanne could be so silly. "The hour of your birth can mean the difference between Libra with Virgo rising and Libra with Aries rising! Rising sign is a third of your fate, along with sun and moon. It gives us the houses, and which planets are in them. It tells us so much more than your simple planets. It can make all the difference, and pinpoint terribly important influences. I would always hope for a time of birth, rather than be left with nothing but sun sign. So, tell me your birthday, and where you were born, if you would be so kind. Sometime in October, I think, yes? Early October. Possibly the first week, or even very late September."

Suzanne couldn't help but to blink. "Why, that's quite correct. My birthday is the second of October."

"Ah. Same as King Richard III."

"Oh dear."

"Indeed. So you see the importance of detail and accuracy in a chart. There are far more than a few hundred personalities and destinies. To leave out time of birth would be disastrous."

"It was half past eight in the morning, thereabouts. Just after sunrise." Suzanne hoped Richard had been born late in the evening.

Esmeralda nodded, as if she'd known it all along. "Of course. Scorpio rising; I can see it in your eyes. What year, then?"

"1625."

At this the old woman seemed surprised again. "Truly? You're that old? I would not have guessed."

"Thank you," said Suzanne, not entirely certain it was true, but hoping it was. She watched as Esmeralda rose from her chair and went to a stack of books nearby. She leafed through one for a bit, then when she found what she wanted, she reached for a scrap of paper then went looking for something else. After a busy search she found a quill and a bottle of ink. Then she cleared a bit of the table, drew her chair to the spot, and sat down to work.

On the paper she drew a circle, and sectioned it into twelve pie pieces. Quickly, looking to the book and back, she drew small figures in the circle's pieces and made notations beneath it on the paper. She rose several times in search of other books, then sat to work on her paper. Suzanne sat, ignored, for many minutes, and sipped her chocolate patiently.

Finally Esmeralda rose from her work, took a deep breath, and said, "There we have it!"

"Me in a nutshell?"

"You and your past, present, and future."

Suzanne felt a twinge of discomfort at that. Though she'd not been harmed by the earlier prediction, she had a mild feeling it might be not a very good idea to meddle with fate. Particularly since her situation had been improving so well this past year or so, and she had no desire to rock that particular boat. She said, "What does it tell you?"

Esmeralda drew her chair closer to where Suzanne sat, laid the paper on her knees, and began. "Well, you've Scorpio rising, and so you appear more dangerous than you actually are."

"I'm not dangerous?" Suzanne didn't know whether to be disappointed by that.

"Not so much as you appear." She examined the paper some more, then said, "I see that you're an intelligent woman. Most Libras are."

"King Richard?"

"Intelligence doesn't necessarily mean a good heart. You, I can see, have Venus in Taurus, and that is your ruling planet. 'Tis also the ruling planet of Taurus. You're a lover of love, and yours is a stalwart heart. Virgo moon, so you don't give love or friendship freely, but once given you never take it back. You can be depended upon."

All that touched Suzanne in a carefully hidden spot. The men in her life had been enormous disappointments at the very least. She pressed her palms together between her knees, forced herself to breathe normally, then said, "Go on."

Esmeralda wasn't looking at her, and so didn't see how

this reading was affecting her. She continued, "You've had a struggle, probably in childhood. Close family members have given you difficulty in the past. I see . . . violence."

Suzanne had to shut her eyes, and said nothing.

Esmeralda continued, "Yes, the opposite sex has always been a trial for you. You were—" She looked up, and stopped short. Then said, "I'm sorry. Shall I stop?"

Suzanne said, "Violence, yes." Her father had beaten her often during her childhood, and she hadn't seen him, nor anyone else of her family, since before Piers was born. But that wasn't why she was here. She added, "What of now?"

"You attract other people who are dangerous. The same influences that brought you hurtful people in the past are at work in your life now."

"I should expect to be beaten again?"

The old woman shrugged. "I cannot say, but the risk is there. I can say it may or may not be by those close to you. That is not in the chart."

"How did you know I was beaten by someone close to me?"

Esmeralda had to think over the answer to that question, her palms against the paper in her lap and her eyes cast upward. Then she drew a deep breath, looked over at Suzanne, and said in an utterly straightforward tone, "Who else? You were not raised in Southwark, that is plain. You lived as a middle-class woman, with middle-class manners. The roughness you present as one who manages a troupe of actors—and as an actress yourself—is learned. I didn't need to see your chart to observe that. I must assume that if you lived with violence in your childhood, it was at the hands of someone close. The logical assumption is that it was your father. Am I correct?"

Suzanne had always thought herself a skilled observer of

behavior, but found herself awed by this woman. She didn't wish to answer, for the assessment was quite correct. She shifted in her seat and reached again for her chocolate. Another sip of that soothed her, and she replied, "Yes." That was as much as she would confess, and she said, "Please, continue with the matter at hand. What of the boy?"

"Have we a natal date for him?"

"We haven't even a name for him. I was hoping you might give me some indication as to where to look for that."

"In your chart? That question would be more specific than is truly possible. God hides certain things even from those of us able to read the stars."

In spite of her current frustration, Suzanne thought that might be a very good thing. She said, "Well, then is there an indication of what the influences will be for me during the next month or so? Perhaps that would give me an idea of where to begin my investigation."

Esmeralda nodded once to confirm she understood, then leapt to her feet in search of another book. It happened to be at the top of a nearby stack. Paging through it, she sat back down next to the paper with Suzanne's chart, and quickly came to the page she sought. "Very well, then. We have . . ."—she made a humming noise and muttered to herself—". . . Mercury retrograde . . . no . . . Neptune . . . no . . . riches." She slapped a palm against the page. "Ah. I see you will come into the presence of money. Great wealth. Are you expecting to gain an inheritance or a windfall of any kind?"

Suzanne shook her head, though her heart skipped at the thought of suddenly gaining great wealth.

"Then you will be in the presence of someone else's wealth."

That was nothing particularly noteworthy. She saw Daniel often, and he had more than a few guineas to his name these days. He was an earl, after all, and well aligned with the king. "More than usual?"

"Enormous wealth. Refined folk. Very much more than what you might be accustomed to. Very proper people."

"Proper people would be something new to me, to be sure." During her years as a tart she serviced a great many members of the peerage, and none of them had ever struck her as having any better moral sense than a jackal.

"There you have it. Look to the ruling classes in your quest for the identity of the boy."

"Thank you, Esmeralda. I hope this steers me in the right direction." Suzanne drained the last sip of chocolate from her cup, then rose. The old woman set aside the book and the chart, and rose also.

"Best of luck with all this. Do beware of the violent men."

"Always, I assure you. Good day, mistress."

Once again in Thread Needle Street, Suzanne fell into deep thought about the boy and what Esmeralda had said. Ruling class. Perhaps she was right. The child had certainly been beautiful. Besides comely features, he had an air of sureness about him that bespoke a privileged background. His manners had been smooth. Cultured, not learned. Surely the old woman had been right. Suzanne would need to ask Daniel about this. And wouldn't that be a study in frustration, to get him to help her with a task he didn't want her to do in the first place?

She stopped walking, and looked at where she was, as she realized she hadn't cut across Cornhill Street as she should have to head home. She stood in Bishopsgate Street, where it crossed Thread Needle. A turn to the right would take her in the correct direction, back across the river, and her detour would only have been a slight one, but to the left she realized she was not very far from Dunning's Alley, where she'd grown up. She'd not been there since she'd left at the age of seventeen. It was the only place in London she dared not go, and until today she'd always made great detours to avoid this section of Bishopsgate.

For a long moment she considered her route. South toward the bridge, home. North and not very far, the home she'd fled. She gazed northward along the bustling throughway thronging with pedestrians, carts, sedan chairs, and carriages. The words of the old woman returned to her. Esmeralda had known there was violence in her past. It wasn't an uncommon thing, but nobody else had ever brought it up to her before, because it was so common among the people she knew. Nobody thought it all that noteworthy, and they all got on with their lives, as did she. She'd thought she had forgotten those days, first in the scramble for survival and more recently in the peace that was her new life in the theatre, but now memories swarmed over her like bees. She wanted to run away from those sharp, painful thoughts.

At the same time curiosity leapt into flame from the embers in her heart. It had been twenty years since she'd seen that house or anyone in it. Nobody had ever come looking for her. Nobody had ever tried to speak to her again. She wondered who of them might still be alive. Two older brothers, two younger sisters. Mother. And the father who had never valued her, for being a girl.

Her chest tightened, and she took a step to the north. What if she went there? What would she find? She took another step. Would anyone still be there? Her oldest brother, Benjamin, more than likely. Would Father or Mother still be alive? The more she wondered the more surely her feet moved her toward her old home, and soon she was walking as if she'd meant to go there all along.

Dunning's Alley was more of a close than an alley. The narrow street led from Bishopsgate Street, back in among a row of narrow houses that, like most other houses built in the past two centuries, leaned out over the street for the sake of gaining space inside. A fairly good-sized close lay at the other end of the street, where four houses stood around a square in which a single tree grew. It was an oak, and hadn't changed terribly much in the past twenty years. Perhaps a little taller, but it had been tall all her life. One torn limb stuck out, ragged, over the paved close. It looked like it had come off a few years before, and its raw end was dark and rotting.

Her father's house stood on the north side of the close. Its door was blue now, rather than the brown it had been before, and may have been freshly painted. Or perhaps she just saw it that way since she'd expected the tired, old brown shade and the blue was far brighter. All in all, the place seemed cheerier than she remembered. There was a sharp twinge of envy, which she couldn't explain. Envy for a house? She'd hated it as a child. This was a place where pain was an everyday thing, where nobody spoke unless spoken to, as if Father were the king in his domain. Nobody in the house, not even Benjamin, wanted to attract his attention, for it was never good.

Many women lived that way, but Suzanne knew not all, and she also knew it was not how she had ever wanted to exist. When she was old enough to understand that certain people did not have to fear being beaten, when Daniel had shown her that another sort of life was possible, she had determined for herself that she would get away from that man who had made her hate herself as much as he hated her.

She looked up at the windows, which were shuttered against the winter cold though there was little wind here in the close. She could remember playing under this tree as a child. Never climbing it, though she would have liked to follow her brothers up it and see the world from high in its branches. She thought they could see all of London from up there. Little girls weren't supposed to climb trees, and she was told if she did so she would never find a husband. It was so terribly important to her father that she find a husband! All her life, everything she was taught or allowed was aimed at securing a husband and freeing her father from the burden of her upkeep.

The peek hole in the blue front door opened for a moment, then closed. The door then opened and a woman stepped into the frame to look out. "May I help you?"

Suzanne shook her head, then looked toward the alley exit, ready to flee rather than answer questions, but she hesitated. Nothing ventured, nothing gained. She turned to the woman and replied, "I'm sorry to bother you, but I am looking for a family named Thornton."

The woman was young, perhaps a few years older than Piers, but not many. Her attire was plain brown without adornment, and that identified her as Puritan, or at least leaning in that direction. She said, "My father bought this house from Master Thornton nigh on ten years ago."

"Jonathan Thornton?"

A shrug. "I truly cannot say."

"An old man, or a younger one?" Suzanne wanted to know whether her father was still alive, or if the house had been bought from her brother.

Again, however, the young woman held up her palms. "I'm at a loss to help you, mistress. 'Twas nearly a decade ago, when I was only a girl, and I never saw those who lived here before. My father has since passed, and now I live here with my younger brother." She was quick to add, "I'll be married within the month." Lest Suzanne think she was a spinster.

"I see." Suzanne couldn't tell why the lack of information disappointed her, except that it had been a hard decision to come here at all and now she had nothing to show for her effort.

"I can tell you he was a married man. Beyond that, I know nothing."

Suzanne nodded her thanks, though the information told her nothing. Benjamin hadn't been married when she left, but he could very well have been by the time the house was sold. And even had her father been alive to sell the house himself, it had been so long since then that he wasn't necessarily still walking the earth. So she knew little more than she had before she came, beyond that her family had gone.

"Again, my apologies for the intrusion. I thank you for your help, and I wish you a good day."

"God bless you, mistress. I hope you find what you seek."

That took Suzanne aback somewhat. The kindness in the woman's eyes spoke of a sympathy that was alien to Suzanne and not entirely appropriate to this encounter. As if the woman knew something she wasn't telling. She said, "Thank you. Do you know what I seek?"

She shook her head. "You appear as if you've lost something very important to you."

Sudden, irrational tears rose, and Suzanne swallowed them. What she'd come for couldn't be so important. Letting it become important to her would be a disaster to the peace she'd found in her son and the life she'd carved for them both during the past two decades. She forced a smile. "Not so important, I think. But thank you for your help." With that, she turned and headed quickly for the alley, lest the woman try to speak of it further.

Chapter Six

Suzanne didn't relish the conversation she now needed to have with Daniel. He was her only connection to things upper-class, and though she'd once met the king, it had been through Daniel, and Charles was unlikely to remember her face even less than a year later. Daniel was her best hope to follow Esmeralda's suggestion, but he was certain to balk at doing so. She decided to take a more conventional route to real evidence first.

It was possible the boy had been thrown from somewhere on the south end of the bridge, near the mill. If so, there was a good chance someone had seen it happen. She went there in hopes of finding someone who had seen something.

This process, surely, must be why Constable Pepper disliked his job so much. Though the law required that witnesses to crime step forward to give testimony and sometimes even apprehend the offender, and though most of London was populated by folks who thought it great fun to involve themselves and tell what they'd seen and heard, there were some crimes and criminals that struck fear in the heart of the average Londoner. Southwark was not like Whitefriars, where authorities feared to tread and nobody ever witnessed a crime. Folks in Southwark were as law-abiding as anyone could be living among the lower and working classes. But it was understood that one respected the privacy of one's immediate neighbors, particularly if they qualified as friends, and one did well to fear anyone who would commit a murder.

At the bridge, Suzanne paused beneath the Southwark gatehouse and looked up at the heads on pikes above. There were a few belonging to those who had been recently executed for the murder of Charles I, in various stages of rot. One or two were nearly skulls, and showed grinning teeth, appearing utterly unrepentant and even a little arrogant in curled, decayed lip. One had tilted back on its spike and gazed sightlessly at heaven, and another had slumped forward, staring hard at the street as if judging each Londoner who passed beneath. Most of Southwark was unconcerned about the details of crown politics, and so Suzanne wasn't sure exactly who these had been, but she figured they deserved what they'd received. In her opinion, regicide was an even worse crime than homicide, for it struck to the very heart of law and order. Killing a human being was terrible enough, but murdering the king brought war, disorder, and destruction to the entire kingdom. Furthermore, that particular war had taken Daniel from her. Her personal loss during the exile of the crown and the King's Cavaliers was incalculable.

Suzanne proceeded onto the bridge and began looking about, assessing the people she saw and examining the layout of the buildings at the southern end to find a spot where the scenario of murder might have been played out.

The jumble of houses and shops lining the roadway was as disorganized as was the rest of London. Some of these buildings had been here since the end of the twelfth century, and like the rest of London they tended to reach out over the street farther with each successive storey upward. Since the nature of any bridge is that it is a throughway, a stream of traffic moved continuously amongst the buildings in both directions. Some vendors cried their wares, but the percentage of those who stopped to buy were fewer than elsewhere. Suzanne approached the side of the bridge to locate the mill, for that was where the archway through which the body had floated was located.

The mill didn't seem much like one, since its wheel was well below the roadway and out of sight. The building appeared just as any other, and to know it was at work grinding wheat and barley corn into flour one had to go inside to find the turning stone. It wasn't until Suzanne did so that she could hear the mechanism, for the commerce, the traffic, and the current of rushing water in the river below quite drowned it out. Workmen in plain linen aprons hurried about their jobs, their hair, clothing, and every exposed part of them heavily dusted with flour and crusted with dirt and chaff. Suzanne wondered why they bothered with the aprons.

A woman behind a table near the front filled small orders, took money, and made change. More than likely she was the proprietor's wife, and by her air of authority Suzanne guessed she might be the one who truly ran the business, while her husband operated the millstone. The master would be deeper inside the workings of the place, supervising the grinding and bagging, and putting together the larger orders for transport to great houses, and smaller towns in the countryside. He would have less time than his wife, and possibly insufficient business experience to attend to the more delicate matters of dealing with the public.

Suzanne approached the proprietor's wife, who greeted her with a wide, sunny smile and said, "Good day to ye, mistress!"

"Good day to you as well."

"How much flour can I get for ye?" She absently swiped and slapped her clothing, as if suddenly aware she was covered in white powder. Everyone and everything here had a thick or thin dusting of it, and her apron was covered with dry flour as well as damp smears.

"I'm afraid I haven't come for flour today." Nor any day, for Sheila did all the cooking and procuring. It had been years since Suzanne had not had a cook, and even before that she'd also had no kitchen and bought most of her food prepared by street vendors. "I come to ask about a murder that happened near here three days ago."

"Which murder? There's been three nearby of late." She spoke with confidence, as if she knew everything about all of them and only needed clarification so she could sort them out.

"A boy in a blue dress."

The woman nodded in a *say no more* fashion. "Oh yes. That one. Everyone's talking about the boy who drowned."

Suzanne's heart fell. Plainly this woman didn't have the facts, and might tell her anything to appear in the know. But she pressed onward, in hopes of gleaning a tidbit that might shed light. "What do you know about him?"

"Oh yes, everything, I vow. We get the gossip in here,

and so there's nothing I can't tell you about what happened. They found him just below the bridge, don't you know. Caught up in the flotsams at the bank, he was. Floating facedown, they say. Wearing a dress prettier than mine." She gestured to the flour-permeated linen work dress she wore, and her smile widened at her own jest.

"He drowned, you say?"

"He certainly did. They say he drowned when he fell over the side up thataway." She now gestured toward the upstream side of the bridge. "He was pushed, they tell me. Right over the side, then *kerplunk*, straight into the water. Died instantly, they say."

"I thought you said he drowned."

"Right. He drowned instantly."

Even had she not seen the stab wounds on the victim, Suzanne would not have thought it likely he'd simply been pushed over the side like that, and nobody drowns "instantly." The few spots where throwing him over might have been possible had a wall high enough to make it difficult to shove an unconscious body into the river, and never mind tossing a kicking, screaming boy over it. "Who told you this?"

"Everybody knows it. 'Tis all over."

Suzanne wished she could eradicate all information from the earth that was "common knowledge." She replied, "So it was some patrons who came in here and told you this?"

The woman nodded.

"Do you know of anyone who saw it happen?"

She thought that over for a moment, then shook her head. "No. Like I said, everyone knows what happened. I figure the constable has got the culprit all locked up by now."

It was easy for the public at large to assume things were being taken care of, and that everything they heard was truth, for their lives were narrow enough that most things in the world could be categorized as someone else's job. Only those whose job it was to collect details and make sense of them cared whether what they heard was true and plausible. She said, "I'm afraid he doesn't. I've been charged with collecting information about what happened. I wonder, is there anything you could tell me firsthand? Where were you that night? Could you have been here after midnight three days ago?"

The woman shook her head. "Afraid not, my dear. We close up at sunset. Lock this place up tight, we does, or the folks tramping this way and that over this here bridge would rob us blind."

"You don't have anyone to guard it? An apprentice, perhaps?" *Someone who might have witnessed something amiss?*

"Nah, nobody. Our last apprentice worked out his contract, then went home to his family last summer. We've nobody since then to stay the night and watch over our wares."

"So you don't know exactly when or where the murder happened?"

The woman shook her head again.

"Do you know anyone who may have seen it happen?"

She thought a moment, her sunny smile disappearing into a rather folded-looking expression that made her face seem toothless, though it wasn't. "Well," she ventured slowly, "there's a pie seller on the bridge who may have seen it. At least, he's the one who first told me about it. He came in here, all excited-like, and told me the whole story."

"Where is he today?"

The woman gestured vaguely to the north, farther across the bridge. "Just a bit up thataway. He's always there, selling them pies. Good pies, they are. Makes them himself, and buys his flour here, he does, so I know he has a care for ingredients."

Suzanne thought she might know whom she meant, and they were excellent pies. Though she didn't know his name, she'd seen him often in her frequent crossings and tasted his wares on occasion.

"Did he say he'd witnessed the incident?"

"No, but he had a lot to tell about it he'd heard elsewhere. I figure he knows something."

Suzanne's hopes were not high on that account, but she nevertheless bade the woman good day to go in search of the pie seller who might know something.

First she had a look at the two nearby spots on the bridge where only a wall stood between the street and a precipitous drop to the rushing water below. At the upstream side what she found discouraged the idea that the murder had occurred on the bridge at all. It was a corner where even in the daytime sunlight was scarce. Tucked away from the roadway, the place was dark at the moment, and at night would be pitch-black. She saw no sconces for torches, nor braziers of any kind.

It would be the perfect spot to kill someone, but only if one could see what one was doing. And not only was there no source of artificial light here, but she remembered the night of the murder had been so thickly overcast there was no possibility of even momentary moonlight. The buildings to the north and south of this spot were built with overhangs that at three stories blocked the sky in any case.

Then there was the wall itself. This bridge had taken decades to build during the late twelfth century, and though it was worn by hundreds of years of weather and calamity, it had been well maintained during its lifetime, and this wall was as solid as any in London. Furthermore, it was higher than she was tall. Not that she was so very tall, but even a

large man would have had to struggle to throw a person—
even a small, deceased person—over it.

She looked down at the stone beneath her feet, where the
accumulation of rubbish and natural detritus was kept to a
minimum by publicly paid bridge maintenance. Though
there was some buildup of leaves blown from the shore and
things dropped by people crossing the bridge, for the most
part the area was clear. She looked for any indication of past
violence, and found nothing to appear even suspicious. The
stone was swept regularly, and drainage was not a problem
here. The area was clean and dry, and though she found some
very old stains, there was nothing to suggest anything untoward had happened here recently. No blood puddle, no
bloody footprints, not even a footprint or scuff mark in the
small amount of rubbish directly beneath the wall. Nothing
on the wall, either. Nothing about this spot caught her eye
to make her think there had been a struggle here.

She stood in the spot, like in an eddy away from the
stream of bridge traffic, and the thing other folks called
"intuition" did not tickle the back of her head as it might
have. Nothing about this spot bothered her and made her
want to ask questions.

A look at the other side of the bridge was equally fruitless,
for there was no spot that gave public access to the bridge
wall close enough to the bank as to let a dead body lodge
where the boy had been found. The closest open wall on this
side was well over the stiff current that would have carried
anything dropped from it nearly out of London.

She sighed and moved farther onto the bridge.

The pie seller owned a cart he parked near the center of it.
The cart held a large iron box with a drawer beneath where
coals on a tray kept the box and its pies warm. The savory smell

of them made her realize she'd missed eating dinner, and her stomach gurgled loudly enough for the pieman to hear.

"Ah, mistress! You sound as if you are in need of one of my fine pies! Come, have a taste! Only a single farthing! If you don't think my pies are the best you've ever tasted, I will give you your money back."

Suzanne knew his game. The sample pies for a farthing were small indeed, and very, very good. A full-sized pie cost more, and though they were also good they were not as tasty as the samples. Nevertheless, she bought a full-sized pork pie for three farthings and bit into it with relish. With the paper it came in, she wiped gravy from her lip and savored the meat and pastry as she chewed. As usual, there was perhaps a bit more gravy than necessary, and an excess of onions because onions were cheap, but the pie was hot, fresh, and well seasoned with salt and pepper. That she was hungry as well made it so much more delicious.

The pieman turned his attention to other prospective customers, but attended to her again when she spoke. "This is an excellent pie, good man, and well worth the price. But for another farthing I would have some information."

"Information I got, mistress. Ain't nothing I don't know about this bridge. 'Tis a small community, the folks who live in this here street. I know them all."

"Very good, then. I'm told you're knowledgeable of the murder that happened at the south end of this bridge some days ago."

"Oh, I know all about that. They found a boy down there, just downstream. They think he was thrown. Just was heaved over the wall upstream, and landed in the water. It's the mill wheel what got him. Caught him under, and drowned him, it did."

"Did you see who threw him in?"

The pieman shook his head. "I were at home asleep then."

"Not making pies?"

Now he laughed. "No, my wife does that. Gets up and bakes them all up so's I can bring them here and sell them."

"And then she sleeps while you're here?"

"No, she works for a weaver during the day." His brow furrowed at this strange line of questioning, and he seemed to think her questions a bit silly. Her next question was aimed at clarifying why she would want to know so much about his wife's sleeping habits.

"Do you live nearby? Did your wife see who threw the boy into the river?"

Again the pieman shook his head. "We live up thataway." He pointed with a thumb over his shoulder toward the north end of the bridge. "Neither of us saw anything."

"Do you know anyone who saw anything? Who told you about what had happened?"

He thought hard for a moment, then said, "I don't recall exactly who first told me of it. It seemed everyone was talking about it all at once. Some folks buying pies, mostly. I couldn't tell you their names."

"I see." All rumor and conjecture. No real facts, other than that a boy in a dress had been found dead along the south bank of the Thames. Facts known by everyone who had witnessed the discovery, and nobody to be found who might have seen the crime itself. "Have you, perhaps, seen anyone lurking about the dark corners of the south end of the bridge?"

"No."

"Have you ever seen a boy near here wearing a blue dress decorated with lace?"

The pieman shook his head. "Nothing like that around

here. I would have chased him off if I had. Don't want nothing like that around my cart. Bad for business."

Suzanne was sure it would have been, but her sympathy was strained. His "information" was worthless, though she gave him his farthing regardless. He'd at least been generous with his time and as forthcoming as possible.

So the bridge was entirely a loss, and the only information she'd garnered was that the likelihood of the murder having taken place there was extremely slim. The area was not suitable for the scenario of the violence evidenced by the body she'd seen, and nobody seemed to know anyone who had seen anything. Since she couldn't place the boy on the bridge at all, she needed to look elsewhere for witnesses.

Next she went to the stairs along Bank Side, upstream of the bridge, for that was the place most likely for the body to have entered the water, between the bridge and the bend in the river. There were fifteen of them, from the Old Barge House Stairs by the bend to the Pepper Alley Stairs just above the bridge. She began there, because the farther upstream the body had entered the water, the less chance there would have been for it to reach the bridge unnoticed. Somewhere along that bank someone might have noticed it or it might have snagged on an obstruction as it did when it reached the bridge.

Everyone she found at the Pepper Alley Stairs knew exactly what everyone on the bridge knew, which was the common knowledge disseminated by those who had found the dead boy. There was nothing new to be learned there, so Suzanne moved on. All afternoon she chatted with boatmen and bargemen. Some were happy to stop and chat, while others evaded her questions and forced her to follow them up or down the steps that led from the top of the bank to the edge of the water. As the afternoon wore on, her feet grew sore and her legs stiffened with cold and exertion. She wanted to give up, and told herself she would find nothing, especially since the farther upstream she went, the fewer people she found who had even heard about the murder. But each time her thoughts wandered in that direction she told herself this was the only way to find any tidbit of information that might give her a direction in which to look. Just then she had nothing but a vague indication of rich and powerful people, and no way to know what had happened, let alone who had done it. So she pressed onward in search of someone who may have glimpsed something. Anything.

The Bank End Stairs were the closest to the Goat and Boar, and they were her best hope for a witness. Here was where her intuition niggled her, where she thought the murder might have happened. This was where a witness, if there were one, might be found. The four previous access stairs had produced nothing, but she had high hopes for this one.

Bank End were the stairs at the very downstream end of Bank Side, and downstream of them were clusters of buildings that overlooked the river directly. No street ran along the bank below Bank End. It was dark, having no brazier or torch sconce, and anyone using the stairs after dark would need to bring a torch themselves or depend on dim, distant bits of illumination from barges, moon, or stars. It was the main reason these stairs had been a favorite place for clandestine rendezvous with Daniel back when she'd believed he loved her, the other reason being its proximity to the Goat and Boar. Since there had been no moon or stars the night of the murder, Suzanne knew the stairs must have been quite dark without a torch or candle.

Now, in the waning, overcast afternoon light, Suzanne

descended the stairs carefully, looking about for anything amiss. A barge was readying to dock, carrying only a few passengers and some few crates of cargo. The bargeman called out their location, and one of the men on board was gathering his satchel and a small box in preparation to disembark. The barge touched the quay just as Suzanne reached it herself.

A man in rags sat propped against the bank wall, holding a stoneware jug between his knees and singing drunkenly to the winter wind that raced down the riverbed at a fair clip. His lips were bluish, and his fingers red with cold, though he wore several layers of filthy clothing. She addressed the drinking man.

"Good afternoon, good fellow. May I have a word with you?"

He peered at her a moment, apparently decided she was a friend, and graced her with an enormous, toothless grin. Not one tooth in sight, and his gums were a patchy white and dark purple. "Right," he mouthed more or less. It came out something like *whie.*

"I wonder, do you spend much time here?" She'd never seen him before, but often men with no homes drifted here and there all over London in search of somewhere to sleep where they might not freeze to death during the winter. Clearly this man did not feel the cold so much as a more sober man might, and was a fine candidate for falling asleep and never waking up. Since it had only been a few days since the murder, she thought it might be possible this man had been here that night.

He replied, "I come here to watch the boatses race. I loves to watch the boatses." With one finger he pointed out toward the water, and ran it horizontally as if indicating a very fast boat racing downstream.

"Were you watching those *boatses* here three nights ago?"

He frowned in concentration and sucked in his lips as he calculated three nights. His mouth became a thin, lipless line over which his nose hung and nearly touched his chin. Then he garbled, "Dunno. Can't remember." *Dunnocanmemer.*

"Might you have seen a boy in a blue dress come down here one night?"

He shook his head. Then he remembered his jug and took a drink. He wiped his mouth with the back of his already soaked sleeve. Then he took another drink and stared at an anonymous spot on the stone quay in front of him.

Suzanne realized she wasn't going to have anything useful from him, and turned her attention to the barge, where the passenger was just disembarking.

"Good man!"

The passenger looked to her, but didn't stop.

"Good man, may I have a word with you, please?"

"I don't care for any company today, thank you." He continued walking.

She walked with him, keeping just ahead of his pace, and graced him with a disgusted twist of her mouth, then said, "The truth of it is, neither do I, and I'll thank you to have some respect for a woman looking only for information."

"You've no vizier. I thought you were a whore." The curl of his lip told her he still thought she was one, but now he thought her a stupid one for not being a professional.

"Be that as it may, I am charged by the office of the constable to find a murderer, and I wish to ask you some questions if I may."

Just short of the stairs, he stopped walking, set down his satchel, and turned to face her. "Very well. What do you wish to know?"

"Do you come to these stairs often? Might you have been here three nights ago?"

"No. I don't come here often, and the last time I was on these stairs was a fortnight ago. Is that all you wanted to know?"

"Where were you three nights ago?"

Now he frowned. "I think that is nobody's business but my own." He picked up his satchel and turned toward the stairs to proceed on his way, and she let him go. He irritated her enough for her to want to detain him and annoy him on principle, but that would be a monumental waste of time and energy. She watched him climb the stairs, then turned her attention to the barge at the quay.

The bargeman was watching her. "Bold of you to be out and about on your own, I say."

"I'm an adult, and I carry a dagger." The last was untrue, but she didn't much like the look of this man. He had a dodgy air about him, and a constant habit of glancing sideways that made him appear shifty. Not unusual for those who worked on boats, but she'd never felt comfortable around men like this.

"You're looking for someone who did a murder?"

"I'm in search of someone who may have seen it happen."

"I may have seen it."

"Do tell?" She had no faith in his honesty, but was prepared to listen just in case. "What did you see?"

"Got any money for this information?"

"Tell me what you saw, and I might be able to persuade the constable to provide you a reward."

He sucked some air between his teeth, then said, "Awright, then. I saw a man down here three nights ago kill another man."

"You witnessed the entire murder, but didn't tell anyone?"

He shrugged. "Weren't none of my business, were it? And besides, I weren't coming here. I was passing these here stairs at speed, a-heading downstream, you know. And I looked over at the quay and saw a man killing another one."

"Two men?"

"Oy, right. Two men a-going at it, then one grabs the other by the neck and throttles him." The bargeman held up his hands to demonstrate, and he shook the imaginary neck of the victim. "Done him just like this, you see."

Once more Suzanne's heart sank as she realized this story was as faulty as all the others she'd heard that day. This one was probably intentionally false, as well. "What was the victim wearing?"

"Why, he was wearing breeches and coat, just like everyone else who comes out at night."

"And the murderer?"

"Breeches and coat."

"What color?"

"Couldn't tell you. They were too far away, and it were dark."

Dark, indeed. Dark enough that unless this man's barge was about to dock he wouldn't have been able to see much of what went on at the quay. She raised her chin and gave him a more gracious smile than he deserved. "Thank you, good man. I'll relay this information to the constable, and he will be in touch with you regarding your reward."

The bargeman grinned and returned to his work, pushing his barge into the current and proceeding along his way. It never occurred to him that she would need his name in order for the constable to find him with his reward. Suzanne watched him go and was glad she probably wouldn't run into him again.

Then she turned back toward the stairs to leave, and slowed as she spotted a blackened torch lying on the quay, just where it met the wall behind the stairs. She went to take a closer look. It lay atop a bit of rubbish that had collected beside the stairs, hard to see in the pile of equally dark refuse. It was larger than an ordinary handheld torch. It looked more like the sort that belonged in a sconce outside a shop or tavern. She also saw that some of the rubbish in which it lay was burnt. A circle of char surrounded the head of it, and the wall beside it was also blackened by fire. It appeared the torch had been thrown aside and had landed where it lay, charring the things around it.

This niggled the back of her mind. Someone had brought a torch here, and recently. She gazed up at the Bank Side above, and began climbing the stairs to it. The niggling at the back of her head was growing into a full-sized hunch.

At the entrance to the alley in which stood the Goat and Boar, fewer than a hundred yards from the Bank End Stairs, she found the sconce that ordinarily lit it was empty. That torch was gone and had not been replaced.

She looked back at the stairs, and wondered whether it meant something, or meant nothing at all.

Chapter Seven

"I'm told that I should look in the direction of the ruling class," she said over a late supper that night. She'd quite recovered from her rather upsetting afternoon, and tucked away her conversation with the young woman in Bishopsgate Ward so that she would forget it quickly. Now she focused on Daniel and how to draw information from him.

He chewed thoughtfully on a piece of beef, ready to chase it with a nice bit of Sheila's Irish bread. He lounged in his chair, entirely at home in Suzanne's quarters in the rear basement of the Globe. He did, after all, own the building, and she was there by virtue of a business partnership between Daniel and her son. Though restoring the theatre had been her idea, and she had brought Daniel, Piers, and Horatio together to form the new troupe and its venue, by law she had no ownership or rights to anything. Piers was her legal guardian, and all her business was done through him and with his approval. Though her only power in this venture was her son's regard for his mother, her relationship with Piers was good and that power was formidable.

Suzanne never let her lack of legal standing get in her way regarding Daniel. Nor did his social rank give her much pause, for it had always been a factor in their relationship and she was accustomed to it. She knew exactly how much influence she had on him, for she was the mother of his only son, and though he did not acknowledge Piers, he was vulnerable where the young man was concerned. Suzanne had spent the past year and a half exploring that soft spot, and was prepared to poke at it again today.

In reply to her comment, he said, "Were the boy ruling class, it would be a touchy thing indeed. No family of good standing would want it known they'd produced a sodomite. Particularly one who sold himself in Bank Side." His tone expressed his extreme disgust, and she guessed he was still uncomfortable about his encounter with the boy several nights ago.

"I wonder whether you know of a family who's had a young son go missing recently."

"If I had, I might not say so to you."

She pretended surprise, and paused in cutting her meat. "For what reason? What have I done to be used so ill?" Her tone was mildly chastising, with a slight shading of humor. It wouldn't do to turn this into a battle of wills.

He shrugged. "You can be overly aggressive when on the scent in an investigation."

"I have had my reasons."

"In any case, you've never had the problem of being too discreet. You've an unfortunate knack for whacking away at a problem and letting chips fall where they may. For what reason are you investigating this? I think it would be best for all if it were simply tucked away with the rest of London's assorted evils. The place is depraved, and there's nothing for it."

Suzanne chuckled. "Listen to you, talking about London and depravity! You, who spent all that time in France, and who brought much of French thought with him when he returned!" Her voice lowered to a conspiratorial whisper. "You, who were so ready to fall into bed with a stranger that you couldn't even first determine the gender of your prospect!"

A deep, red blush crept up Daniel's face from his neck, and Suzanne feared she might have gone too far. But he said, "I might not have had any interest in what I perceived as a perfectly natural and willing girl, had I thought I would have been welcomed by you later in the evening."

"I'm certain your wife would have welcomed you."

"My wife is beside the point." Suzanne understood that his complaints about Anne were facile whining, and that he enjoyed her bed regularly. Certainly more regularly than he had while exiled in France. Now he reached across the small table and touched her free hand, which lay flat on it. "I would prefer you above all others, were you nearly as willing as that misguided boy."

She knew that to be untrue. Though he would be perfectly happy to have a romp with her if the mood should ever strike her, she knew he preferred nobody. At least, he didn't prefer her over anyone. Except, perhaps, a boy in a blue dress and blonde wig. She felt he was putting on a show for her. A demonstration of his manliness. She withdrew her hand. "Don't worry, my lord, I understand that you prefer women over boys, and that your error that night was a fair mistake. Anyone might have been flattered into not noticing his hands. Or his extreme lack of bosom. There was, after all, a great deal of lace at his neck."

He also withdrew his hand, once more embarrassed. She wished he would have enough maturity to not have to prove himself with every woman he encountered. She thought he would sulk now, but he said in a tone that was quite reasonable, "Why is anyone investigating the murder of a sodomite? Who would even think it a crime?"

"He was human, Daniel." Anger bloomed in her breast, like a bloodstain across a bodice from a heart wound, and she swallowed hard. "One doesn't need a special reason to want justice for a young boy. Why are you so hateful?"

"They are an abomination."

"God's creatures."

Daniel fell silent, and took a bite from his bread. More silence filled the room as he chewed. Suzanne watched his face as he struggled with himself on this subject. Rather than speak and give him a chance to sidetrack her, she waited until he would speak next. Finally he said, "I don't understand that sort."

"Neither do I, but I do understand that there are things of God's earth I can't be expected to understand, which are therefore impossible for me to judge."

"Of course not. You're a woman."

She fell silent and sat upright in her seat. Her eyes narrowed and hardened.

He said, sulking, "Very well. I don't understand you, and therefore cannot judge you." He waved her on to continue. "Go on."

She said, "It is all right not to judge, and in fact Jesus tells us we shouldn't. I can be bewildered by some behavior and still want justice for a boy who was stabbed, mutilated, and thrown into the river like so much rubbish. God made him what he was, and I am not to say why. But it was a man who made him dead. *That* much I can know is unjust. That much I am confident to judge."

Daniel emitted an affirmative though grudging grunt, and sounded as if he could be coming around.

So she pressed. "I wonder whether there is someone among the peerage, or close to it, who has a son nobody has seen recently. Whom do you know might fit that description?"

"We don't all know each other intimately, you know. And some are more private than others."

"I realize that."

"I certainly don't know all their children, either."

"Of course not."

"Besides, nearly everyone has children who are off in various forms of fosterage or schooling."

"Of course. But have you heard anything unusual?"

Daniel thought hard for some moments. Then he shook his head. "I don't know. There are so many who send their children here and there, for education or to simply get them out of the way. To France, to the countryside . . . one never knows where the offspring are—or sometimes who the offspring are—even if one is friendly with the parents."

"Someone terribly proper, Esmeralda said. Someone very high up."

"I can't—" Daniel stopped short, staring into the middle distance, remembering. "The Earl of Dandridge has a son about that age who was recently sent to France."

"Good." Suzanne nodded, pleased Daniel was now co-operating. "Any others?"

Daniel shook his head, then said, "Wait." His head tilted, as if he were listening carefully to a dim memory. "Wait.

There is another. It was months ago, though. Duke of Cawthorne." He nodded. "Yes, Jacob Worthington, Duke of Cawthorne. He has a son that age, and by all accounts the boy has been in the country since last summer."

"And you think our victim could be this boy? But if he's been away for months, how was he killed in London?"

Daniel shrugged. "I wouldn't hazard a guess. But you asked about absent sons of high-ranking gentlemen, particularly high-ranking gentlemen who are of extremely proper families. Cawthorne is a Puritan of the purest stripe. Never a word but in praise of God, and never a whisper of scandal about his entire family. Ever."

"That strikes me as . . . unnatural."

"Indeed."

Suzanne determined to arrange visits to the families of the duke and the earl.

THE next morning, as Suzanne set out to visit the western end of London, she was exiting her rooms when there came a shouting from the upstairs dressing room, two stories above the stage level. She knew it was the dressing room, because the voice was Liza and Suzanne couldn't tell what she was saying. Were she in one of the rooms closer to the basement, Liza's voice would have carried clearly enough for everyone in the 'tiring house to hear and understand every word.

Then came Wally's voice, in full, manly tenor, and Suzanne realized they weren't rehearsing. She sighed, and hoped Horatio was in the vicinity to calm them down. At the very least to keep them from scratching each other's eyes out.

She fled through the rear exit, hoping not to be dragged

into the actors' conflict, and found Ramsay waiting for her in the alley outside the rear door of the theatre. He lounged against the wall of the building across the narrow way, facing the Globe entrance, and when he saw her he regained his feet and presented himself at attention. "Good morning, my dear Suzanne!" He was bundled inside a bulky sheepskin coat, and today he wore breeches and tights against the sharp January weather rather than the kilt he usually preferred. His hat was broad brimmed, but old and had lost its shape so that the brim drooped. Bad for fashion, but good for warmth. Even a true Scot such as himself must appreciate warm clothing when he could get it.

She stopped short, quite surprised to see him lurking here. "What are you doing here in the alley, Ramsay? Why did you not come inside and out of the cold? Have you been here long?"

He glanced at the theatre door, then back at her. "Not long. I've come to escort you through your day. I'm told you're hot on the trail of a murderer, and I aim to make certain you don't share the fate of the victim in question."

She made a vague shrug, as if shaking off the silly thought. "I don't see any danger ahead for me today. In fact, I am headed for some rather genteel neighborhoods. I need to speak to some folks in Pall Mall and Westminster. I must see the Earl of Dandridge, who has a new estate in Pall Mall, and I'm told the Duke of Cawthorne maintains his London residence in Orchard Street."

Ramsay's eyebrows went up, and a not-quite-stifled smile curled the corners of his mouth. "Westminster? Are you sure they'll let you in? Or even walk down the street?"

"Not at all. I rather expect the moment my foot touches

the ground there a wild pack of palace guards will rush at me with pikes and demand to know my business. And further it is my firm belief the presence of a large, loud Scot would only hinder my chances at going unnoticed." She headed off up the alley toward Maid Lane, where she could flag down a carriage for the ride across the river and around the bend in the Thames to the wealthiest part of London.

"You injure me, my lady." Ramsay pressed a palm to his chest as he fell into step beside her. The icy cobbles beneath their feet caused much slipping, and Suzanne was forced to take his arm to steady herself. He pressed his free hand to hold hers secure, and made certain she didn't fall. He continued, "I would stand ready to do your bidding. I wish only your safety."

"Nonsense. You wish to occupy my bed."

"That as well, but it can wait for a more suitable moment. And speaking of that, have you considered my offer?"

"I've been considering it, but cannot tell whether I am ready for marriage. You know I rather enjoy my new life, and already have too many men taking credit and money for my efforts."

"I assure you, I wish no credit for anything I haven't done myself. Were you my wife, I would laud your accomplishments to the heavens."

"That's very well, but marriage is a rather high price for praise I should have in any case. You could do that without having my lifelong commitment. I wonder what you could offer me I don't already have on my own."

"You did mention bed . . ."

"I have had all of that I care for, thank you very much, and also without the Lord's blessing. With few exceptions, it's pretty much all the same, once all is said and done. Since William left, I find I don't miss it." She was careful not to mention the one time with Daniel only a year ago, which at her age she'd found entirely too casual, and given his attitude she didn't particularly miss being with him anymore, either.

"But you haven't had me."

"And what would be so special about a romp with you? Have you parts that are unlike other men? A secret knowledge of technique that has gone undiscovered by the rest of humanity since the beginning of the world?" She kept her tone light and humorous, lest she hurt his feelings. Her wish was to keep him at bay, not to chase him off with mean words, for she enjoyed his company and didn't wish to lose it.

Ramsay chuckled, impervious. "Were I to reveal my parts to you, you might faint at the sight." That brought a delighted guffaw from her, and she let him continue, which he did eagerly. "Why, my member is so large, and so vigorous, you could hardly contain it."

"I don't suppose I could."

"However, I suggest you try. You'll never know what you might accomplish unless you try."

That made her laugh again, giddy in the chilly morning. They arrived at the street, and Ramsay waved down a carriage for hire. It stopped, and the driver leapt from his seat to open the door. Ramsay and Suzanne climbed inside and sat. She ordered the driver to take them to Pall Mall, and sat back for the fairly long ride. Ramsay settled in next to her, and had the good grace to not take her hand in his. Instead he crossed his legs and folded his hands in his lap. She likewise folded her hands in her own lap.

"It hasn't escaped my notice that you are still here."

He agreed cheerfully, took her hand from her lap, and kissed the back of it. "Aye. I'm most noticeable."

"I can't take you inside with me when we get there."

"Assuming they let you inside and they don't set the dogs on us."

"Well, we'll see what happens when we get there."

"Aye. Won't we, though?"

Chapter Eight

P all Mall was the newest neighborhood in London, suddenly fashionable since the return of the king. Previously
it had been a park where the ball game of that name had
been a popular pastime among the upper classes, and now
it was a scattering of brand-new and unfinished houses of
bright brick and new-cut stone, each surrounded by newly
dug gardens and sparse-grown lawns. One of those belonged
to Daniel, and as they passed it Suzanne stared hard to see
whether his wife was in. She wished she could hate Anne,
but had found it impossible. Most likely, everyone found it
impossible to dislike her, for she was beautiful, graceful, and
treated everyone she met with respect. Sometimes Suzanne
even thought Daniel didn't deserve her.

Today there was no sign of Anne at Daniel's house.

The house belonging to the Earl of Dandridge was by no
means the most elaborate in the street, but inspired enough
awe in Suzanne and Ramsay that they both had to gawk out

the carriage window as they approached up the circle drive. Ramsay was the only one with a comment. He said, "Och."

Suzanne agreed. The stone in this house was so new, the hewn corners so sharp, they appeared able to cut flesh. Daniel's house had been built only six months ago, but even it wasn't this precise.

When the carriage stopped, Suzanne stepped down from it. Ramsay followed, and offered his arm to Suzanne.

"No, Ramsay, I think you should stay here and wait for me."

"I would much rather accompany you."

"I think it would be better for me to go alone. You can be very intimidating to some."

"And that is my best feature."

"I thought your member was your best feature."

"Oh, aye, it is. Should I draw it out and render them all speechless?"

She pretended to think on that a moment, then shook her head and said, "No. I'm here to get them to talk, so that would defeat my purpose, I'm afraid. Just stay here and make certain our driver doesn't wander off or drink too much from his flask."

Ramsay glanced over at the driver, then said, "Very well, my lady."

"Stop calling me that. It impresses me only with your eagerness to flatter. It doesn't help your case."

"Then by all means I will stop calling you that, you yeasty whore."

"That's better. Now wish me luck."

"Good luck, you unprincipled tart."

Suzanne laughed. "Very well, you may call me a 'lady' if you must. But only when we're alone."

With a grin he said, "Alone? Something to look forward to." He retreated to the relatively warm carriage and graced her with a handsome smile that made her smile in return. Then she faced the front door of the earl's house, and wiped that smile from her face as a servant opened it to see who had just arrived. Suzanne approached in all seriousness, having arranged her face into a somber and sympathetic expression. She might be bringing bad news, and even if the murdered boy weren't the earl's son there were certain to be tense and upsetting moments during this meeting.

"Good day," she said. "My name is Mistress Suzanne Thornton, working under the authority of Constable Samuel Pepper of Southwark. I have an urgent matter to discuss with the earl, if I may."

The manservant gazed at her stupidly for a moment, then said, "Southwark?" It was as if he'd never heard of the place and would consider mention of it beneath him if he had.

"Yes. Is the earl available for a short interview? This shouldn't take long at all."

"The earl?" The man seemed dumbfounded anyone from Southwark would be so bold as to ask for an interview.

Suzanne's voice took on an edge of impatience. "Yes, good man. It's a matter of utmost urgency. It involves his son." She didn't know the name of the son, and wished she'd looked into it before coming here. This wasn't her first time to wish she'd prepared more thoroughly before an interview, but there was nothing for it now but to forge ahead and hope for the best.

"His son?"

Exasperation rose. "Yes. His son."

Finally something sunk into the man's head, and he gestured that Suzanne should enter.

Inside the door was an entryway larger than any Suzanne had ever seen. Doors gave egress to either side, and a stairway with a curved banister led to an upper floor. The newel post at the bottom was intricately carved and highly polished, brand-new and with nary a mark of use on it. Her hand, of its own accord, reached out to lay a finger on it, just to know it was real and not some magical thing created by faeries. The servant bade her wait, and so she waited, still and silent.

The wait was long enough for her to understand her time was not particularly valued, but she remained still and listened to the various household noises. There were voices in a distant room, and a single shout that must have come from the kitchen, for it was accompanied by a banging of copper pots and a clatter of what may have been wooden utensils. The smell of sawdust still permeated, even though the house was warm, with hearths everywhere busily burning wood.

Eventually the servant returned, followed by a handsome peer in his thirties or early forties, distinguished though wigless and wearing a velvet lounging robe. The servant announced him, and introduced her, then disappeared so expertly and discreetly Suzanne only looked up from her curtsey to see he was no longer there. The earl peered at her, frowning.

"What's this I'm told about a problem involving my son? You're aware he's in France?"

"That is what I was told, but something has arisen and I must inquire after him. May I ask, when was the last you heard from him?"

"Why, we had a message from him only a few days ago. He tells us all is well. Tell me what is the matter." He seemed intensely concerned about his son.

"He's near the age of twelve or thirteen?"

"He's fourteen years old. Why do you want to know? What could the constable in Southwark have to do with him?"

"Could you describe him to me?" Fourteen years old was perhaps older than the boy she'd seen, but one could never tell for a certainty with children.

The earl's temper began to unravel. "Now hear me, good woman, I demand to know what the matter is you've come about. What of my son?"

"I'm sorry, but there's been a murder, and we're afraid the victim may be one of the nobility. If you could tell me what your son looks like, then perhaps we can rule him out and your worry will be over."

Without hesitation, the earl said, "He's got bright red hair, like his mother. Tall for his age, and somewhat hefty as well. His nose is covered with freckles, and his eyes are a light hazel color." An edge of panic came into his voice. "Tell me, does your victim fit that description?"

Suzanne sighed, both relieved and dismayed. "He does not. This boy had dark brown hair, and was quite thin."

Tears rose to the earl's eyes, and he placed a hand over his mouth. "Thank God. He's all right, then?"

"He's not the boy we found several days ago. I'm terribly sorry to have disturbed you, my lord." She executed an especially deep curtsey to express her sincere regret.

"It's quite all right, mistress." Plainly the earl was relieved it was someone else's child who had been murdered.

"I'll leave you to your business, and again I am sorry to have given you a turn."

The earl nodded, and gestured toward the door. "Good day to you, then. And I wish you success in your investigation."

She thanked him and left. Now she had to do the same to the Duke of Cawthorne in Westminster.

While Pall Mall was London's newest neighborhood, Westminster was one of its older ones outside of the ancient walled city. Orchard Street was named for orchards that once belonged to St. Peter's Abbey near Westminster Hall, which trees had been taken down to make room for expensive houses. In addition to being an old neighborhood, it was stultifyingly wealthy. Ramsay hadn't exaggerated much when he'd spoken of having dogs set upon them. As their carriage approached the house belonging to the Duke of Cawthorne, huge, old trees shaded the road. Other houses lined the street, in high style and quietly assured of their superiority. Suzanne found herself looking up and down the street as the carriage hurried along it, half afraid of having attracted the notice of those whose business it was to eject the riffraff from the area. Unlike the areas of London to the east, where people came and went at will and often anonymously, this place was impermeable. Unassailable. Inviolable.

The duke's mansion was a stately gentleman of brown brick, smaller, perhaps, than the showier houses in Pall Mall. This neighborhood may have been the less fashionable this year, but it was well established by old families, particularly those who had come through the interregnum in the good graces of God and Oliver Cromwell. This house was bare of unnecessary ornamentation, and though the garden seemed adequate and might bloom up nicely in the spring, there was no statuary at all and no color to speak of anywhere other than black trees, brown grass, and white ice. The structure was impeccably maintained, but was entirely brown. The carriage stopped in the street directly in front of it. Its driver opened the carriage door for Suzanne.

She stepped up to the magnificently large and solid, though plain, brown-painted door and tapped with its knocker. The wait for someone to answer was interminable. She was on the verge of trying again when the door finally opened to reveal a manservant in black livery. More plain than plain, with not even a white collar or sleeves to relieve the severity of the costume.

The footman said, "Good morning," and gazed expectantly, as if he'd asked a question and expected a pertinent reply.

"Good morning. My name is Mistress Suzanne Thornton. I wonder if I might have a word with his grace the duke." The footman's eyes glazed over and a hard line came to his mouth, so that Suzanne could see she wasn't going to get anywhere with him. So she added quickly, "It's regarding his son. I'm afraid I have some very bad news." She wasn't certain of it, but let this man believe she was, so that he would take her seriously and let her in.

It brought raised eyebrows, but the manservant yet hesitated. Suzanne needed to be better convincing. She continued, "I am here at the behest of Constable Samuel Pepper, who is investigating a murder."

"Whose murder?"

"I cannot say. I must speak directly to his grace, if you please." Her tone suggested she would speak to his grace even if the footman did not please. And she certainly wasn't going to tell him that the reason she couldn't say who had been murdered was that nobody knew his name.

The footman thought about that for a moment, then gave a slight nod of his head in lieu of a bow, said, "Wait here," then retreated to the house and closed the door.

Suzanne looked back at Ramsay, who stood by the carriage while the driver tended to his horses in the cold. A light sprinkling of snow was in the wind, and white flakes danced like faeries around him.

Again, the wait was interminable. Cold made inroads into Suzanne's clothing, and she shifted her weight back and forth to keep the blood moving in her feet. Her teeth began to chatter, though she struggled to make them stop.

Finally the door opened again. She might have sworn the footman appeared disappointed to find her still there, but he recovered quickly and swung the door wide for her to enter. She stepped inside and began blowing on her fingers to warm them.

The inside of the house was quite toasty. A short entry hall led to a large parlor in which a good-sized hearth held a merrily burning log. A stack of similar logs stood by, ready to feed the fire. The footman told her to wait, and he disappeared through a door at the end of the room. Suzanne immediately thrust her hands toward the fire to warm them. Slowly feeling returned to her fingers.

She looked around the room. Everything about this place spoke to her of security and established authority. People who had been wealthy, and secure in their wealth, for generations. Portraits on the walls honored family members past and present with the work of highly skilled and highly paid artists, and that work had been set in costly frames carved in rich woods or layered in gold. The furniture was perfectly kept and gently used, impeccably clean, and though old was not worn. A vase of hothouse flowers stood on a deeply polished wooden table, and the spring scent mixed oddly with the winter smell of burning wood.

The portraits covered the walls from ceiling to chair rail, seemingly random because of size, but she could see they were arranged somewhat chronologically. The south wall appeared to contain subjects dressed in Elizabethan costume, and the next had more modern, Puritan attire. She turned, looking for the most recent family members. They were behind her.

The largest of these paintings appeared to be of the duke, though she supposed it could have been an old picture of his father. The Puritan fashion of dress was so plain it was difficult to tell how old the clothing was. This face was stern, frowning. It was the portrait of someone whose main concern was the authority he held over others in the world. She'd found in the past that most of the peerage were overly concerned with controlling others. It was what gave their lives meaning, and very often was more important to them than the wealth that usually accompanied the power. She would need to tread carefully with this fellow, lest she find herself in trouble with the crown over a minor slip in protocol.

Then she noticed a small painting in the lower right corner of the wall of contemporary paintings that drew her eye. This one was very finely wrought, almost small enough to be a miniature, but not quite. It portrayed two subjects. A pair of boys, one a couple of years older than the other. Both with dark brown hair, and both with smiling eyes and ruddy cheeks that bespoke good health. The artist had quite caught the joy in them both, which shone from the picture like a light. Suzanne's breath caught, for she recognized the younger boy as the poor child that had been found floating in the river. She had to turn away, lest tears rise and she be caught having to explain them to the duke.

The wait this time was even longer than at the door. Every so often she would look up at the duke's portrait and wonder why these people always thought it so terribly important to put her in her place. This was so unnecessary. She knew well her place, had been taught it all her life, and hardly needed to be reminded. She thought of Little Wally, and just then she envied him his utter insouciance toward society and decorum. Ramsay, as well. Had he accompanied her into the house, he more than likely would now be encouraging her to go home, and suggesting the duke should engage in a physically impossible sex act. However, having seen the picture of the victim hanging on this wall, Suzanne had a keen interest in learning anything she could about the boy and his family.

Finally the door to the rest of the house opened, and the footman entered to announce the duke. His purpose was to give Suzanne a chance to stand and not expose the duke to the sight of her sitting in his presence, but she hadn't sat while waiting and only turned toward the door with a mild expression, neither smiling nor frowning. The duke entered the room.

He was a large man, broad shouldered and burly enough to mitigate his mighty efforts at elegance. Like everything around him, his attire was plain, but of terribly expensive fabric and cut. His robe hung with a perfection that spoke of expert attention to his frame and the way he moved, but it was black and collarless. He wore no gold, silver, or jewels, not even any rings on his fingers, no signet that might show his rank. His slippers bore no decoration. Not even did his face have adornment of beard or moustaches. His hair was thick and virile, a dark brown, graying at the temples in the most genteel way. He was well scrubbed, smoothly groomed, and his hair had the perfection of a marble statue with nary a strand gone astray.

His eyes were equally stone-like. Flinty. Suzanne looked

into them, and had to wonder whether this man had a soul. Surely there must be one in there somewhere, but she wasn't seeing it. His visage shook her to her toes, and she had to force herself to continue looking at his face and not at the floor.

He said, "What is it you want? What of my son?" His voice was deep and gravelly, and she guessed he'd often used it for shouting down his opponents in Parliament.

It struck her that, for a father so concerned about the welfare of his son, he'd kept her waiting a remarkably long time.

She curtsied as deeply as was called for, and she replied, "I've come to ask you about him. I believe he is about the age of twelve or thirteen. Is that correct?"

"Paul is twelve. He's not in London. He's with his mother's cousins in Kent, for nearly three months now."

"Have you heard from him recently?" Certainly not within the past week.

"We had a message from him just yesterday."

"May I ask when it was sent?"

"Three days before."

Suzanne knew he was lying, and it put her on her guard to know exactly why he was avoiding the truth, and precisely what truth he was avoiding. He continued with a soothing smile on his face, which did not lend credibility to his story, coming from the man in that portrait behind him. It was almost as if the painting were the real expression of himself beneath the façade he presented to her in the flesh. "Said he's well, and enjoying his studies. Being the younger son, he will do well to join the clergy. He's a talent for it."

Certainly that was another lie. The boy she'd seen in the Goat and Boar had little religious thought in his head, if any, and fit too naturally into the role he'd played with Daniel to be anything other than the sensual creature he'd professed. She turned to the portrait of the two boys, thinking, then turned back to the duke. "I'm afraid something terrible has happened to him, your grace."

The duke now abandoned his smile, but otherwise his expression did not change.

She went on. "Your younger son, the one in that portrait there"—she gestured toward it—"has been killed."

Now the hard line of his mouth matched the portrait. "How do you know this? Who are you?"

"As I explained to your man earlier, my name is Mistress Suzanne Thornton. I've been asked to help in the investigation of the murder of a young boy. He is the younger of the two in that picture."

"You're certain?" He glanced around at the painting of his sons, then back at her. "There's no doubt?"

"I saw the body," she said, without mentioning she'd also seen him alive the night before.

The duke seemed to stand straighter, but his expression remained stony. He said, "Tell me what happened."

At that moment the inner door opened and a woman entered. She was a bit younger than Suzanne, and quite a bit younger than the duke. "Jacob," she said to him, and Suzanne guessed this was the duchess. She appeared to want to say more, but hesitated when she saw their faces and sensed the tension in the room. She looked from one to the other, puzzled. Finally she said, "Jacob, what is the matter?" Worry deepened the lines in her face so she suddenly appeared older than she was.

"Leave the room," Jacob ordered his wife as he would have done a servant.

"I think not." She knew something very wrong was afoot, and stood her ground, though her hands clasped each other with white knuckles and pale fingernail beds. She looked from her husband to Suzanne, then back, waiting for one of them to tell her what was the matter.

"I said, go." He didn't raise his voice, though his anger at being contradicted could be heard in it.

"I shall stay, Jacob." She turned to Suzanne and said with softened voice and utter politeness, "Please continue, mistress."

Someone else might have waited to speak until the woman had obeyed her husband and left, but Suzanne thought the duchess deserved to hear this conversation. She deserved to know exactly what had been said rather than to hear what her husband would deign to tell her later. She said to the duchess with as much sensitivity as was at her command, "I'm afraid your younger son, Paul, has been found dead, your grace. His body was pulled from the Thames three days ago."

Blood drained from the woman's face. "Paul?" She tossed a glance to her husband, then returned her attention to Suzanne. "Paul? No. It can't be. He's in Kent. He cannot possibly be in London." She turned again to her husband, as if asking him to confirm her words. He said nothing, so the duchess continued to Suzanne, "It cannot possibly be the same boy. You're mistaken." She nodded to affirm her own words, as if that was all it took to change the truth and all would be right again.

Suzanne chose her words carefully, and kept her voice as gentle as she could while insisting she was not mistaken. "I'm afraid it's true, your grace. I wish with all my heart I could be wrong, but I see that portrait there is the very boy I saw pulled from the river."

The duchess shook her head, and her mouth tried to form words, but none came. She looked to her husband again, her eyes pleading him to say it wasn't so.

The duke said in a tone somewhat gentler than before. "Please leave the room."

She shook her head again, then said to Suzanne, "Tell me what happened."

Suzanne looked at the floor to organize her thoughts and decide how much detail to include in her story. As she cleared her throat to speak, she knew she would have to tell all to get the right answers to the real questions she had. She began with the discovery of the body.

"Three days ago, a washerwoman discovered a body floating in the river. Some boatmen plucked it from the water. It was found to be a young boy, approximately twelve or thirteen years old." She paused for a moment to assess the reaction so far, and the duchess seemed to be taking this with as much calm as could be hoped for. So Suzanne continued, "The boy had been murdered."

The duchess gasped. The duke was as still and hard as the marble statue he'd seemed before.

"Also, I must tell you, he was wearing a dress. He'd been disguised as a girl."

This statement brought no reaction from either of them. Plainly neither was surprised by the revelation that their son liked to wear women's clothing. This struck Suzanne as odd, though she reflected perhaps it shouldn't. More than likely they knew their son better than anyone other than the servants, and were aware of his predilection for dresses. But she made mental note of it and continued, exploring and noting their expressions. "And I'm terribly sorry to have to tell you this, but the body was mutilated."

"He was eaten by fish in the river?"

"No. His . . . an appendage had been cut off." She felt it unnecessary to mention the piece had not been lost, or where it had been found.

The duchess laid a hand over her mouth, and her eyes welled up with tears. "Oh!" The duke was looking at the floor now, and his expression was unreadable. The duchess said, "How do you know it was our Paul?"

"It isn't. It can't be," said the duke. "Paul is with your cousins." He was still looking at the floor.

Suzanne said, "I'm sorry, but I saw the body myself shortly after it was taken from the river."

"How did you know to come here? You never saw that picture until now. How did you recognize him and know he was our son?" Her tone accused trickery, but Suzanne understood the duchess was grasping at straws.

Rather than implicate Daniel, and to avoid admitting she'd acted on the advice of an astrologer, which might have sent these people into a Puritan tizzy about heresy and the abyss, Suzanne committed the sin of bearing false witness, saying, "A bystander recognized him. I cannot recall his name. But regardless of how I came here, there is no doubt the victim was the younger boy in that painting there." She gestured to the small one with the two boys.

The duchess looked at it, saw her youngest son, and the realization finally came home. Her mouth opened as if to cry out, but no sound came. Only a struggle to express the unexpressible. Finally a strangled noise came, a hopeless cry that spoke of killing grief. She didn't take her eyes from the painting, and sank to her knees on the floor.

Her husband bent to steady her and to keep her from going all the way down. He supported her as she drew a breath and emitted a heartbroken sob, finally closing her eyes so that tears ran down her face.

Suzanne hadn't anticipated having to bring this news to the boy's mother. She'd only imagined talking to his father, and now was sorry it had been necessary to tell the duchess. She knelt beside her and took her hand. Almost insensibly, the duchess gripped Suzanne's hand in both of hers and held on as she sobbed. Suzanne said, "I'm sorry," and repeated it over and over.

The duke said, "You've accomplished your mission, mistress. I think you had better leave now." The anger in his voice was copper clad.

Suzanne gently retrieved her hand from the duchess's grip, and stood. "Your grace, of course there will be an inquiry to find your son's killer."

"I said, leave. Immediately." As if summoned, the manservant entered the room and stood ready to escort Suzanne from it.

"Yes, your grace." Suzanne knew she would have to attempt questioning him later, and didn't relish it, but she also knew she would get nothing further from either of the Worthingtons until they'd calmed down. "I'm sorry to have brought you this terrible news. May God give you strength." Then she curtsied appropriately and allowed the manservant to see her out.

When she exited the house, Ramsay was lounging in the carriage chatting with the driver who sat above. He leapt to attention and hurried from it to help her up the steps and inside. "What did you learn?" The driver came to close the carriage door behind them, then prepared the horses to leave. Suzanne and Ramsay settled into their seats. She wished for a lap robe, for the carriage was terribly cold and the emotional scene she'd just left gave her that much more of a chill.

"I'm afraid I learned very little beyond the name of our victim. He was their youngest son, Paul. They'd thought him safe with cousins in Kent until just now. They hadn't even known he was missing."

"No message from the cousins?"

"Apparently not."

"Not very conscientious of them, I'd say."

"Indeed." Suzanne thought that over for a moment. "Not very conscientious at all." Surely they should have sent a message as soon as he'd left Kent, which would have been at least a day or two before she'd seen him in the Goat and Boar even if he'd arrived in London that very morning. A message so important, sent a week ago, would certainly have arrived before now. All in all, those cousins of the duchess didn't seem adequate guardians of their ward. As the carriage started up and rolled down the wide street, she said, "There were a number of things that bothered me about the parents."

"Such as?"

"I cannot say. Only . . . some bits simply don't fit right, and I don't know for a certainty what they are or how they don't fit."

"Intuition?"

"People tell less with their mouths than they do with their bodies as a whole. Sometimes we women understand things men can't, because we pay attention to things other than the obvious."

"Then you should know how the bits don't fit."

"I will. I must first think on what I've seen."

Chapter Nine

When Suzanne and Ramsay returned to the Globe,
they found Daniel's carriage standing at the front.
The horses had been blanketed, so Suzanne knew he'd been
waiting some time. He was sure to be in a testy mood. She
bade Ramsay good day and thanked him for his company
that morning, then readied herself to talk to Daniel about
what she'd just learned.

He stood when she entered her sitting room. "There you
are." By his tone he was impatient that she'd kept him waiting so long, but he didn't actually say so. He knew her well
enough to understand that had he voiced his complaint, she
would have merely pointed out that he'd not had an appoint-
ment with her and she could hardly be held responsible for
his inability to find her at home. He could fuss and whine
all he wanted. She would not feel the least guilt, nor would
she ever arrange her day around the off chance of a visit from
him. Certainly, in that way lay madness.

She agreed, more cheerfully than he, "Here I am." She removed her gloves and handed them to Sheila, then her cloak, and the items disappeared into her bedchamber with the maid. Suzanne gestured that Daniel should sit, and she took a chair opposite the sofa where he sat. "I've been to see the Duke of Cawthorne."

"And what did you find?" His tone was wary, as if expecting bad news.

"You were right. The victim is their youngest son, Paul."

He grunted and shifted in his seat. This was indeed bad news. "I could be right about nothing, for I told you nothing. I never said he was their son; I only said their son was not in London."

"You're absolutely correct. It was Mistress La Tournelle who told me the boy was of the upper class."

"I hope you're not going about telling people I said the duke's son was a sodomite. I never did."

"Not to worry; I kept your name entirely out of it."

"You should be warned Cawthorne is nobody to take lightly. He's among the peers who are prone to treat the king as their lackey, as if we controlled the kingdom rather than he."

"Well, Daniel, you must admit that Charles is dependent on money you in Parliament deign to give him. You are more powerful than you think."

"Cawthorne is among a tight clique who are apart from the rest of us. Even I wouldn't want to cross those who are so powerful they have no regard for Charles. Caught between the king and the Puritan Parliament, I often feel powerless. Neither fish nor fowl, I am often alone in my efforts at anything."

"As I said, Daniel, so far as he and the world are concerned, the body was identified by a bystander whose name is quite forgotten. You needn't worry."

"Still, I wish you would keep entirely out of it yourself. It's not seemly, I think."

She sat up, pretending offense. "It seems to me that, with my background and experience, there should be very little I could do that might for me be termed 'unseemly.' It's not as if I had great social standing to protect."

"You have an association with me."

"One you keep as hidden as possible."

"Nevertheless, I wish you would have a care about how things appear. I can't have you running around town—"

"You don't *have* me at all."

"You know what I mean."

"No, really, I don't. Tell me what you mean."

He paused a moment, to calm his rising anger, and to think through his reply. Then he said, "I own your theatre. It's known we have a relationship."

"What is known is that you have a business relationship with my son. What I do may reflect on him, but you have no responsibility regarding me. In fact, you've gone to great lengths to distance yourself from me in the eyes of society. There is little chance of me ever embarrassing you. I could strip naked and swing by my heels from a chandelier in the king's privy chamber, and it would mean little to your reputation."

"Well, no, that might actually enhance it."

"In any case, you see my point." Her lips pressed together at the memory of the day he'd told her to never visit him in his quarters at Whitehall, for fear his wife might learn he was Piers's father. She was forced to accept his wish, but every day was sorely tempted to reveal their secret. Now her irritation over it harshened her tone.

"Nevertheless, I don't think it's advisable to continue with this investigation."

"What do you think will be revealed?"

"What has already been revealed is bad enough."

"That you are a chamberer and not so very particular about whom you invite to your bed?"

Daniel blanched. "He was extremely well disguised."

"Not so very well I couldn't tell he was a fraud from where I sat. You had an arm around him, if I recall."

"I did not."

"You did."

Daniel opened his mouth to protest, but she overrode him. "And even were he a girl, taking him upstairs would have been low behavior any way one might look at it. Even as a girl—"

"He presented himself as a tart."

"I am of the school of thought that deems patronizing whores of any age is an unseemly activity for a Christian gentleman, no matter how wealthy, powerful, or handsome."

"Men patronizing whores supported you well enough."

"Which you did not. And 'well enough' is a matter of opinion. Besides, that boy was only twelve years old."

"As a girl he looked older."

"That's no excuse, and in any case even as a girl he never appeared more than fourteen or so. Still too young for anyone other than an arranged fiancé, but particularly so for a man about to turn forty."

"If you thought so, then why didn't you mention it?"

"I am mentioning it now. Though I shouldn't have to. I am, after all, not your guardian. In theory you should be responsible for your own behavior, and adult enough to know when you're acting the fool."

That poked a sore spot, and his eyes went wide for a moment. Then they narrowed and his brow knotted in a frown.

"A man should be able to do what he likes with his person and his money."

"I would rather enjoy listening in when you explain that to your Presbyterian wife. And won't her equally Presbyterian brother the duke—who has no love for you in any case—be enchanted with your thoughts about the freedoms of men relative to respect for his sister?"

He fell silent for a moment, then said, "Is that a threat?"

"Is what a threat?" She couldn't imagine what he meant.

"If you dare speak to Anne of this—"

"Don't be silly. I don't care whether you bang a hundred whores." Not to mention that she'd thought it over carefully months ago, and decided that Anne was a sweet woman and didn't deserve to hear that bit of bad news. All in all, Daniel was an adequately attentive husband, their life together was as pleasant as could be expected for an arranged marriage, and telling Anne about his dalliances would only hurt her in ways that would do no good. "I have no claim over you, and don't wish to exert one." It was a lie, but she only knew it in moments when she was most candid with herself. "But that doesn't mean I am sanguine about your need to have every woman who glances your way." Were she ever honest with Daniel, she would admit she'd much prefer that he would choose her over the others. But after more than twenty years of sharing him with his wife, mistresses, and assorted nameless professionals, she knew there was no hope of ever being his only love. So she closed off her feelings and pretended they didn't exist. The terrible thing of it was that she sensed he knew her heart in spite of her caution, and he often touched it or skewered it according to his whim.

There was a long silence as they both realized they'd quite gone off the subject and had nothing else to say in this particular argument. Then Daniel said, "Very well. I'll take your word for it you will keep my name out of your investigation."

"It should go without saying."

He nodded, possibly because any further words might turn as ugly as the others. "So, then, what do you intend to do about this boy?"

She sighed, relieved he'd accepted she would continue with the investigation. "I must learn how young Paul Worthington progressed from his father's mansion to the Goat and Boar. Via Kent, it would seem."

"What will that tell you?"

"Well, he was wearing the dress when he was killed. Someone who knew him in that dress became angry enough to stab him to death."

"Why angry? Perhaps it was a robbery. He was soliciting, and more than likely had a pocket full of cash beneath his skirt."

She shook her head. "Though there was no pocket, as one might expect of someone selling his body, it could be that the men who fished him out of the water took it. Or else he had a handler who relieved him of his proceeds periodically throughout the night. But regardless of that, the killer must have been very angry, to have cut off the willie and stuffed it in the boy's mouth. A robber at the very least wouldn't have bothered. Lord Paul didn't die for his night's takings."

"Then, what?"

She thought for a long moment, waiting for inspiration. She let her mind wander as it often did, skipping down various paths without guidance. Then she blinked and peered at Daniel. "What did you feel when you discovered you had your arm around a boy and not a girl?"

"I never had my arm around him."

"Very well, no arm. Tell me what you felt when I told you he wasn't a girl."

Daniel shrugged. Plainly he was reluctant to revisit that moment. But she pressed.

"Tell me, what did you feel? Embarrassment, of course. What did you feel toward him?"

"Nothing."

"Not nothing. And that's not what I'm getting at. What emotion did you feel when you saw he was a boy who had fooled you into thinking he was a girl? A girl attractive enough to make your willie stiff."

"It wasn't stiff."

"As you say. Tell me what you felt."

"Very well, anger. I was angry with him."

"Right. Of course you were angry, as any man would be who was not a sodomite. By attracting you to him, he put you in a very dangerous spot. Had I not warned you, and had you taken him upstairs to use him as a girl, and had there been anyone to see it whom you could not trust with your life, your very existence could have been at stake if an enemy in Parliament ever decided to make a case against you with the crown for sodomy."

Daniel paled. Apparently he hadn't thought of that possibility.

She continued, "At the very least your reputation would have been forever marred."

He nodded. "I was extremely angry to learn I'd been betrayed."

"Betrayed" might have been a stronger word than Suzanne would have used. "Fooled" would have suited better, in her opinion, but she kept that to herself for the moment. She said, "But, being who you were, you weren't angry enough to hurt him for it."

"What do you mean?"

"Being the sort of man who will bed any creature that breathes—"

"Not just any creature."

"Very well, human creature."

"Suzanne—"

"Being as flexible in your preferences as you are, Daniel, you had no desire to kill him and took the incident with enough humor to do no more than blush and chuckle."

"That I did. I saw no need to make a huge fuss over the thing. I was happy to let it die down and be forgotten."

"Right. But what about the sort of man who is not so flexible? What about a man who would be terribly offended to even be approached by a sodomite? The sort who might think it reflected badly on him, and who would be horrified to think anyone might think *he* was a sodomite himself. Would such a man be moved to kill?"

"Of course. And few would blame him."

"I would."

"You're a tart yourself, and as you've said, you've no reputation to protect. A man whose entire life and livelihood depends on being seen as a man—a man in control and not subject to . . . unnatural practices—who would want to avoid a conviction and possibly execution for sodomy, would be justified in killing anyone who sullied his reputation."

"A boy."

"A boy who apparently was sophisticated in the ways of fornication, and who was quite old enough to have understood the danger in which he was putting his clients."

Suzanne made a small humming noise of concession that

was nonetheless noncommittal, then said, "I'm certain someone encouraged him to do what he did. Surely he never decided for himself to seduce men by presenting himself as a girl. Surely there must have been someone else guiding him in it."

"Well, I suggest that might be a direction to take in your inquiry. Find the men who patronized young Worthington that night, and you'll find your killer."

Suzanne sighed. "London is large. It will be like finding a needle in a haystack."

Daniel shrugged. "The boy was pretty, and most convincing. Your haystack might very well be stiff with needles. It will be a question of which is the one who saw him last."

Some voices rose from the stage area outside the basement window in Suzanne's kitchen. The window opened onto the below-stage area where a trapdoor at center stage gave egress for actors, who came and went from below-stage through another trapdoor, to the room above Suzanne's quarters. That was the green room, where actors ready to perform awaited their time onstage. Situated as she was, most afternoons Suzanne could hear everything that went on in the theatre, and now there was a row started up onstage. She listened as it moved from the stage to the 'tiring house, then to one of the upstairs dressing rooms, and decided she needed to address the situation.

Suzanne excused herself to Daniel and said to the maid, "Sheila, do serve Daniel some dinner, while I calm the actors." She rose to leave. "I'll return shortly."

"Aye, mistress."

Upstairs in the first dressing room, she found Liza and Wally shouting at each other. Several other actors sat around listening, and Horatio had just preceded Suzanne into the room.

"What in bloody hell is going on here?" Horatio's booming voice bounced from the close, wooden walls and hushed
everyone in the room. When he had everyone's instantaneous
attention and they all gaped at him in silence, he continued,
"I said, what is going on? What has you two at each other's
throats?"

Liza and Wally glared at each other. She was in her costume for *Twelfth Night*, though that night's performance
wouldn't go on for another two hours. Wally hadn't yet
donned his own costume and face paint, and so appeared
slightly alien to Suzanne, who always pictured him in full
female regalia. Today he had on no paint, and his light brown
hair was free of wig and oddly masculine at shoulder length.
His square jaw made him even somewhat attractive as a
man. However his attire appeared, though, his stance was
his customary hipshot, pseudo-feminine pose. Chin up,
hands out and palm-down as if resting on a farthingale, he
gazed down his nose at Liza as if he were a duchess and she
a cinder girl.

Liza, for her part, fumed at him with as much disgust as
was at her disposal, which was considerable with her fiery
temper learned on the streets of London's old city. Suzanne
could almost see the steam rising from the top of the girl's
head. She pointed to Wally and shouted, "He—"

"*Lower your voice, if you please!*" shouted Horatio even more
loudly.

Liza fell silent for a moment, frowned at Horatio, then
proceeded in a much more appropriate voice. "He says he's a
better woman than me!"

"I only said I am the better choice to play a woman
onstage." He lowered his chin and gave her a withering stare.
"And I am."

"I'm a real woman."

"I'm a real actor."

She hauled off with her hand to slap him, and Horatio grabbed it in one fist to hold her back. She staggered, thwarted.

"Stop!" he ordered. His enormous hand held her in a solid grip.

She struggled with him, but he was too big and too strong for her. He held her hand in his without much effort at all, until she gave up and stopped trying to get away. Then he let go of the hand. She held it to her chest and rubbed the sore knuckles.

Horatio said to Wally, "Why do you antagonize her? You know she's a temper."

"She's an arrogant witch. She thinks all that is necessary to play a character is to be one. She's no thought for how she presents herself onstage."

Suzanne commented, "I think she's rather good." Wally frowned at her, and she added, "Though I think you are also an excellent actor, Wal. But you should give Liza her due."

"She's a no-talent whore."

Liza responded with, "I've got talent." She was a whore, and had no qualms about it. Her great dream was to be one of the dozens of actresses known to have bedded the king. So far she went ignored by Charles, but she was young yet and held out hope.

Wally said, "She thinks being a woman is better than knowing how to play one."

"It is."

"How can you even believe that? You, who clop across the stage like a horse, and bray like a mule!"

"You, who prance across the stage like a wood nymph and whose voice is shrill and false as a tin whistle!"

"I'm believable as a woman!"

"Only because the audience has never seen a real one on the stage!" Voices were rising again.

Horatio cleared his throat in a threat to shout them down again. They fell silent and looked to him as if he could settle the argument. So he did. "Neither of you is a better choice than the other."

Both Liza and Wally opened their mouths to protest in unison, but Horatio cut them off. "Depending on the role and on the play, but mostly on how that play is interpreted by the master of the troupe, which in our case is myself." That made them both clamp their mouths shut and frown, waiting to hear what he meant by that. And he obliged. "Not every production of a given play has the same tone or style. Just as each individual performance is unique among others in a run, each cast brings its own flavor and character to the script. A creative master of the troupe will consider how all the actors work together, and how their own characters will fulfill the characters they play. There was a time when all women in a play were given to be played by small men or young boys. I've played many a witch and nurse myself in my day, and I vow I was as good an actor as a woman as I was as a man." He nodded to Wally, who shifted his stance and glared at Liza as if he'd been vindicated. "However, the new idea of having real women play the women characters is an interesting style choice I applaud. 'Tis a fresh perspective on an ancient art. I would go so far as to say we are lucky to live in these times when such a monumental change is here for us to explore." The last he said with a broad stage flourish of his hand.

Wally interrupted in a voice dripping with contempt, "'Tis French foolishness, and the king only wishes to plunder the ranks of new actresses for his bed. That's what exploring is going on."

"And good for him!" Liza shot back. "He gives some mighty excellent gifts to them as gets picked!"

"But fucking the king doesn't make you a good actress."

"It would make me a rich whore."

"Which you are yet neither, and are unlikely to ever be."

She raised her hand again to slap him, and Horatio prevented her once more by grabbing her hand as Wally took a step backward to avoid being smacked hard. Liza struggled again, trying to wrench herself free so she could chase Wally down and hit him.

"*Both of you!* Stop this now, or I'll recast both your roles and neither of you will be playing a woman on my stage ever again." Liza stopped struggling, and Wally crossed his arms. Horatio continued, "If I hear one more word from either of you on this, I will carry out that threat and you'll both end up looking to the king and his brother for work."

Wally said under his breath, "I at least have worked with both royal companies."

Liza muttered, "Prick!"

He responded, "Cunny!"

Horatio let go of Liza's hand. "There, that's better. Go quietly and don't let the audience ever know what you're really thinking. Step out onstage and act like lovers. Show me which of you is the better actress." He waved his hands at them. "Go, now. Shoo."

Both Liza and Wally left the room, and the rest of the company watched them go.

Suzanne said to Horatio, "Tonight's performance is going to be strange, at the very least."

"Not to worry. If either of them ruins the show over this,

I'll carry out my threat. Neither of the royal companies would put up with that, and so I will not, either. There are too many men eager to play women who have been put on the street because of the king's preference for women onstage, and more to come, I'm certain. We won't be crippled by these two."

Suzanne went downstairs to prepare herself to leave for Bank Side, where she would begin her search for that haystack needle.

Chapter Ten

W hen she left through the rear door, she once more
found Ramsay at his post, waiting for her.

"Diarmid, it must make for a terribly boring day to stand
there against the wall, waiting for me to emerge. I say, you
really ought to come inside if you want to see me."

"And let you slip away without me?"

"For that, I could have gone through the front entrance
had I wanted to avoid you."

"Will you?"

"No. So really there's no point in you wasting your day
waiting. Come inside and amuse yourself watching the
rehearsals until I emerge." She glanced around the empty alley
for who might be listening, then said in a lowered, confidential
voice, "You might even find yourself tapped to play Olivia or
Viola, should Liza or Wally annoy Horatio much further."

Ramsay laughed out loud at the thought. "Aye, Horatio
would adore me as a great, loud, strapping Olivia!"

"Well, it is a comedy after all."

He chuckled some more as he fell into step beside Suzanne heading down the alley toward Maid Lane. "And where are we off to this evening?"

"Bank Side."

"And who to question?"

"Anyone who appears likely."

"Then I expect 'tis an excellent thing I am here, for you know the Bank Side is filled to overflowing with murderers and charlatans." He was joking, but Suzanne knew there was always a grain of truth in all humor. Twisting falsehood was pointless and never funny. She took his arm and they walked toward the river.

The sun was just throwing sunset colors when they arrived at the Goat and Boar. Still a little early for the regular crowd, who generally descended on the public house once the Globe performance was finished. But there were a few patrons sitting around the large table, and Young Dent was supervising the roasting joint on the fire. It hadn't been there long, and still was quite pink on the outside. Supper wouldn't be available for another hour or two. Dent turned the spit and fixed it in place before moving on to other duties.

Suzanne watched Dent move through the room at his tasks. A hunch came over her. Though he'd insisted he'd not remembered a boy in his tavern these several nights ago, she wondered whether she'd only miscommunicated her questions to him. She'd asked after a boy, but Dent may have thought he'd seen a girl.

"Dent!" Suzanne called to him as she removed her coat and muff. "Bring us your best wine and two clean glasses if you please. And one for yourself, as well. Come sit with us for the moment; I wish to have a chat."

Dent, unaccustomed to being asked to sit with his customers, appeared less than comfortable with the suggestion, but after a moment's hesitation nodded nonetheless and went to do her bidding as she sat herself at a small table near the hearth. Ramsay removed his own coat and took a seat next to her.

Dent brought the bottle and three glasses, and took the empty chair next to Suzanne. Dent was in his twenties, having taken over the Goat and Boar when his father had died a couple of years before. He was thin and tall, and when working never stopped moving. But at rest he was as calm as anyone, and set his hands in his lap. Ramsay poured wine into the glasses, and they drank. Dent looked expectantly at Suzanne.

"Dent, I wonder how your memory is of four nights ago."

"I've an excellent memory of most things, should I take notice. And I notice much. However, I prefer not to blather things about. It would make for a reluctant drinking crowd, should word get out that I gossip too much. I could find myself lonely, and I like hearing the gossip of other people, you understand."

"Yes, quite. But there's something you might help me with."

"You, personally?" He glanced at Ramsay, who furrowed his brow and gave his head a slight shake as if to indicate his presence meant nothing; that he was only there to keep Suzanne company. So Dent returned his attention to Suzanne. "Right. I'd be glad to tell you anything I know."

She replied, "Very good. You remember four nights ago, when there was such an unusually large crowd here?"

"That same night as when you was asking after that boy yesterday?"

"Yes. That night."

"Indeed, I do. It was quite a crowd, it was. I wouldn't care to tell you how much silver I took in, lest word get out and someone think to rob me." His grin was wide. It must have been a large windfall indeed.

"Do you remember a young girl? There was a young girl in here that night, wearing a very nice blue dress decorated lavishly with lace."

"There was a lot of tarts in here that night. Seems they can smell a crowd with money, and they come to help me sell the ale and relieve the wealthier patrons of their burdensome purses. I daresay I may have had the short end of that particular stick, having only food and drink to offer for sale." He snickered, a rather odd, snorting laugh. Always one to mind his own business, he rarely laughed in the presence of his patrons, and Suzanne was struck by the odd sound. She found it amusing in itself, and never mind his tired joke.

"Do you remember the girl in the blue dress?"

"I do. She was a lively one, that girl. Like a lady, she was, but as forward as the most brazen whore you'd care to meet."

"Did you see her with anyone that night?"

"I seen her with nearly everyone that night. She bounced from one man to the next, and disappeared several times, then to return and attach herself to someone else. She must have made quite a lot of money."

"Where did she go whenever she disappeared?"

Dent frowned, thinking, and looked over at the door. "Don't know as I could say for certain. Most of the girls take their patrons upstairs, and for that I get a portion of their fee, depending on how long they spend. But that girl in the blue dress never did." He raised a finger as he remembered something. "Now, some of the girls, particularly the uglier ones who don't command much of a fee, they'll take their men outside, to the dark corner of the alley up that way." He gestured in the direction of the dead end the nameless alley outside made against the blank wall of a warehouse that stood in the next street over.

"It was terribly cold that night."

Dent shrugged. "Any man so sensitive to cold will pay to go upstairs or do without. Them as don't feel the cold so much, and with little cash, will take what they can get. It's generally quick in any case. Nobody lingers about. The girls lean up against that wall so's they don't dirty their dresses too much. 'Tis cheap for the patron and quick for the whore, so she can go a great many times in an evening and she doesn't spend so much effort negotiating her fee and securing a room. Some of 'em gets on their knees for it, so's they can spit and not have to clean up after. A cup of ale to wash it all down, and they're ready for another go. And I get to sell 'em the ale. All in all a tidy arrangement, from where I stand."

Suzanne knew all that. She'd done it herself many times in the ever more distant past, and in this very tavern. But, knowing that the "girl" in question had been a boy, she now saw the practice in a new light. Lord Paul could get away with pretending to be a female prostitute by using his mouth. Very handy, and as engaging as he was, as Dent had said, he probably made a great deal of money at it.

"Do you remember any of the men she was with?"

"You mean, other than Throckmorton?"

A grin curled one side of her mouth. "Yes, other than he."

Dent thought for a moment, but Suzanne could tell by his face there wasn't much hope of a name. He shrugged. "I can't say as I can remember any faces. There was so many in here that night I'd be hard put to even remember you were here if you weren't asking me about it just now."

"It's quite all right. I can't expect you to remember everything. Any recollection of faces at all? Not necessarily ones that girl was with. Anyone who was here late in the evening after I left, who might have seen her leave with someone."

"Oh, certainly. There was Big Willie and his friend, Warren. They both stayed late, as always, playing for tips. They get little money, usually, and like to drink theirs, so they had no truck with the whores. But they threw back their share of ale during the night, and Willie played until the place was empty, even after Warren packed it in. He'll remember who all was here."

Hope grew for Suzanne. Willie was a good friend, bright, and observant. For a shilling he would be able to tell her the names of everyone present during the entire evening. "Very good, Dent. Thank you for your help; Willie is just the sort of person I was hoping could tell me something."

Dent nodded and stood as Ramsay paid for their wine, and he and Suzanne gathered themselves for the trek to Willie's rooms near the bear arena.

It was a bit of a walk, and in the winter darkness was quite cold. But the streets were not empty, and the torches that lit the entrances to various eating, drinking, and whoring establishments guided their steps along the cobbles. The heat from them took the sharpest edges from the cold night air in the narrow streets as they passed.

Willie lived in a single room in a tenement very near the arena where people were entertained by bears fighting dogs set on them. Tonight could be heard a great deal of shouting from it, and beneath that was the snarl and roar of animals fighting each other to the death. Beneath that was the similar roar of men egging on the fight. Suzanne didn't think very highly of the sport. The bear always died, and some-

times a dog or two, which—even aside from the cruelty—
she thought was awfully predictable and not particularly
interesting. The wagering was too complicated to be her idea
of fun, and so there was nothing about bear baiting worth
her while. She and Ramsay hurried past the arena doors,
looking for the small entrance to Willie's room.

It was a basement door, down several steps from the
street. Suzanne had been here before, and more often than
not an unusually deep puddle lurked beneath that bottom
step, deceptively deep and a danger to good shoes even for
one wearing pattens. Ramsay held her hand to keep her from
slipping as she stepped down, tested the bottom, and found
no puddle. More important, she found no puddle frozen into
a sheet of slippery ice. So she finished her descent and
knocked on the door.

There was no answer, so she knocked again. Still no
answer. The room had a window up at the street level, so
Ramsay helped her back up the steps to look. No candle was
visible inside the room, and it was far too early for him to
be asleep. Willie wasn't home.

Suzanne muttered an unladylike curse, and said to Ramsay, "He's out, I'm afraid."

"Have we any idea where?" Ramsay stared across at the
cluster of men loitering outside the arena entrance. None of
them was Willie.

Suzanne thought a moment. "He's not at the Goat and
Boar, so he must be playing his fiddle somewhere. Horse
Shoe Alley. He likes the corner of Horse Shoe Alley and Bank
Side." It was back the way they'd come, and past the Goat
and Boar. She took a good, long look up and down the street
here, and neither saw nor heard a little man playing a fiddle.
Big Willie always gathered a crowd when he played, and the

only such crowd in this street was more interested in bears and dogs than in music. Suzanne and Ramsay pulled their cloaks tighter around them and set off once more.

Snow began to fall, in tiny flakes that flitted about inside circles of torchlight like moths around a flame. Suzanne and Ramsay walked more quickly, and their breath came in puffs of vapor. The cold made inroads into her clothing, and in spite of her heavy cloak and muff a chill came on her. The cold air wafted into her skirts as she walked. She stuffed her hands deep into her muff and pressed it into her belly, but she only became colder. Before long she began to shiver. Even walking didn't warm her enough against it.

Ramsay saw it, and opened his coat to draw her into it. At first she hesitated, but realized it was only going to become colder if she refused the invitation. She was cold natured, and so was susceptible to it, while most men were hot natured. Ramsay, as large and vibrant as he was, had heat to spare and a coat large enough for them both. It would be no hardship for him to lend her some warmth. So she stepped close to him, inside the coat, and let him warm her with his body.

On the corner of Bank Side and Horse Shoe Alley they found Big Willie and his fiddle, standing in a circle of light around a large brazier. Suzanne was thankful for finding him and for the warmth of the fire. She greeted him as she thrust her hands toward the burning wood and pitch. "Willie! I'm so glad we've found you!" She rubbed her gloved hands together and blew into her cupped palms, then put them next to the fire again.

"Good to see you, as well, Suze. I was just about to give 'er up for the night. This weather is playing the devil with my fiddle. Can't keep it tuned for my life, says I."

"I quite agree. It's not a night for anyone to be about." She rubbed her palms together and flexed her fingers. Too bad Willie hadn't packed it in earlier; it would have saved her a bit of walking and quite a lot of shivering. She sighed as the warmth of the fire unclenched all her muscles.

"So, what did you want me for, if you don't mind my asking?" Willie took the opportunity for a break, set his fiddle into its case and shut it, then stuffed his hands into his armpits beneath his coat. The gloves he wore for playing had no fingertips, so his fingers must have been quite cold.

"Young Dent tells me you might be able to remember what faces were to be seen at the Goat and Boar four nights ago."

"Right, everyone was there. Including yourself and Master Ramsay here." His expression and tone asked why she didn't remember herself who was there.

"I mean after we left, and you and Warren were playing for tips. Dent tells me you lingered quite late."

Willie nodded. "You know I keep an eye on the crowd. Always looking out for a tipper, and knowing what tunes each one likes." He tapped his forehead and winked. "I got a list in my head, goes back twenty years, it does."

"You know everyone in Southwark."

"I know everyone who visits here from across the river, as well." He nodded toward the Thames behind him.

"Except the girl in the blue, lacey dress at the Goat and Boar four nights ago."

"Including her. And she weren't no girl, neither."

"Quite right. What do you know about her? *Him.*"

"He was the one they found floating in the river, wasn't he?"

"He was. I'm looking for his killer."

"He showed up just the night before he was killed. Can't tell you his name, though."

"He was Paul Worthington. Son of Jacob Worthington, Duke of Cawthorne."

Willie's eyes went wide. "God blind me! You don't say!"

"I don't, actually."

He nodded, and touched a finger to his brow. "I got ya, Suze. Nobody'll hear it from me."

She knew they would, but she hoped he would keep her name out of it, at least for a while. "In any case, what did you see that night? Regarding Lord Paul? Who was he with?"

Willie shook his head. "I seen him with a great many men that night, including our own Throckmorton. Nearly split a gut to keep from laughing out loud at that one, I did. Had his arm around the little tart, he did, and thinking he would have a bit of—"

"In any case, Willie, who else had his arm around that very young boy?"

Willie frowned as he concentrated. "Well, there was Warren. And Young Dent." Suzanne's eyebrows raised to learn this. She would have to ask Dent about that when next she saw him. For now, she let it pass as Willie continued, "There was one or two whose names escape me."

"Describe them to me."

"One was a sailor I'd never seen before."

"Plenty of sailors to be found in Bank Side. Doesn't exactly narrow it down for me." The wharves were just across the river, and men from the ships docked there often ended up in South-wark for the bears and bulls, and of course the whores on Bank Side. The Goat and Boar was a natural place for them to collect for ale, whisky, and wine. "What did he look like?"

"Well, he were some'at average. Medium height, not too

fat, not too thin. Plain-looking. Brown hair, I think, though he wore a cap down low so it was hard to tell."

"Nothing to distinguish him from other sailors?"

"Well, he were missing a hand, that one."

"Which hand?"

Willie had to think on that a moment, held up each hand in turn as if weighing them, then raised his right hand as he remembered. "His right. I'm sure of it."

"Good. Go on."

"Well, then there was one who appeared terribly fancy. All silk velvet and brocade, and a great, curly, long wig to make the king fall on his sword for envy. He carried a silver-topped cane, though he never appeared to need it for more than decoration. More trim than average, and he moved a bit like a cat. All smooth-like, and that."

"Did Lord Paul take either of these men outside?"

"Both of them. Though with the sailor it was more like the boy had talked the patron into it, and the rich fellow appeared to demand the boy accompany him. They knew each other, I think, or at least they spoke to each other as if they did. And with the rich fellow the boy seemed less like a girl. Like he was dropping the pretense just a hair."

That very much interested Suzanne. "What did they say?"

"Couldn't make out the words. Only the tone, and I could see their faces."

"How did they act? How did the boy act toward the older man?"

"As I said, they plainly knew each other. The boy was all smilin' and that, though I must say he never stopped smilin' no matter who he was talking to. But he seemed especially happy to see the fellow with the cane, and when he was directed outside he went willingly."

"But it was different from the other men."

"Right. Can't put my finger on why. Not really."

"Was that the last time you saw the boy?"

Willie shook his head. "No, he returned not long after, and resumed his quest for men with money."

"Did you ever see him go upstairs?"

Willie shook his head again. "No, if he left the public room, it was to go out to the alley."

"Did you happen to notice the last man he was with that night?"

"No, I can't say as I did. There were some more, but I took no notice of who they were, nor could I tell you which one was the last one. The strange boy in the blue dress didn't tip, so he wasn't exactly the center of my attention. Just, sometime during the evening he stopped coming back inside."

"Quite all right, Willie. You've given me something to work with here." She looked to Ramsay. "Next we go across the river to the wharves and hope to find a sailor missing a hand."

"In the morning," said Ramsay.

"Right." The thing to do now was to go home and get some sleep. Ramsay walked her safely to the Globe, all the way to the basement apartment. As they descended the steps, she wondered what villain he expected to encounter so deep in the structure. At the door, she turned to him, looked up at his face, and once again was impressed by his height. He was most likely over six feet tall. Taller than Daniel, certainly. Even taller than Horatio, who towered over most people she knew. And Ramsay was far more handsome, and had real hair of his own instead of a wig. Just then she couldn't help smiling up at him, like a silly girl less than twenty just discovering a new love.

That thought sobered her, but though her smile dimmed his did not. He said, in a voice and accent that mocked the very suitor he claimed to be, "Well, I must say I had a lovely evening, and enjoyed your company very much."

She couldn't help a chuckle at that. "It was a charming stroll through the city. We'll have to do it again sometime."

"I am at my lady's disposal."

"In the morning, then, and don't be late. And do come inside when you arrive."

His voice went soft. So terribly soft she would have cuddled up inside it, were that possible. "Verily, I would want naught else but to come inside."

For a long, suspended moment, she thought he might lean down to kiss her. She would have sworn he leaned toward her. But then he came to his senses and stood straight again.

She said, "There's no need to give yourself a chill loitering in the alley. Knock and have Sheila let you in."

He cleared his throat. "Right." Then she let herself into her rooms and closed the door behind her with the feeling of having escaped something dangerous.

Chapter Eleven

The next morning a knock came at the entrance to Suzanne's rooms in the Globe basement, and Sheila went to admit Ramsay, who presented himself for service.

Suzanne was in the midst of a breakfast of bacon and toasted Irish bread, sitting at the table at the inner end of her sitting room. She gestured to the single chair opposite. "Do sit and let Sheila bring you some food."

Ramsay sat, but waved off Sheila with a shake of his head. "None for me, though I thank you. I've already had my fill of mutton pies from the street vendors this morning."

Suzanne made a face. "I don't know how you can tolerate those nasty pies. Naught but suet and gristle, in my experience." For her they were also a reminder of the worst days, when she'd had no roof over her head and ate what she could buy, steal, or cajole from those vendors.

"Not all of us are lucky enough to have a good maid who

is also a wonderful cook." He threw Sheila his most charming grin, which she rewarded with a deep blush and a smile.

"Then you should eat here instead."

"I would have breakfast every day here, and before rising, if you wished it."

Suzanne smiled at her own folly for having invited the too-forward comment. She replied, "Do have a piece of toast. Surely you have room for that."

Ramsay said, "Thank you, I do." He grinned again at Sheila, who hurried off to fetch a plate of toast.

Another knock came, and Sheila returned to answer it. In came Horatio, his wig askew as ever, and he stood in the sitting room appearing agitated. "I hate to disturb thee so early, niece, but there is a matter of significant importance I wish to discuss, and of late I've been hard put to find you in." This matter must be dire, for Horatio had slipped into the quasi-Elizabethan thee-thou that was his habit when upset. During the interregnum he'd adopted it for the sake of mocking the Puritans in power, who had outlawed theatre and forced him to take his art to the streets. He'd been arrested once for performing, and therefore had little love for Puritans and Presbyterians. His devout Catholicism made him impatient with Protestants in general, but he had a special dislike for those who attacked the love of his life, the theatre.

"I apologize, Horatio. I've been occupied with other things these past few days." She gestured to the room to indicate the lack of others demanding her attention, and added, "You can see I've some time to myself at the moment, so tell me what I might do for you."

He drew himself up to his full, considerable height, his

arms straight at his sides in an attempt to still the uncontrolled gesticulating that was another sign he was upset. His fingers splayed and flexed, for he was never able to control them no matter how hard he tried. His deep, booming voice was barely under control, but Suzanne was certain he could be heard in the stairwell outside. "We need to talk about Liza and Wally."

Suzanne sat back in her chair and laid her hands on her lap. "Haven't they quit snapping at each other?"

He shook his head. "Every day it's a struggle to keep them from blows. I've tried to make them understand the behavior is not acceptable, and they swear to me they will refrain in future, but then the very next performance is a nightmare of bad blood. 'Tis but a matter of time until they fall out onstage and become the laughingstock of London theatre." His mouth pressed closed hard enough to make a white line around his lips, and his eyebrows bobbed as another factor came to mind. "And I will become a laughingstock. I can hardly bear such a thing, and will not. I must recast if they continue on this way."

"I quite agree, Horatio. It's untenable, and you shouldn't be expected to suffer it."

That calmed him somewhat, and his fingers stilled. He seemed to breathe more easily. "Yes. 'Tis untenable, I quite agree. I must recast, then, and in all haste. I thank thee for thy assistance." He turned to leave, but Suzanne stopped him.

"No, Horatio." He turned back, and she continued, "There's no need for recasting, I think. Perhaps there's some way to avoid that."

"I don't see how, my niece. They are like two dogs in a ring. They circle each other, then one attacks, then the other responds. 'Tis only a question of who attacks first. A couple of old spinsters fighting over a widower couldn't be more hateful. I've complaints from the entire cast."

"Then I must have a chat with them both."

"I've attempted it, and have had no success."

She thought a moment, considering the possibilities for action. She could threaten the two, but that had probably already been tried. It would seem the atmosphere of togetherness she'd worked hard to instill made them feel their positions with the company were inviolate. They might not believe Horatio when he said he would recast their roles. Or perhaps something else was at work here. Some sort of fear or other insecurity. She would have to think on it and decide on an action to take.

To Horatio she said, "Let me speak to them. Perhaps I can find a way to convince them it's in their best interest to get along with each other."

"I tell thee, 'tis impossible. They hate each other and will not reconcile."

"Let me try. Give them to the end of the run, and see if they will change their behavior before we do anything rash. It won't sit well with the rest of the company if we are too quick to exclude our players. This is the first such situation we've had, and everyone will be sensitive to how it's handled."

Horatio at first appeared to want to resist agreement, but finally nodded. "Very well. I bow to thy higher authority and good judgment. Speak to them, and if they persist in their disruptions I will exclude them from future productions."

"Eminently fair, in my opinion."

He nodded again, then bowed in almost the same motion.

"Good day, my niece." Then he made his exit without the aid of Sheila to show him the door directly behind him.

Ramsay said, in a low, slow tone, "Excitable fellow."

"He controls it. He's actually an excellent actor, and his vision for the Shakespeare is perfect for us. He puts his soul into this company, and I can understand why he's upset when two of his actors appear to be making the play less than it could be."

Yet another knock came, and Suzanne wondered who else might need her attention so early in the morning. The sun was barely up, and she knew few who were such early risers. At least, she'd thought she knew few. She and Ramsay paused in their conversation once more as Sheila went to answer the door.

In stepped Constable Pepper, who greeted her with a voice hoarse with the catarrh she'd seen developing on his last visit. He coughed, causing her to step back. He removed his hat and looked from Suzanne to Ramsay, then back to Suzanne as she stood to greet him. She gestured him to the upholstered chair nearby, and they both sat. He appeared dismayed. Plainly he'd hoped to find her alone with her maid. "I need to speak confidentially, Mistress Thornton." He coughed again, this time covering his mouth with a fist.

Suzanne glanced at Ramsay, who gazed blandly at the constable. The Scot said nothing, waiting to see how this would go before making a comment. Suzanne said, "You may speak freely, Constable. I have complete trust in him."

"I must insist."

"So must I. Since you have come all this way so early in the morning, my educated guess is that the matter at hand is far more important to you than it could possibly be to me. Therefore, I invite you to either tell me your business or return to your office where your brandy awaits. I will proceed with my day as well." Sheila brought a small plate of toast, set it before Ramsay, curtsied, then returned to the kitchen.

Pepper reddened some, shifted his considerable weight, then glanced at Ramsay once more before speaking. "It is about the Duke of Cawthorne."

Suzanne sat up straight, and a charge of alarm fluttered in her gut. This couldn't possibly be good, for Pepper to have heard from someone other than herself that she'd interviewed the duke. "What of him?"

"He summoned me this morning, before the sun was even up. Without the least consideration for a man who works hard every day, he had his driver put me in a carriage and haul me all the way to Westminster. I don't mind telling you, it distressed me greatly."

Suzanne flinched with suppressed laughter at the suggestion Pepper ever worked hard. Or worked at all. She replied, "It must have been an unbearable ordeal."

"My heart nearly stopped, I tell you! And so when I arrived he dressed me down right proper for sending you after him to question him about his son. Of course I assured him I had done no such thing, and furthermore I told him I couldn't imagine where he'd gotten the idea I had. He told me you'd said it when you'd come to grill him yesterday. Surely you did not, and he simply misunderstood you." He frowned at her and waited for a reply. Plainly he expected it to be in the affirmative.

Since Suzanne hadn't actually grilled the duke, and in fact had not named Pepper at all and therefore could not have even suggested he'd sent her to grill Cawthorne, she felt perfectly justified in saying, "I did not." How Cawthorne had even learned of her association with Pepper puzzled her.

"As I told him. In any case, the duke insisted you had, and further pressed that you be admonished to cease all enquiry on the matter."

"He did?"

Pepper nodded. Then he took a deep breath, leaned toward her, and said in a plaintive tone, "Now, I pray you, please tell me what on earth he means. What matter?"

Suzanne had to stifle a laugh as she realized Pepper had gone all the way to Westminster, spoken to Cawthorne, and returned to Southwark without the slightest understanding of the matter at hand. No wonder he was distressed and confused. She said, "He means the boy in the dress who was murdered."

Pepper straightened, thought about that for a moment, then said, "I see. And what about him?"

"The boy in the dress has turned out to be Cawthorne's youngest son, Lord Paul."

The light of understanding went on, and Pepper repeated with less irony, "I see. Are you certain of it?"

"Absolutely and without reservation. There was a portrait of the victim on the wall of the duke's house. I couldn't be more sure the dead boy was his son."

"And you questioned him in the matter?"

"I informed the boy's parents he was dead, and further described the condition in which he was found."

Pepper blanched. "Oh dear. Perhaps you shouldn't have done that."

"They needed to be told." And she had needed to learn who the boy was and how he came to be wearing a dress, but telling Pepper that would only lead the conversation into the gray area of how she'd come to be in the duke's house to begin with. Better to circle that subject entirely and depend on the constable's laziness to not have it brought up.

"But it might have been advisable to spare their sensibilities regarding the condition of the body."

"They would have learned it eventually. Better to hear it from me early on, so steps could be taken to limit public exposure, than to hear it by rumor after too many unsympathetic people had seen the body and gossiped about it."

Pepper had to concede the point, and nodded. "Very well, then. In any case, I am here to inform you that you're not to investigate this any further. Your involvement in the boy's death is at an end. The crown and the magistrate are satisfied that we've learned all we need to know, and I am no longer pressed to find the killer."

Suzanne, for her part, still felt pressed. "But that killer is still at large in the city."

"Better to let him go than to make an enormous public brouhaha that will only embarrass the duke and break the heart of his wife, the boy's mother."

"You would have a murderer go free? What of justice?"

"God will sort him out, I vow."

"And if he murders again before God gets around to punishing him?"

Pepper's lips pressed together, and his voice took on an edge of frustration and impatience. "Alas, there is nothing I can do about that. Cawthorne has made it clear he doesn't wish any further inquiry. The victim was his son, and so I intend to abide by his wishes."

"You mean, he's a duke and so you intend to abide by his wishes."

"That as well." Pepper was making no bones.

Suzanne was stymied for a response to that, and so fell silent. Ramsay wisely remained equally silent.

Pepper rose and restored his hat to his head. "So I see we are all in agreement and you well understand the situation. I bid you both a good day." He turned to glance at the door but a few feet away, then said, "I'll see myself out." And with that he took his leave.

Suzanne frowned into the middle distance, thinking, while Ramsay chewed on his toast as he waited for her to say something. She weighed in her heart her possible responses to this turn of events. Could she let go of the investigation? Should she? Could she face the day each morning, knowing a murderer was loose in the city and that she might have the ability to apprehend him?

Finally Ramsay swallowed and said, "You're going to keep looking for the killer, aren't you?"

She focused on his face and nodded. She had no choice if she were to live with herself.

Having finished breakfast, Suzanne and Ramsay bundled up in cloaks, gloves, and muff to venture out to the docks along the river in search of the one-handed sailor mentioned by Big Willie. Rehearsal was in progress on the stage and in pockets of open space here and there about the theatre. Suzanne noticed Little Wally running lines with Matthew and Louis on the ground in the pit, and decided to have a chat with him about Liza. She asked Ramsay to wait for her by the entrance doors, and approached the cluster of actors.

"Wally, might I have a word with you for a moment?"

He turned to address her, in full femme though he wore his men's street clothing. "Why yes, mistress. Whatever your heart desires." He strode as gracefully as a queen to follow her to the other side of the pit, out of earshot of the other two men, seeming to float above the gravel and leaving nary a footprint. Suzanne couldn't help but look at his feet to make sure they were touching the ground. They were, of course, but one couldn't know it by watching him move. He stood, poised like a dancer, and waited for her to speak.

"Wal, I hope you know I value you as a member of this troupe. I believe you've brought a great deal of talent and skill to our production of *Twelfth Night.*"

His gaze dulled and a line appeared between his eyebrows, which was his way of frowning. "I detect the approach of a 'however.'"

"Nonsense. I offer my praise in all sincerity. I have nothing ulterior to say. Wally, it is because of my high regard for your abilities I come to you for help."

He eyed her with palpable skepticism. She pressed on and hoped he would believe her.

"My dear, I understand there is a conflict between you and Liza concerning the relative merits of your talents."

"She's a sow."

"Be that as it may, I find myself in a bit of a bad spot concerning that conflict." Liza was perfectly capable of being sow-like when angered, and so Suzanne didn't care to argue the merits of Wally's accusation. She continued, "I need help from you with her."

"What sort of help could I possibly give? I've no control over her attitude toward me."

"I mean, I think her attitude is hurting her portrayal."

Wally suddenly dropped his overtly feminine stance and set his hands on his hips to lean toward her in a conspiratorial attitude. His voice became a harsh, masculine whisper.

"I've been saying that all along! She thinks of herself as the end-all because she's got a cunny and I don't, and she doesn't realize that it takes more than bits of flesh to portray a character!"

Suzanne nodded as she saw she might be getting somewhere with him. "So you see what I mean."

"Absolutely! I keep trying to tell her that, but she will never listen. All she can do is go on about how she's a 'real' woman." A note of grief entered his voice, and it struck Suzanne he might wish he were a woman. She couldn't imagine anyone wanting to give up the freedoms he owned as a man, but she laid it down as one of the many mysteries of life.

In any case, she hurried to present her suggestion and hoped it would be accepted and carried out. "Wal, I wish you would do something for me."

"Whatever my mistress would have of me."

"I would like you to help Liza become a better actress."

He shook his head and stepped back. "Oh, I don't think I could."

"She's talented enough. All she needs is some guidance."

"She won't listen to my guidance. She thinks she knows all and doesn't need any help from anyone."

"I think she'd listen to you if you approached her properly."

"Like, how? I've never had anything from her but ugliness."

"Ignore the rude remarks and defensive posture. Start with admiration. Let her know you think she's already good at the work."

"But she's not."

"Pretend. You're an actor. Act. Let her think you admire her work, then slip in some bits that you think would improve that work. After all, this craft is an ongoing process.

Nobody ever comes to where he can't learn something new. You'll agree with me that the objective of every truly great actor is to make each performance better than the last."

Wally nodded, agreeing, though Suzanne had no idea whether he'd ever thought it before. It was something she'd always felt true, but she was a very different sort of performer from Wally. Nevertheless, he seemed to at least understand what she was saying.

She continued, "So approach her in that spirit. As if you were inviting her into a secret club of actors who are highly skilled and extraordinarily talented. That she might have the greatness of Kynaston or yourself, and that what she desires can be learned."

He thought that over for a moment, then nodded again. "I see what you mean. Trick her into becoming skilled."

"It would certainly be a benefit to the troupe if everyone in it were equally skilled."

"We would be, had the French not meddled in things the way they have, letting women onstage and all."

"Well, I'm afraid we can't put that genie back in the bottle, and we've got to live with how things are. In any case, can I count on you to help me in this? For the troupe?"

"Of course, my mistress." He resumed his feminine stance and curtsied without benefit of skirt.

"Thank you, good woman." Suzanne nodded and smiled, then bade him good day and went to collect Ramsay once again where he awaited her by the doors.

SUZANNE'S decision to keep looking was vindicated that very morning. She and Ramsay had just stepped onto Maid Lane when there arrived a carriage unfamiliar to anyone at the Globe. A plain, black carriage came to a stop directly in front of them. The horses were fine animals and matched in every detail, though none of the tack bore any ornamentation. Even a funeral carriage would have had black crepe at the windows and headdresses for the horses, but this had none of that. Suzanne sensed its occupant would be equally fine and equally plain. Suzanne waited as the coachman descended to open the door and help his passenger down the steps. A glance back at the theatre entrance told Suzanne that Matthew, Louis, and Wally had come to see. They stood in the open doorway, staring.

The passenger was the Duchess of Cawthorne. She bore an unhappy frown as she looked about at the unfamiliar and bustling street. It seemed too much for her long-sheltered sensibilities. When she spotted Suzanne, her brow smoothed some to see a familiar face.

"Mistress Thornton," she said, sounding somewhat relieved. "I'm so glad to find you here." As if she had been in terror of having to make her way into the theatre and seek her out by herself. "Come." She gestured them toward her carriage, and had a glance at the crowd by the theatre doors. "I wish to speak to you in confidence." Another glance at the onlookers, and she appeared to fear an attack from ruffians. The actors gawked, with little understanding they were frightening her.

Suzanne might have had a dry comment about this being a day for speaking in confidence, but she refrained from saying it. Instead she said, "By all means, your grace."

The coachman held the door and helped the women into the carriage. Ramsay followed. Suzanne, Ramsay, and the duchess settled into the seats, and the coachman was ordered to drive.

"Where to, your grace?" the coachman spoke through a vent near the ceiling.

"Just . . . anywhere. Not too far. Find a circle and simply make a loop if you can." Had they been in Westminster, she might have ordered him to drive through St. James's Park, but in Southwark there was no equivalent circuit. The driver would simply have to wander aimlessly as best he could in unfamiliar territory.

"Yes, your grace." The carriage lurched into motion in the cobbled street.

The duchess addressed Suzanne, though she kept glancing at Ramsay as if she felt odd to ignore him. "I've come to make a plea for your help." This last she directed at Ramsay, and it appeared he was the one she thought could help her.

Suzanne leaned in and raised her voice a little to direct the woman's attention away from him, for he had no authority in any matter involving Suzanne. "What may I do for your grace? I am at your service."

The duchess finally settled her attention on Suzanne and said, "I wish you to continue your investigation of my son's murder." For a moment her eyes clouded and teared, but she brought herself under control and continued, "I want his killer to be found and brought to justice."

"You're aware that the duke has requested there be no investigation?"

She nodded. "Yes. I overheard the discussion my husband had with the constable this morning. Jacob has a bit of a temper, I'm afraid. He's a terribly devout man, but his one great fault is that he can't help raising his voice when he's angry. So I heard every word he said, though I heard nothing said by the constable. After he left, I had a talk with my husband, and I confess it was not a terribly graceful one.

When I requested he rescind his hasty order, he began shouting again. It was all I could do to keep from bursting into tears. But over the years I've become accustomed to his histrionics and I was able to keep from breaking down. However, I failed to convince him of my terrible need to have justice done for my baby." The duchess welled up, and her nose began to turn red. A gumminess entered her voice as she continued, "He was adamant the investigation come to an end. He said it would only cause gossip, and that it would hurt him in Parliament. He said there would be things said that would hurt me." She looked straight into Suzanne's eyes. "Are you a mother?" Suzanne nodded. "Then you know there is nothing that will ever hurt me more than my son's death."

"For me it would be unthinkable."

The duchess sighed and dabbed her eyes with a handkerchief. "In a sense, it's made me free. I'm no longer afraid of Jacob. No matter how he treats me ever again, he cannot do worse to me than has the man who murdered my boy."

Suzanne felt that a man who couldn't assert authority without shouting and violence was a weak leader to be disregarded in any case, but kept that thought to herself. She said, "The constable came to me this morning and ordered me to desist."

"I would have you continue, even against my husband's wishes."

"You would publicly defy your husband?"

"Certainly not. I wish you to defy him." A slight smile twitched at the corner of her mouth, and Suzanne took the comment as a slight humor. "Seriously, Mistress Thornton, you realize I cannot appear to be a disobedient wife, and have no authority to ask you to disregard the duke. However, I hope you might find your way clear to somehow discover who murdered my baby."

"I should stumble across him while walking down the street?" Suzanne also smiled as she indulged in some humor of her own.

The duchess responded with a slight chuckle. "I'm certain we would all adore it to be that easy. I would that you might continue with discreet enquiries. As much as you can, without too much ado."

Suzanne could see the duchess knew little about how investigations were carried out, and was naïve about the devastating power of gossip. But she leaned forward and said in a low voice, just loud enough for the carriage occupants to hear but mindful of the coachman sitting above, "Your grace, I assure you I've already decided to continue with the investigation."

The duchess sat straight, drew a deep breath, and nodded as she once again had to struggle against tears. "Thank you. God bless you."

Suzanne took this excellent opportunity to glean as much information as she could from the victim's mother. She needed to know the story of Lord Paul's trip to Kent, and how he might have ended up back in London. "Do tell me, your grace, what was your son like?" She hoped to learn something about the boy's penchant for dressing like a girl.

Now a wan smile crossed the duchess's face. "Oh, he was the sweetest little boy! Never raised his voice, even as boys are wont to do. Always a kind word or gentle touch. I love both my sons equally, but I daresay, if I had a favorite it would have been Paul."

Suzanne remembered the gentle girl-like creature in the Goat and Boar that night, and knew what she meant.

The duchess hugged herself and gazed out the window at the huddled houses of Southwark passing by. It took several moments for her to find words for her thoughts, then she said, "Since yesterday I've had horrible visions of how his last moments must have been. He must have been so frightened." Tears fell again, and she repeated, "*So frightened.* I should never have let Jacob send him to my cousins. I should never have let my baby out of my sight."

Suzanne asked, "How long ago was it you sent him to Kent?"

"'Twas three months ago. We thought some time with my cousins there would be beneficial to him."

"In what way?"

Now the duchess pressed her lips together and was silent, thinking hard. Suzanne spoke to help her decide what to say.

"Your grace, every bit of information you give me could be helpful in tracking down the killer. I never know what tidbit might lead me down the right path. Why was your son sent to Kent?"

More tears came. Finally the duchess said, "It was Jacob. My husband wanted him away from London."

"Why?" Though Suzanne could guess, she needed to hear what the duchess would say.

"Jacob never liked Paul terribly well. As a small child Paul was never lively like other boys. He didn't care for the rough-and-tumble games they enjoyed. Jacob thought him weak. As Paul grew older, he seemed even less like a boy. He had mannerisms that were so like those of a girl, he infuriated Jacob. My husband tried to break him of those habits, but it seemed the harder he tried to make him stop behaving like a girl, the more Paul avoided the world of manly things. The duke said horrible things to our son. Called him names, and there were great shouting matches between them. Jacob accused him of doing things with men and beasts he was too young to even know about yet. And as Paul grew in size and understanding, he became angry with his father. And afraid, which only angered Jacob more. Finally the two of them could no longer stand to be in the same room. We'd always sent him to Kent in the summer, but this year when he returned he simply could not be civil to Jacob. He would have been thirteen next month, and so Jacob began talking about sending him away to university. Oxford. Instead I convinced him to send Paul back to Kent, and there my cousins could continue his education."

"And he would be out of sight of London society."

"Jacob was ashamed of him. And 'tis true there are few in gentle society who would have accepted him. It was a quandary. I wanted what was best for him, and didn't wish him to be hated by our friends and equals. But also I never wished him to be away from me."

"Do you know how he came to return to London?"

"No. All these months I thought he was safe in Kent. I missed him, of course, but I took solace in thinking he was safe and away from the temptation Jacob feared so."

"What did the duke fear?"

"That Paul would fall in with sodomites. He was certain it would happen, and in fact often accused our son of it. He tried to beat it out of him, and only I understood that his nature was immutable. All Jacob accomplished was damage. Like removing the red from an apple; what you have left is a mutilated apple."

Suzanne knew well the futility of beating children, for she'd taken a great deal of damage from her own father. She asked, "Who went with him? Did he have an escort, or was he alone?"

"We had our coachman take him."

Suzanne glanced up at the small, grated window in the coach wall above the duchess's head. "Him?"

The duchess addressed the window and raised her voice to be heard over the rumbling of the carriage. "James?"

"Aye, your grace," came the attentive voice from above.

"Please be good enough to tell me which of you it was who delivered Lord Paul to Kent in October."

"That were Thomas, your grace."

"Not yourself?"

"No, your grace."

The duchess murmured to herself, "Well, that's unfortunate." Then she said to Suzanne, "Thomas was let go a number of weeks ago." She raised her voice to the driver again. "James, what was the problem we had with Thomas, do you remember?"

"I'm afraid I never knew, your grace. He was here one day and gone the next, so far as I ever knew. I had the impression he'd absconded, and am a mite surprised not to have heard there were anything missing from the household. Truth be told, your grace."

Suzanne said, "Did he simply leave? Or was he let go? Did he say why he was going?"

The duchess frowned and said half to herself, "I'm certain he was let go, though it's possible I've just assumed it." Her look was somewhat sheepish. "I confess it's terribly careless of me to not know what has happened in my own household.

Thomas has been gone since just after the New Year, and I've assumed Jacob had things well under control regarding the staff. I suppose I should ask him what happened with Thomas."

"I would like to have that information, should you be able to obtain it without mentioning my name."

"Of course."

"Have you heard from anyone in Kent since Lord Paul left your house?"

The duchess thought hard on that, and as she failed to remember any communication from them, a line appeared between her eyebrows. "No, I'm afraid we've had no letter from them."

"Is that the usual?"

The duchess shook her head. "No. And I'm ashamed to have not realized it before. We should have expected some sort of communication from them, even a short note."

Suzanne nodded. She'd also thought it quite strange that Lord Paul's parents had not known he was in London. She asked, "When he went to Kent, did Thomas return in a timely manner?"

"He returned most speedily, I'd say. I'd have thought he would have been gone another day, but he never lingered. We thought him conscientious to have discharged his duty so efficiently." She once again addressed the driver. "James, Thomas returned from Kent in such a timely manner . . . Did you ever hear whether there was a reason for it?"

The driver was slow in answering, then said, "He never said, your grace, I'm afraid."

"I should have thought he might have lingered a day, to rest the horses and himself."

Again the driver paused, then replied, "I'm afraid I've no thoughts on that, your grace."

"I see. Thank you, James."

"Aye, your grace."

The duchess seemed satisfied with the driver's answers, but Suzanne didn't like his reluctance to speak. She wondered whether Paul had even left London on that trip.

Chapter Twelve

Suzanne would have liked to question the driver further, but had been warned against grilling the duke, and she assumed that extended to his servants. It wouldn't do for the driver to mention such an interview to Cawthorne. The next thing, then, was to search down the one-handed sailor Willie had mentioned the night before. Rather than return Suzanne and Ramsay to the Globe, the duchess had her driver take them across the river to the wharves where stood the seafaring ships downstream and the lesser barges and transports upriver. First they searched the Three Cranes Wharf and Dowgate above the bridge, then below it the Billingsgate Dock. It teemed with commerce.

As Ramsay and Suzanne set foot on the wooden dock, she kept a sharp eye on her surroundings for the sake of safety. It was good to have a big, brawny escort by her side. The last time she'd been here she was attacked, and didn't care to have that happen again. She saw very few women on the dock, all whores and beggars. The men were seafarers with few local ties and little incentive for civil behavior. There were no gentlewomen in sight, not even ones awaiting male relatives.

Suzanne began her search for men with a missing hand, as she had at the other docks upriver. She held out little hope, for as had been pointed out earlier by those she'd queried, the very nature of a sailor was to not stay long in one place. But it had been less than a week since the man in question was seen at the Goat and Boar, and she felt a slim hope he might still be in London.

The dock was a busy, bustling place. Built of solid, sturdy wood, so solid the footfalls of people walking on it sounded as on a cobbled street, the dock had room to accommodate a significant number of very large vessels, and an ample lane down the middle for ships to enter and leave. One such ship was leaving now, towed and steered by two rowboats, its sails furled entirely until it would reach navigable water. Suzanne couldn't help hurrying for a better look at it, wishing she'd caught it earlier, lest her quarry be on it. She scanned the gunwale, though the one-handed sailor might have been anywhere else on that ship, and watched it as it moved like a fat duck, swaying slightly when it reached the current of the Thames, out of her reach so that she might never know whether she'd just missed the sailor who could have been a witness or a murderer.

She slowed and looked around. Ramsay had kept sight of her, and now followed her closely once more. "Ramsay," she said in a slightly distracted voice as she scanned the crowds of men, "do ask someone whether they've seen a one-handed sailor."

Ramsay was also looking, but staring in a particular direction. "No need, Suze. I see one now."

She spun to see where he was looking, then turned in that direction. "Where?"

Ramsay pointed with his chin. "There. He's carrying a large sack of corn. Or something. Caught it with one hand, and steadying it with the arm that has none. 'Tis his right hand that's gone, as Willie told us."

Suzanne saw the sailor with the sack perched on his left shoulder, and her heart leapt. Just as Willie had described him, he was average in height and weight, and had brown hair to his shoulders. He wore a coat that was new enough to mark him as either more successful or more sober than most sailors, and his breeches and tights bore no holes at all that she could see. The corn sack he carried appeared to be filled with other sorts of objects, probably his personal belongings. He was walking toward the river, his gaze glancing over each boat as if in search of a particular one. She hurried in his direction, and Ramsay came after.

She fell into step next to him, and greeted him with a warm smile. "A pleasant afternoon to you, good man."

He kept walking, but looked over at her, then to front again. "Thank you, I've no need for company at the moment, and no cash to spend on it today, either."

Though her first impulse was to make a ribald joke in response, she held it back and said instead, "You misunderstand me, young fellow." The sailor wasn't particularly young, but he was younger than she and so she thought to enhance her authority of age. "I've nothing to sell, but rather am buying."

That caught his attention, and he stopped walking. He set his burden down on the boards and focused on her face. She remained smiling. He asked, "What is it yer buying, and for how much?"

"Information, if you have it." She reached into the slit at

the side of her skirt and into the pocket tied at her waist beneath it, to draw out a shilling.

"If I ain't got it, I expect I can get it fer ye." His gaze was glued to the coin she held.

"If you don't have this information already, I don't want it. I'm looking for a man who was in the Goat and Boar across the river in Southwark some five days ago. I wonder whether that could be you."

He nodded. "Aye, it were. I were there some nights ago, though I couldn't say fer certain which one. Sometimes I lose track of which day is which, I'm afraid. I hardly ever need to know when Sunday comes, and so they all just sort of jumble together like 'at."

"And you left with a girl."

"I did, fer true." He nodded, and glanced down at the coin in her hand like a dog eyeing a bone.

"Which girl was it?"

"Oh, they all look alike to me." He shrugged, a careless shoulder shake that rippled the length of his body. "There's no remembering which girl I took out to the alley."

"Try to remember, for 'tis aught but your memory that makes you important to me."

"Blue dress. With lace. Pretty girl, she was. Talked a mite too much, though. Kept askin' about how I lost my hand." He held up his stump wrapped in a blue rag in case she hadn't noticed it already.

"Did you stand her against the wall, or did she go to her knees?"

The sailor blinked, surprised. "A little personal, don't ya think?"

Suzanne gave him a *don't have me on* sort of smile and said, "She was a whore and you a paying customer. This is strictly business, and not so very personal at all in the end. Which was it?"

The sailor shrugged again. "On her knees."

"You never felt up under the dress at all?"

"I tried to, but she were terrible shy about it."

"That's more than likely because she wasn't a girl at all. That was a boy in that dress."

The sailor gawped at her and forgot about the coin. For a moment he seemed speechless, then he laughed. "Naw. She weren't."

"She was. *He* was. His name was Paul Worthington."

The sailor shook his head hard, and glanced around as if afraid of who might be listening in and think he was a sodomite. "No chance of that. I woulda known." His face was turning a dark red, and his eyes took on a rather wild, angry expression. Clearly he was shocked to learn the truth about the whore he'd bought the other night. Dismayed, as well. He was not happy to learn he'd been with a boy.

Suzanne decided he could not be the murderer. This man's surprise was obvious and real. He had not known before now the girl in the blue dress was a boy, and so could not have been the one who had stabbed and mutilated him. She handed over the shilling, and it disappeared into a pocket, though a puzzled look knotted his brow. "Thank you, good man. You've told me what I needed to know."

"Which was what, if you don't mind my askin'?"

"That you're not a murderer." She gave a slight curtsey by way of thanks, and ignored the man's even more surprised expression. "Good day to you, and thank you again." She took Ramsay's arm and headed for the street.

"Aye, mistress, I'm at yer disposal. Anytime ye like," came the sailor's voice after them.

On the walk back across the bridge to Southwark, Ramsay said, "What did we accomplish, then?"

"Not much, I'm afraid. We know the sailor isn't the murderer, and so we've ruled out exactly one man in all of London who bought whores that night. Now we need to look for the well-dressed, catlike fellow whose name escapes Willie."

"There were plenty of other men in the Goat and Boar that night. Could have been any of them who guessed the whore in the blue dress was not a girl. Daniel, for that."

"One step at a time, Diarmid. Let's find the most likely candidates first. And I think we can rule out Daniel. Just a guess, but I don't think he did it."

"You're certain?"

"Well, how about we give him the benefit of the doubt until we've reason to believe otherwise."

"I dunno. He's a pretty dodgy character, don't you think? Perhaps we should keep an eye on him."

Suzanne laughed and slapped his coat sleeve.

THAT evening Suzanne waited in the backstage area as the cast of *Twelfth Night* came offstage. Spirits were high, for it had been a rousing performance and the happy ending of the comedy always left the cast as giddy with amusement as their audience. They chattered with each other and with guests who accompanied them to the green room, where there was sometimes food and drink to be found. It was customary for guests with money to sometimes treat actors with bottles and baskets, and often the entire backstage area turned into an enormous party after a performance. Less so for The New Globe Players than for either of the royal troupes, but even this group had some loyal middle-class followers who liked to bask in reflected glory, however dim it might be. Tonight several bottles of fine wine stood on the table against the far wall, and there was a board of French and English cheeses for nibbling. Lively conversation filled the room, and Suzanne came to try the wine.

It was rather pleasant. She enjoyed a rich, dark wine, and drank happily of this. As she sipped, a man she didn't know well came to talk to her. His was a face she'd seen before but had never put a name to. He appeared a low-level crown functionary of some sort, in his late twenties or so. He owned an oval face with soft features, topped with an enormous, showy wig that must have cost him several pounds. He was the sort of backstage guest who wished to be part of the theatre but had neither the talent and discipline to be an actor nor the wherewithal to be a patron. A hanger-on of the worst sort, taking up space and contributing nothing. He sipped from a glass of the wine, smacked his lips loudly, and said to her, "This is excellent wine, mistress."

"It is. I wonder who sent it."

He looked around the room, then pointed in the direction of a conversation cluster. "That fellow, I believe. The one in the green."

It was Horatio he referred to. Plainly this fellow was pretending more familiarity with the troupe than he possessed. Though Suzanne knew Horatio would never have spent his money on wine for the troupe, she only nodded and took another sip. She found it common in men younger than thirty or so that they pretended expertise beyond their true experience. She also found it tedious beyond measure.

This young man seemed at least sensitive enough to know he was getting nowhere with the wine discussion, so he changed his tack. "I hear through the grapevine that you spend your time investigating crimes." The young man seemed to thrum with curiosity, as if he'd been waiting all afternoon for a chance to ask her about it and the assay into the wine had been merely pretext.

She peered at him, and with a smile gave a coy tilt of the head. "So you hear? Who told you that?"

"A little birdie. Actually, several little birdies." He gestured at the room in general. "You're not quite the talk of the town, but murmurings grow. It's rumored you work on the sly at the behest of the local constabulary."

"Rumored?"

"Indeed. Though I suppose you won't be doing it secretly for long, if enough people talk about it."

"People such as yourself."

He only blinked at her, and didn't reply.

"Who let you in on my little secret?" She hadn't thought it so clandestine, but she was certainly surprised anyone would care to talk about it much. But then, some people had so little to do that any sort of gossip was exciting to them, no matter how unimportant.

"I was in my office several days ago, when some men came in to have their pay. They were talking amongst themselves about it. Said you were asking around about the murder of a boy wearing a dress."

"Did they say the name of the boy?"

This fellow shook his head. "No, they didn't seem to know it. Only your name. And the constable's. They said it was the constable of Southwark who had brought you to view the body. Said you were quite the authority in the situation, asking questions and demanding answers as if you were Pepper himself."

Well, that particular rumor certainly wasn't going to sit

well with the constable, should he hear she was attempting to usurp him. She supposed she should expect another visit from him before long if this kept up. She said to the guest, "One shouldn't put too much store in gossip."

"Do you mean you aren't asking around about the murdered boy?"

"I mean Constable Pepper has no need of my help, and is perfectly capable of doing his own work." That he never actually did it was beside the point. She assumed he might be capable, were he ever to bother himself.

The young man in the expensive wig snorted, as if that were the funniest thing he'd heard all day. Suzanne ignored it, and cast about for another subject to discuss, to wrench the conversation away from Samuel Pepper and the death of Lord Paul. However, he dragged it back where she didn't wish to go.

"A boy in a dress! I say," he said. "Something should be done about the sodomites in London. I vow, it's become so that one can't feel under a skirt without running a risk of having a handful of willie for one's trouble!" He chortled at his own jest as he took another sip of wine.

Suzanne had no reply to that, never having attempted to put her hand up someone else's skirt, and not terribly pleased with men who did so uninvited. They seemed to think it a birthright of some sort.

The young man continued, "I can't say as I'm particularly surprised someone decided to kill him. It must have been quite a shock for the patron to find his money gone for misrepresented goods. I certainly would not have been amused."

Suzanne's attitude went dry and took on an edge of disgust. "You spend a great deal of money on whores, then? By your tone I suppose you've been cheated many times. If so, then I would have to wonder whether you actually seek out tarts who are more boyish than the rest? Perhaps you are attracted to men and simply don't realize it, or are unwilling to admit it even to yourself." She sipped her wine and watched his face flush nearly the color of it.

His voice lowered to an ugly, disgusted growl. "I despise sodomites, and would not suffer them to live. The law says they should hang, and I quite agree with it. They are not men. They are an abomination."

"And perhaps they might feel the same way about you."

He gazed darkly at her for a long moment, then excused himself and went to speak to someone else. The sense of relief in Suzanne was palpable. The tight band constricting her breathing loosened, and she was able to sigh over such hatefulness.

About then the crowd was thinning as the actors and guests began leaving for their evening's entertainments in the local taverns and the bull and bear arenas. The animal fighting carried on all night, and so those who worked in the theatre often liked to have their relaxation there. Suzanne finished her wine and considered whether she would go to the Goat and Boar or stay in with her Aristotle. Or else the writing of her own play, which had become less of a pastime and more of a possibility for her future. These days she occasionally fantasized she might become a playwright like Shakespeare or Marlowe, lauded for her witty dialogue and fascinating plots. Other times she realized her fantasy seemed most plausible when she'd had a bit of wine.

She set down her glass for Christian to collect later when he tidied the backstage area before bed, and turned to leave. Directly behind her, she was a bit startled to find Little Wally, who murmured her name barely loud enough to hear.

"Yes," she replied. "How are you this evening? It was an exceptionally fine performance today, I must say."

"Thank you, mistress." He gave a quick curtsey, from habit, though he'd changed to street clothes appropriate to his gender. Then he continued, "May I have a word, Suze?"

"Always, Wal. I am at your disposal."

He hesitated, appearing to search for words, which made her more curious about what he would say. "You understand, mistress, that I've come to respect your thoughts on some things. Since joining the Players, I've known you to be reasonable about certain particular subjects that concern me greatly. That is, I think I can trust you."

She smiled, mildly since she would rather not appear to be laughing him off. "What concerns you this evening?" There was a dire note in his voice, a seriousness uncharacteristic of him. It made her attend closely, curious about what was on his mind.

"I have heard about your investigation."

"Not a well-kept secret, I'm afraid. You should know I've been told by the constable to desist."

His face fell in disappointment. "You're no longer looking for the man who murdered the boy in the blue dress?"

"How did you know I was? Constable Pepper came here to recruit me, but I don't recall announcing any details of our conversation." So far as she had known until some minutes ago, only Daniel and Ramsay were privy to that particular information. Had Sheila, who overheard everything, been gossiping to the actors? That was quite unlike her, and Suzanne had known her for years. She made a mental note to find out why everyone seemed to know her business.

He shrugged. "Not to put my nose where it doesn't belong, but I thought it was common knowledge. You know

Southwark is nothing but one enormous grapevine. Everyone in the cast has been chattering on about it, since the thing happened. So, have you given up the chase? I was rather hoping . . ." As his voice trailed off he gave a slight, wondering shrug by way of finishing his sentence.

"Why do you ask? Have you something to tell me that might help?"

He hesitated before answering, then said in a bare whisper, "You know they hate us." His lips had gone even more thin than usual, and the tightness of his voice was grim.

Suzanne lowered her voice as well. "By 'us' I think you mean sods, am I right?"

He nodded, then glanced around to see whether there was anyone nearby listening in. There were only a small cluster of actors and their guests in chairs on the other side of the room, and Christian cleaning up a spill on the floor near the door. They were all quite absorbed in their own talk and laughter, enjoying themselves and the evening, paying no attention to anything outside their warm circle of friendship. He leaned in to whisper, "We must be terribly careful."

"I've never thought you to much care whether anyone considered you one of them. I thought you were a free spirit, not tied to any social convention that didn't suit you."

"'Tis one thing to give the appearance, and quite another to give proof of it that might be used to bring charges. I am an actor, so my true nature is never of great importance to anyone and the world thinks me harmless and amusing. I may behave as I please, for in the greater scheme of things nobody takes seriously anything I do or say. But I ever avoid serious talk, and especially I do not make open confession outside a certain circle of acquaintances. Many people think me a sod, but they would be hard put to give proof of it in court, and I believe everyone rather prefers it that way. Particularly, I do."

"I see. And so what would you ask of me?"

"Do find this man who has murdered that boy. I implore you."

"I would like very much to do that. But I find myself somewhat stymied. I must move more discreetly than I am accustomed, for the boy's father has ordered me to stop. It's been made clear to me there will be repercussions if I persist, and only the boy's mother has asked me to continue. And yourself, of course."

"What did you learn before the order came?"

"Only that the victim was selling himself at the Goat and Boar the night he died, and that he was probably murdered by one of his clients."

Wally shook his head and his agitation grew. "It could have been anyone. Any man who could see the boy was not a girl might have killed him for it, and furthermore would have not thought it a crime. A great many men would not think it a crime, and in fact might boast about it. You can't assume the killer was anyone who even knew him or met him before."

"Then even more I am at a loss, if I have nobody to suspect or must suspect everyone."

Wally sighed, and his expression of frustration agreed with her feelings on the subject. He rubbed finger and thumb at the corners of his mouth.

She continued, "What has me truly puzzled is how Lord Paul came to sell himself in a public house. He was supposed by his parents to be in the country with cousins. Who took him from his home in Westminster and brought him here?"

A light sparked in Wally's eyes. "I know of a man who could help you to learn that sort of thing, but I would warn you to beware of him. He is a purveyor of women and children. He operates in the Haymarket, and I know he has been known to use boys. He himself is a pederast."

Suzanne had never heard of a harlot's attendant managing boys, which quite surprised her, for she'd thought she'd been entirely familiar with the seamy side of London. Of course she knew men often bought boys, as they ever bought anything that could be obtained, but the practice had always been so removed from her experience and so hidden from public sight that she simply had not thought about it much. All in all, she realized that since she wasn't a man, she knew very little about how men went about buggering each other. She said, "Could you tell me the name of this man? Does he maintain a house?"

"He's Mordecai Higgins, who can be found in the Westminster Haymarket, but his actual location varies often. Do not approach him in search of a boy, for he will melt into the city streets without leaving so much as a spot of oil. He's known publicly for procuring girls, and only a man who has been given entrée by a fellow sodomite will ever find him by asking for a boy. You must present yourself as in search of an ordinary harlot's attendant and nothing more."

"Very well."

"And never forget that he may well be the very man you seek for the murder. I assure you he would not hesitate to murder for the sake of his domination of others."

"I understand." She understood that most homicide was for the sake of domination. Then she asked, "Tell me, Wal. Since the king has returned and London is no longer in the grip of Cromwell's Puritan sensibilities, how is it that sodomites are still so wary? Nobody seems to care anymore what people do in private, and a precious few care what happens in public. Why do you hide?"

A puzzled look came over Wally's face. "Why would anything have changed for us? The king is not one of us, and in fact is so much a womanizer he must be especially horrified by us. He would have us all hang and not feel the slightest qualm about it. We are as hated by libertines as we are by Puritans, and must fear everyone."

"I see."

"Do tread lightly in the Haymarket, Suze. I rather enjoy working for you and would hate to hear of you floating in the river."

"Thank you. I think I would rather dislike it myself."

Chapter Thirteen

I t was now well after sunset, and though she would have liked to stay in with her writing that evening, instead she dressed to make the trip to Westminster and the Haymarket. Tonight she wore the men's clothing she preferred for days she spent at home, thinking the breeches and tights might give the effect of an ambivalence of gender that might help her fit in. Where she wore a dress in public to look respectable, here she needed to seem less respectable.

When she exited her quarters, she found herself confronted by Ramsay, who sat on a lower step of the stairwell outside her door, cleaning his fingernails with the tip of the small Scottish dagger he called a *sgian dubh*. She stopped in her tracks and gazed at him without speaking, wondering how she would get past him without having to bring him along.

"Good evening, Diarmid."

"Where are you off to, this fine night?" He smiled in

greeting, as if they'd just met on the street and he was asking out of idle curiosity. He returned the *sgian dubh* to its
customary place beneath his shirt.

She thought of lying to him and telling him she was
headed for the Goat and Boar, but knew he'd only ask to go
with her then. It wouldn't do for him to accompany her to
the Haymarket, and she couldn't simply slip away from him.
"How did you know I was leaving?"

"Christian overheard you and Wally talking, and he ran
to my rooms straightaway to tell me you planned to go to
the Haymarket tonight."

In that case, there was no lying to Ramsay in hopes of
getting rid of him. She confessed, "Yes, that is where I am
going. And I must go alone."

"You cannot. I won't allow it. 'Tis far too dangerous."

"That can't be helped. I must find and question a man
called Mordecai Higgins."

"Who is he?"

"A harlot's attendant. I'm told he might be able to tell me
something about how Lord Paul ended up in the Goat and
Boar when he was supposed to be in Kent."

Ramsay stood, and continued to block the stairs. He set
one foot on the bottom step, hands on hips, and bent his
head toward her to emphasize his words and his greater size.
His tone was even more firm than before. "As I said, 'tis far
too dangerous for you to go by yourself. I shall accompany you."

"You'll frighten him off; I'll never find him with you by
my side."

"Then accept that you'll never find him. I'd rather you
failed to find the murderer than to offer yourself as a new
victim."

"Diarmid, I must go."

"Then you must allow me to go with you. I willnae budge from this spot unless you agree to let me follow you to the Haymarket."

She thought that over for a moment. There was no other exit from that part of the basement, unless she wanted to climb out the kitchen window to the sub-stage. Besides being less than graceful, it also would not get rid of him. He'd only meet her on the stage at the trapdoor and follow her from there. She said, "Very well, follow me, but not closely. Come behind me, and keep me in sight. Then if there is trouble you may come to my rescue."

"I'd much rather be by your side."

"Of course, you would. But I can hardly stroll into the Haymarket with you right behind me like an enormous guard dog, ready to do damage to anyone who threatens me."

"I wouldn't—"

"Of course, you would. And you'd be a sorry friend if you didn't. Not to mention worthless as a suitor. So I must insist. If you accompany me, you will keep enough distance between us that you will not frighten off my quarry."

He considered that, head tilted slightly to one side, then said with a nod, "Very well."

The Haymarket in Westminster in daytime was a bustling center of commerce filled with shops that sold food, fabric, leather, swords and knives, and many other finished goods. Not far from the newly fashionable Pall Mall, the streets and alleys of the market were a jumble of buildings, some in deep decay and others less so for being adequately maintained. In daytime the cries of vendors and shopkeepers' wives filled the air and there was an energy of profit making that gave the place a sheen of respectability in spite of its aging buildings and pocked pavements.

At night, with the shops closed, the place turned into a collection of shadows crawling with the less fortunate. Windows and doors were shuttered and barred against thieves who made their lives at it as well as thieves who became so only when opportunity presented itself. Some pubs showed light, and men came and went from them, but for the most part the streets were dark. The coach carrying Suzanne and Ramsay trundled down Market Street, and Suzanne ordered the driver to slow. She gazed out the window at the darkness, finding only the occasional single torch at the entrance of a public house. Even those places had little traffic. But she guessed they were where she was most likely to find someone who knew where to find Master Higgins. She ordered the driver to stop, and hopped out before he could come down and open the door for her.

Ramsay rose from the seat, "Suze, allow me to accompany you."

She turned to reply and stopped him from descending the steps. "We've discussed this already, and my mind has not changed. Stay here until I've gone inside. Really, I would prefer you to stay outside."

"Highly unlikely."

"I know. So if you please I must insist you wait a sufficient while before following."

He sighed, and eased back into the shadows of the carriage.

She drew her cloak around her as if it were an armor that might protect her from the danger of this venture. For a moment she wondered why she was attempting something so foolish, but shook the thought away and approached the tavern. Fear would only make her vulnerable to those who could smell it.

Inside the public house she found only a few men sitting at tables and drinking, talking in low voices. Every one of them fell silent at her entrance, and stared at her. She was accustomed to attracting the attention of men in taverns, but this had a feel of hostility alien to her. These men didn't want her here, and made it clear with nothing but a look. She guessed they were talking business they didn't want over-heard, and so she approached the bar where a man who appeared to be the proprietor awaited her with a stoneware jug at hand.

She gave him a cheery smile, as if strolling into a strange public house at nearly midnight were something she did every night of the week. "A cup of ale, if you please, good man."

He took a wooden cup from a shelf behind him, and poured some ale into it. She placed some coins on the board before him, then took her ale to a chair near the hearth, where she opened her cloak to the air and reached out her free hand to warm it by the fire. The men in the room resumed their drinking, the three at the large table near the door with their heads drawn close and their voices a low murmur. Suzanne sipped her ale and let the alcohol warm her on the inside and loosen the knot in her gut.

Minutes later Ramsay appeared at the door and made a direct march to the bar without a glance at Suzanne or the other men in the room. He ordered some whisky, loudly and with commentary about the superiority of distilled spirits over simple ale and wine. The proprietor had no whisky, but offered brandy instead, which Ramsay accepted with robust good humor. He remained at the bar to drink, leaning against it and scanning the room as if looking for a likely conversation to bide the time. Suzanne wished he'd stayed in the carriage; she could feel the tension increase in the room since his arrival. This wasn't going to work.

However, caution to the wind, she leaned over to speak to the fellow opposite her next to the fire. "You. Could I ask you something? I'm looking for someone as lives hereabouts." The man gave her a sideways look, as if turning his face entirely toward her might be a danger to him. She continued, "His name is Mordecai Higgins."

That was all it took. The man stood, set his cup on the mantel over the fire, and hurried to the door, stuffing his hands into his coat pockets as he went.

Suzanne watched him go and realized that though this seemed like a failure, she nevertheless must be on the right track. That man had recognized the name, and more than likely knew something about who Higgins was. It would have been far better had he been willing to share his information, but perhaps there was hope for help from those in the room who had not left. She now looked to them.

The three at the large table stared at her, apparently having forgotten Ramsay at the bar. One of them said to her, "You're looking for Mordecai?"

Hope fluttered in her breast, and Suzanne's outlook brightened considerably. She smiled. "I hear he's a harlot's attendant."

"And what need have you of one of those?"

She cleared her throat as if about to broach a delicate subject, and lowered her voice. "Well, I got me a daughter for sale." An odd light came into the man's eyes, and she hurried to continue. "Hard times have fallen on us, you see. My husband died and left us nothing. I take in laundry, but it's not near enough to keep body and soul together for myself and six children, all between the ages of four and nine, you see."

The expression on the man's face actually seemed to brighten when it became apparent the girl for sale was no older than nine. He disgusted her. It would have been a joy to see Ramsay beat him, and she hoped for it to happen later, but for now she needed information from this man. He said, "Have you any cash? It'll cost you a pound to see him."

She stifled an impatient sigh at his stupidity, and screwed her face into an expression of hopeless desperation. "Oh, if I had that much money I wouldn't need to sell my dear, sweet daughter!" *Stupid, stupid man.* Had she the money—and a daughter—she certainly wouldn't be offering either to a stranger. Not even for the sake of the information she really sought.

The speaker appeared ready to tell her he had nothing for her, but the one at his right elbow leaned over and murmured something to him. Whatever was said changed the speaker's mind, and he said, "Very well. Come with me."

Suzanne rose without a glance at Ramsay, but she could sense the tension in him grow as she followed the stranger out of the public room and onto the street. She didn't dare look behind her to see if Ramsay was following, and only pulled her cloak around her as she walked.

The night cold crept in. The man took her through several streets, and soon they were no longer in the Haymarket area. After some turns, she thought they might not even be in Westminster anymore. They came to a street that seemed especially decayed. It rather looked like Whitefriars, but she knew they couldn't possibly have walked that far. The houses here were old and close together, in a cluster and looking as if they depended on each other for support to remain erect.

They appeared dark and asleep. Her guide descended some steps to a door, and knocked in a peculiar rhythm.

A few moments later came the sound of a bolt being removed, and the door was opened on large, well-oiled hinges that were surely better maintained than anything else about this house. Suzanne and her guide entered quickly, and the door was shut behind them as silently as it had opened.

Before them stood a man in a dress. There was no guessing regarding his sex, for it was not a skillful disguise. He had not the build to pass as a woman, no matter how feminine the attire. His shoulders were wide and muscular, and his beard, though shaved quite close, still showed a dark shadow. His wig was cheap, obviously a man's wig awkwardly dressed to appear feminine. The result was a bizarre mess that stuck out in odd directions. When he spoke, he made no pretense at femininity and his voice was an undisguised baritone. "What do you want?"

Said Suzanne's escort, "I've got a woman here says she's got a girl to sell."

"You brought her here?" Alarm tinged the voice of the man in the dress, and he gawked at Suzanne as if she were a poisonous snake.

The guide waved off the question with an insouciant hand. "She's just a woman. Ain't nothing to fear." *Stupid, stupid man.* Suzanne remained silent and struggled not to show too much interest in her surroundings.

But it was difficult not to stare. This room was well lit with candelabras and sconces, which she noted had not been visible from the outside. A glance at the windows told her they had been painted over in black. Nobody outside this house would know of any activity inside, even to a single lit candle. But there was so much light here Suzanne could see into even the most remote corners. She saw a congested gathering of men and boys in various stages of womanly dress. Some wore nothing more effeminate than foppish men's clothing, beauty patches, and painted faces, and so appeared no more like a woman than many at court these days. Others wore dresses and men's wigs, or no wigs at all. A few were done up as fully and convincingly as had been Lord Paul nearly a week ago. One was dressed as a milkmaid, even to carrying around a bucket. Suzanne blanched when she saw sticky bits of fluid in it that were not quite milk, and the room stank of it. Another had on the costume of a nun, and Suzanne was certain she didn't want to know what dramatic bit he was done up for. Some, she saw, were boys as young as ten or so. Everyone seemed lethargic, some lay about and were entirely unconscious, and a sickly sweet smoke drifted about the room and mixed with the odors of ale, wine, male seed, and other body humors.

Bizarre as it all was, this was an oddly familiar tableau. Suzanne had once been accustomed to such scenes, and realized the only difference between this and the brothel she'd lived in years before was that she was the only woman here and the brothel had been scrubbed a bit more thoroughly. The girls at Maddie's had dressed as bizarrely as these men, and some had been as young as the youngest boys in this room. Never having lived anywhere but London, she didn't know what life might be like in the countryside, but here in the city, where anything at all could be found for sale, men liked their whores young, pliant, and relatively risk-free for disease. She didn't like it, but there was no denying this deplorable scene was nothing new.

Her guide was asking after Master Higgins, and the man

who had answered the door considered the request. He said, "You know he don't like visitors."

"Right, he don't. But this here mistress has got some young ones. The oldest is nine. Not all girls, neither."

The other man looked at Suzanne, who gave a nod and a smile. Her son was well old enough to take care of himself, and so she was perfectly willing to give up children that didn't exist. He said, "Very well. Come with me." He turned to make his way toward a spiral stairwell, and she followed. Her guide tried to follow also, but the other man told him to go home.

Suzanne said, "How will I find my way back to the Haymarket?"

"Not to worry," he said, and declined to elaborate. But as her guide left the building and the man in the dress proceeded up the stairs, she decided there was little choice but to go along and hope to work out the rest of it later.

The room at the top of the stairs was less well lit than below. A single hearth threw light into the room, but there were no candles about, so leaping shadows, like dark, crazed doppelgangers of the room's occupants, covered the far walls and ceiling. A man lounged on a chaise in the middle of the room, half covered by a sheer silk drape, and attended by a young man. The older one wore an elaborate wig of masculine style, long enough for its curls to drape over his bare, shaved chest. The silk covered only his private parts, giving Suzanne the impression it had been drawn over him hastily on hearing footsteps on the stairs. His expression was of irritation and impatience. The young attendant standing behind the chaise appeared dressed as Adam. He wore nothing but a large leaf that may or may not have been from a fig tree, attached to his privates with a string. He had no wig, and his thick black hair was carefully and artfully arranged to appear wild and uncombed. The arrangement was so precise, the sides swept back and the top tumbled forward over one eye, it must have taken hours to achieve. He stood with his arms crossed, his eyes narrowed as he waited to return to whatever he'd been up to.

"What is it, then?" said the testy man on the chaise. He tugged at the silk to be sure it covered enough but not too much. Apparently part of his dignity was to flaunt himself exactly as he pleased. No more, no less.

"Business, my lord." The man in the dress gave a deep curtsey, then he bounced to his feet in ludicrous imitation of a young girl. The floor trembled with his weight.

"What sort of business?"

"This woman's got a daughter she says she don't need."

Suzanne said, "You're Mordecai Higgins?"

He sat up and put his bare feet on the floor. "I am. Who sent you?" His gaze fluttered over the man's garb beneath her cloak, and he seemed terribly interested in it.

Suzanne wasn't likely to bring Little Wally's name to this man, and no longer needed the fiction of a daughter for sale, so she pulled a nearby chair close to the chaise and perched on its edge. She leaned close to say, "I don't really have a daughter, Master Higgins. My name is Suzanne Thornton, and I'm here to learn the fate of Lord Paul Worthington, who was killed some several days ago." All in now, and heart pounding, she awaited his reply and watched his face closely for any indication she needed to flee. She probably wouldn't even make it to the stairs in that eventuality, but she would at least try to escape.

For a long moment there was no reading Higgins's face. He stared at her with an utterly blank expression, and she readied herself to be ejected from the room. Or taken and murdered like Lord Paul, but she hoped she was right about him. She had a sense that this man was not a murderer. Not, at least, the murderer of a young boy who had been worth a tidy sum of money to him.

Finally he made a delicate and utterly graceful gesture to his attendant, who brought him a pair of velvet breeches and a brocade jacket, both of a rich burgundy color that was nearly black in the dim light. Higgins also gave a smooth, insouciant dismissal to the man in the dress, who obediently disappeared down the stairwell. He donned the breeches and jacket, every movement as artful as dance, then sat back down on the chaise and crossed his legs. To his attendant he said, "Be a good boy and bring us some wine." Adam went to comply, moving as smoothly as a fine lady. Higgins leaned forward to speak to Suzanne in a soft, low voice. "I ask again, how did you find me here?"

A lie came to mind, but as she spoke it she realized the lie could very well be true. "A musician friend of mine saw a man fitting your description at the Goat and Boar the night Lord Paul was murdered. He described a handsome, elegant man who moved like a cat. He said the man was not a client, and that the boy knew him and liked him. I asked around about a harlot's attendant who manages boys, and your name quite naturally rose to the top."

"I have a reputation among ordinary folk?"

"I'm hardly ordinary, Master Higgins. I am a tart myself, of long history, and move quite freely among those who know you. I assure you, your name came quite easily to me, and goes no further than myself regarding this matter. Whatever information I might obtain this evening."

Higgins leaned back again as his young servant came with

a tray loaded with wine and glasses and set it on the chaise next to his master. He poured, and handed a glass each to Higgins and Suzanne. Then he left again via the spiral stairs. One deep draught, and Higgins said, "I miss him."

Suzanne wasn't certain whom he meant, then realized. "Lord Paul."

"He was a joy. A delight to have about."

"His mother felt the same way."

"She didn't deserve him. He was miserable in that house, with those horrible, despicable parents. He belonged with us."

"To be exploited?"

"He earned his keep. Just as, I expect, you did in your earlier life."

"I was quite a bit older when I made my choice to leave my father's house." Her *error.* She'd spent many long years regretting her blunder in rejecting a proper marriage in favor of bearing the child of a man who was not in a position to support her. But that was then and was far removed from the subject at hand. She continued, "How did you find that boy, in theory protected by his parents? How did you separate him from his home?"

"Rescue him, you mean. I rescued poor Paul, and separated him from parents who beat him and ridiculed him, and who then exiled him from that home."

"It couldn't have been so bad."

Higgins leaned forward again, and placed his hands on his knees to thrust his chin at her. "You think you know so much? You think you know how it is for a boy to be a stranger in his father's house for being too much like a girl?"

"I know what it's like to be beaten and otherwise ignored for not being born male."

That gave Higgins some pause, and he considered her

words. "Perhaps, then, you can understand why Lord Paul was unhappy at home."

"You think he was happy with you?"

"I know he was. Just as you must have been happier in a brothel than with someone who beat you."

"I must say I'm far better off now, free to make my own decisions, than I ever was in the custody of another, man or woman. But that's neither here nor there. You were seen with Lord Paul that night before he was killed. You were in the Goat and Boar."

"I was."

Suzanne's heart leapt with hope at this lucky news. "What was your conversation with Paul that night? Tell me what happened."

"Naught but an accounting of what money he'd taken in and whether it would be worth his while to return to that public house in future. 'Twas his first time there. We wished to learn what money could be had from the ordinary folk in Bank Side."

"Why was he selling himself as a girl? Surely there's more money to be made from men who would have him and know he was a boy."

"More money from each man, 'tis true. But far more risk. Well enough for a select clientele, but when such men are not readily available or not plentiful enough there is far easier money to be made in an ordinary public house filled with ordinary men who don't look so closely at the women they buy. Very quick, very lucrative, very low risk. And then there is that Paul enjoyed the thrill of fooling them all, as if it were a contest. He loved being thought a real girl, and I think fantasized that he actually was one. He adored the chase, and relished the attention he received from men who fancied themselves the conqueror. He often laughed about it. That boy was very good at it, you know. He was more feminine than most whores who are actually women."

"I know. I saw him before he was killed. It took a sharp, sober eye to tell he was false."

"And what did you think when you saw what he was?"

"It amused me. A male friend of mine had his arm around him, and when I saw my friend was wooing a boy I thought it funny."

"You laughed at your friend."

"For the same reason you laugh at clients who think they're with a girl. It's always funny when someone acts the fool."

Higgins gazed at her again for a long moment, as if thinking something over. He appeared to be reconsidering his original opinion of her. He said, "Do you have any idea who killed him?"

She shook her head. "Some have pointed a finger at you. I was told you are dangerous."

He made a disgusted noise and shifted in his seat. "Bah! Fie on anyone who would think I could do that to any of my boys! Or the girls, for that! Each one is a treasure."

"Each one is worth money."

"I love them all."

"That's not the consensus, unless you mean it in the physical sense. I'm certain you have violated each one personally."

"They're precious people because they're mine, and I let it be known I will protect them with whatever means is at my disposal. I would kill, for a certainty, but never my own! I would personally murder, with my own hands, anyone who so much as threatened someone under my protection." Anger clenched his teeth and his hands balled up in fists. Suzanne began to believe he did miss Paul, in his own, bizarre sort of way. Even more she saw how much she did not understand about this sort of man. It disoriented her and made the world seem shifty and untrustworthy.

She could see this interview was not having the desired result. She pressed the question that bothered her the most. "Tell me, who brought you Lord Paul? How did you know his situation, and how did you steal him from his parents? I don't expect it happened that you met him at a dinner party in Westminster and became fast friends."

"Cawthorne's coach driver. He's one of us. A longtime client. He came to me with the story of that poor boy who wished for a refuge from his father and the beatings."

"The driver, you say? The one who was supposed to take Lord Paul to Kent? Thomas?"

Higgins shrugged and nodded. "I suppose so. His name was Thomas, at least."

"I'm told he was let go. Do you know where he is now?"

"I've no idea where he was supposed to take the boy, and not the slightest notion how he accomplished bringing him here. If you say Paul was sent to Kent, then I cannot dispute that. I knew little about the mechanism by which the boy was taken. I paid for him, of course, and it was a fair penny. But I didn't care much to know how the thing was done. When Paul arrived, he was not unhappy."

"How did he seem?"

"Like anyone starting a new life, he was a bit apprehensive. But we all did our best to make him feel welcome, I assure you."

Suzanne wasn't certain how to view this statement within context. Having observed the scene downstairs, she thought Higgins's idea of "welcome" and "not unhappy" might be a shade different from hers. Her imagination presented a wide-eyed and terrified twelve-year-old. In her mind's eye she saw a trembling child taken from his mother and thrust into a strange world peopled with bizarre creatures who dressed and behaved strangely. However, she had to admit to herself she'd seen Paul that night nearly a week ago and had not had any sense that he was frightened. She said nothing in reply, not knowing what to think. There was something missing in the picture. Something that should have been there but was not, and she couldn't put her finger on exactly what it was. "Did he ask the driver to bring him here, or was he coerced?"

"I only know that Thomas told me of him, then the boy appeared at my door and he was put to work within a week."

"After having been starved and beaten into submission."

Higgins sat up straight, indignant. "We beat nobody here. We don't need to. Flies and honey, you know."

"But it took you a week to bring him around to his new life."

"There were things he needed to learn. We showed him the ropes."

"And whips and chains?"

Higgins laughed, as if she'd made a joke, and she supposed it would have been a funny joke at the Goat and Boar, but not so very amusing at the moment.

She continued, an edge of anger to her voice, "Lord Paul is dead. He didn't need to be. It's my opinion your actions led to his unnecessary demise. You are largely to blame for the murder, and should be held legally accountable for his abduction."

"Fortunately for the both of us the crown is unlikely to pursue the matter."

"Both of us?"

"Had I actually felt threatened by your words, you can be

certain I would never let you leave this house alive. However, since I fear nothing from you I will let you go so long as you never return to Haymarket in search of me."

"You won't help me find the murderer?"

"I have given you all the information I have on this. I've no better idea who committed this crime than you do. Other than, of course, I would point out to you one thing you seem to have overlooked."

"And what would that be?"

"The murder happened in your bailiwick. On the night little Lord Paul was killed, he was among your kind, not mine."

Chapter Fourteen

As promised, Suzanne was allowed to leave Higgins's house without harm. When she stepped out the door it slammed and bolted behind her, and she looked about the nearly pitch-dark street, wondering how she was going to get back to Southwark. It would be a very long walk, in the middle of the night, and a dangerous one for a woman alone. She'd been raped before, and even for a professional it was never a pleasant experience, particularly if the assailant was one who liked to draw blood or leave marks. This was the very sort of situation for which she needed Ramsay, and she wondered what had happened to him. She hoped he was all right.

Just as she began walking, the slap of reins came from behind and the clop of hooves followed it. She turned to find her hired carriage emerging from deep shadow in the alley. Relief washed over her as Ramsay opened the door and hopped down from it. The driver reined in his horses, and

Ramsay helped Suzanne into the carriage with one hand on hers and the other at her waist.

As she settled into the seat and the carriage lurched forward, she shut her eyes against the world and laid a hand against her face. "Oh, that poor boy!"

"What did you learn?" Ramsay took her hand again, and she could tell by his grasp he wanted to hold more of her and more closely, but he only captured the one hand between both of his.

She shook her head. "They abducted him. It was Higgins whom Willie saw in the Goat and Boar that night."

"Do ye think he killed Lord Paul?"

Again she shook her head. "The boy was worth too much money to him. Nobody associated with Higgins would have hurt Paul, for they would have had to answer for it, and dearly."

"Perhaps if the boy tried to escape to his home?"

Suzanne considered that. Might Higgins have killed Paul if the boy tried to go home? Would Paul have wanted to go home? Willie hadn't indicated any resistance in his behavior toward Higgins that night. "I don't think he did. I think he would have been reluctant to return to his father's house."

"Surely you don't think he preferred to sell himself."

"I do. Even when I learned I would have no help from Daniel to raise Piers, I never considered returning to my father. With Higgins, Paul was among people who were at least pleasant to him. Who praised him for being the way he was. He spent his nights pleasing people and making them feel good." Suzanne knew it couldn't have always been so, but Paul had still been new to that life. There hadn't been enough time for him to have realized its drawbacks. "You saw him that night at the Goat and Boar. He was having fun, and no pretense about it. He was good at being a girl, and now he was able to indulge himself with it to his heart's content, and was praised for it. Men gave him money for it. I don't think he tried to get away from Higgins. Not that night, in any case. He was still too new. Besides, the mutilation would have required far more anger than could have been aroused by a simple escape attempt. It would have required the sort of anger and disgust Higgins and his crew would never have had for someone like Paul. He was one of them. They valued him for that. As Higgins told me, and as I've said before, this was done by someone not of that bent."

Ramsay sat back against the carriage seat to think. "You're certain?"

"As certain as I can be without having witnessed the deed."

"Then you're not any closer to the truth than you were this afternoon."

"Don't know whether I'd say that, but it all does seem as if it were coming very slowly." She said thoughtfully, "I've an idea. When we return to the Globe, I'll need to wake Christian and send him on an errand."

The winter dawn was still several hours away when the hired carriage deposited them at the front entrance of the Globe. Suzanne invited Ramsay in, for she knew he wouldn't go home if she told him to. He would more than likely fall asleep propped against the wall of the stairwell, blocking the way in and out. Better for him to have a seat in her sitting room and be out of everyone's way. She was exhausted, having been awake since early yesterday morning, but was too nervous from the expedition to the Haymarket to sleep. Ramsay's eyes also looked haggard, but she knew he would stay with her as long as she required him. "Go wake up

Christian in the green room; he lays his pallet beneath the table nearest the hearth. Bring him to me in my quarters."

"Aye, Suze." He went to do her bidding.

Meanwhile, she let herself into her rooms, quietly so as not to awaken Sheila, and went to her desk in the alcove of her bedchamber. There she took a sheet of her best paper and wrote a note on it in her most careful hand. She hoped it would explain enough without revealing too much. When it was finished, she folded it and sealed it just as a sleepy-eyed Christian presented himself according to Ramsay's request.

"Take this to the Duchess of Cawthorne, and await her reply. The household should be awake by the time you get there."

"Duchess?" Christian went wide-eyed. He was accustomed to carrying messages to and from Daniel's quarters in Whitehall, but Daniel was only an earl, and addressing a duchess was beyond the scope of Christian's imagination.

"The Duchess of Cawthorne. Hire a carriage in Maid Lane, and the driver will know where to take you. It's in Orchard Street, in Westminster." She handed him some coins. "These are for the driver, and don't let him tell you he needs more than this. Give him my name, and tell him that if he insists on more money he may take the issue up with me later today." That would prevent the driver from trying to take advantage of a ten-year-old.

"Yes, mistress."

"Remember to wait for the reply from the duchess, and don't hand this to anyone but her grace. The butler will give you a fair amount of grief, but if I know you it won't sway you from your mission."

"Yes, mistress." A tiny smile of pride curled his lips.

"No matter who might demand you turn it over."

"Yes, mistress."

"If you're asked who is the sender of this letter, tell them the Earl of Throckmorton. Daniel won't mind, and by the time anyone can verify you will have delivered the message and returned with the reply. But most of all, make certain nobody but her grace sees this."

"Yes, mistress."

"Hurry, now."

Christian spun on his heel and ran from the room.

Ramsay appeared at the bedchamber door and tapped on the frame, asking to know what was going on. "What is it we're needing so early in the morning?"

"Just some information. I find myself down a dark alley, with no direction to take, and I need a bit of information in order to proceed."

He stepped inside the room. "Ah." He sounded as if he didn't understand any of it, but was unwilling to question further.

She said, "Come, sit," and gestured to the foot of her bed. "He'll be a while."

Ramsay sat, and looked around. "I've dreamed of this place." His utter seriousness, a truly theatrical deadpan, was comical enough to make her smile. "I can hardly believe I'm here."

"I can hardly believe it, either. Behave, or I'll make you leave."

"How would you have me behave? As a marauder? A thief in the night? You must be clear, for me to know what you would have me do."

"You'll keep your hands to yourself, please."

"To what purpose?"

"So I might feel safe in my own bedchamber."

"How could you ever be unsafe with me in the room?" He laid a hand on the smoothly made-up mattress beneath him. "With me in this bed?" The humor drained slowly from him as he caressed the comforter that covered the bed. She watched him, suddenly fascinated by his large hands, barely aware of his soft voice. For a moment she wondered whether she hadn't been unfair to him by thinking his profession of love was only a ruse to get something from her. Perhaps he had real affection for her and she was throwing it away unnecessarily.

But, no, that was what had always landed her in trouble with Daniel. Every time she had thought he truly cared about her, it always turned out he only wanted to lie with her and nothing more. Most men were like that, and she couldn't bring herself to believe even one of them might do otherwise. Particularly Ramsay, who never seemed serious about anything. She said, "I imagine you would be quite dangerous in bed."

"Only if asked. If you like, I could be as gentle as a kitten. I could show you things you cannae even imagine." He reached over to kiss the back of her hand, then when he looked up his face was very near hers. "I could make you feel so womanly you couldn't bear to be in the presence of another man for all your life."

Her voice became far huskier than she would have liked. "That might make my life terribly difficult."

"Nonsense. I would make a home for you. Give you a house and fill it with everything your heart could ever desire. You would have furs and horses. You could spend your days doing whatever you pleased."

"Except be around other men."

"As I said, you wouldn't want to be around other men."

He kissed her hand again, then tugged on it and drew her from her chair to sit next to him on the foot of the bed. She let him, for her blood was running hard and it felt marvelous. At that moment, though even then she knew she would regret it later, she wanted it to grow. She wanted to see how marvelous it could feel, for she hadn't felt anywhere near this good in an extremely long time. He leaned down, and this time he touched his lips to hers.

Her heart did flip-flops. Ramsay wasn't nobility like Daniel. She knew he was lying about the riches he would bestow on her, for he had none. But since he knew she knew he had none, the lie was more like a story for entertainment. He was an actor, and this was a performance.

He kissed her more deeply, and touched fingertips to her cheek. He kissed her eyelid, then the other. He was the performer, playing the lover.

And she was the audience waiting to be amazed and entertained. She was a maiden in that audience, heart pounding that she might be deflowered by him. All the years of selling herself dropped away and she was returned to the day she'd first given herself to Daniel.

Daniel.

He who had taken her gift, then walked away without returning even the smallest part of it. She couldn't afford to let that happen again.

"Diarmid, no."

Ramsay tried to kiss her again, but she avoided it and focused on the floor so she wouldn't have to look at him and his disappointment.

"No, I can't."

"Not yet?"

She had to think about that, then said, "I don't know. I'm sorry—"

"Och, there's naught to be sorry about. I've stolen a kiss . . . two kisses. I leave to the good and with hope of better next time." He stood, made a leg with a wide flourish of his arm, then straightened with a cheerful smile on his face. Always the performer. "I will wait in the sitting room for the return of young Christian, while my lady sleeps the sleep of the just, alone in her bed."

"Very well, Ramsay. Thank you."

"My pleasure. Truly it is my pleasure." And with that he retreated to the outer room.

Suzanne gazed at the open doorway for what seemed an uncommon long time, and half entertained the notion of calling him back. After all, she was saving nothing, and particularly not for marriage. It would mean nothing for her to invite him to bed with her, and they would sleep the better for it afterward.

But that was the very problem. It would mean nothing. She could mean no more to Ramsay than she had to Daniel, which was not nearly enough. It was better to keep herself to herself and not allow him to take hold of her in any fashion.

So tired she couldn't keep her eyes open any longer, she lay back on the bed and the world went away in an instant.

CHRISTIAN returned with a pounding on the door, and Suzanne awoke to find herself lying on the bed, still in her clothes. She rose and stumbled toward the outer rooms, rubbing sleep from her eyes and circulation back into her face.

Sheila reached the door before her and let Christian in just as Suzanne entered the room. Ramsay was still oblivious, lying on the sofa, and snored like a bear.

Christian burst into the room with the energy that is owned only by children, and thrust a sealed envelope at her. "The duchess wrote you an answer, and she put it in a real envelope!"

Ramsay startled awake, and looked about to see where he was.

Suzanne took the message, and dismissed Christian before breaking the seal. The envelope was indeed a fine one, of smooth, soft paper that felt more like cloth than anything else. It was bleached a pure white that made everything around it seem shabby and dirty by comparison. Absently she took it through the kitchen and onward to her bedchamber. When she arrived and sat at her desk, she found herself followed by Ramsay, who settled himself once more at the foot of her bed. He scratched his head sleepily and ran his fingers through his hair by way of organizing it as he watched her read the letter.

Mistress Thornton,
Many thanks for your efforts. I assure you the duke will not know you are continuing the investigation. There is some news. I have learned that Thomas was not let go, but rather he simply disappeared two days after New Year's. His belongings are not here, and so I suppose he has fled. James repeats to me that he doesn't know where Thomas might be. I have no idea, either, and of course cannot ask Jacob. If I learn anything further, I will send another message via James.

The information you have requested is: February 21,
1649, London, England, shortly after the noon hour.

Suzanne smiled. "Come, Diarmid. We've an errand to accomplish." She rose from the bed and took his hand to draw him with her.

SHE didn't bother to change clothing for this trip, possibly because she balked at removing it with Ramsay anywhere in her quarters. The night had been long and her nap short; she preferred to do her errand and return to sleep some good, long hours.

However, at the top of the stairs she heard a voice in the green room near the upstage entrances that reminded her she had other business to attend to that was equally important. Liza was chattering away to someone, gossiping about one of the other whores who frequented the Goat and Boar. The subject didn't interest Suzanne, but she separated herself from Ramsay for the moment with one raised palm and ducked into the green room.

Liza was talking to Matthew, the both of them having just arrived for the morning's rehearsal. Suzanne gave them each a gracious smile.

"Good morning to you both. You look well."

Matthew chuckled as if she'd made a joke. Liza said, "We are well. We'd be more well, did I not have an entire guinea disappear from my earnings last night. 'Twere stolen from my table at the public house, and I know by who." Anger flushed her face and her lips pressed together.

"I'm sorry to hear that. Perhaps you might consider giving up the whoring and attend to your acting, then?"

"Whatever for? I earn nearly as much banging the drunkards at the Goat and Boar as I do acting in plays."

Matthew kept singularly silent. It was widely known he wished to marry Liza, and it was up in the air as to whether she would continue to sell herself if he did.

Suzanne sat on a chair near the large table at the end of the room. "I think you've a far better future as an actress than as a tart." Liza's tongue was much too sharp to be overly pleasing to her patrons. "And I speak as one who has gone from one to the other. In fact, Little Wally was telling me just yesterday—"

"Little Wally's got naught to say 'bout me." Liza looked to Matthew for confirmation, and he nodded to Suzanne. They'd apparently discussed Little Wally between them. "I won't hear naught from him."

"Well, I can't imagine why you wouldn't want a compliment from him."

"He's a sod," said Matthew, as if that explained everything.

But Liza's brow crumpled. "Wait. A compliment, it was? What sort?"

"Why, he told me he envies your beauty. He knows he's not the fairest actress in the troupe, and he wishes he had your fine appearance."

"He says I move like a pig."

"That's not what he tells me." He'd never said "pig" to Suzanne, so technically it wasn't a lie. But the next was entirely falsehood. "He says he wishes you would help him move like a real woman."

Liza gawped at her as if she'd told her the moon was made of green cheese. "Do you mean that for true, or are you having me on?"

"'Tis true. Every word." Suzanne knew she would burn in hell for this, but hoped God might understand her good intentions. "He knows he moves in imitation of a genuine lady, and would like to know how best to appear like one. What with so many women ascending the stage these days, he fears the audience will expect him to be indistinguishable. Really, he believes his career is in the balance."

"He should, because it is. It won't be very long before he'll not have any roles for being too male to play women and too female to play men. In a way, I feel a mite sorry for him, I do."

Good. Suzanne was making progress. "Then you won't mind helping him. Give him some advice regarding his portrayal. I'm sure he'd be ever so thankful for it."

Liza thought about that for a moment, but Matthew broke into the talk. "I think it would be best to just leave him be and cast women in those roles as soon as the king makes that decree his lordship has been saying he would."

Liza said, "What decree?"

"His lordship Throckmorton says the king keeps promising to make a decree that female roles should be played by women. 'Tis what they do in France, and he thinks them French is all better than us English. Throckmorton says it'll be all women in them roles by Christmas."

Liza said, "Poor Wally, then. He'll be on the streets."

"Like the rest of us when things go against us. Better him than us."

"But he doesn't deserve it. Nobody deserves that. He can't help it."

"He's a sod. He makes his own choices, and lives with 'em just like the rest of us."

Suzanne addressed Liza, hoping to cut Matthew and his

negativity out of the discussion. "You could help him. Perhaps if he were more convincing as a woman, he could continue to play the women's roles. For a while, at least." She knew it would be quite a while before the Players would be able to find enough skilled women to fill all those roles, and there would be work for Wally in her troupe until then. However, it appeared there was a chance Liza would have enough pity on him to stop fighting him.

Liza opened her mouth to reply, but Suzanne added, "But we don't wish to hurt his feelings. I hope you'll tread lightly with your advice. Don't let him think you're correcting him. Let him know you think he's a skilled actor."

"I don't think he's a skilled actor. I think he's the most false—"

"To be sure, you're free to think what you like. But hurting his feelings is counter to what you would be trying to do. Let him think you admire his work, and that you would give him secrets to how women really are. He would be pleased to learn what you could tell him."

"Would he really?"

"I think so." She rose to leave. "Give it a try. I think we'd all benefit from whatever you could show Wally. The better he does, the better we all look. Consider it."

The look on Liza's face made Suzanne hopeful as she left the room and returned to Ramsay, who awaited her just inside the upstage entrances.

"What was that about?" he queried.

"Well, either things will calm down between Liza and Wally, or else they'll murder each other."

He chuckled. "Then you'll know who did it and can dispatch the investigation in no time at all."

She laughed also as they left the building.

The day was not as cold as had been others recently. Certainly not warm, but there was no wind and for the moment it seemed a thaw might be in the air. Of course it was still January and winter would have them in its grip for another two months or so, but for today the walk across the bridge was not particularly unpleasant.

Suzanne rapped on the door of the astrologer's rooms near the Royal Exchange, as Ramsay ducked his head to keep it from bumping the plain wooden brace overhead that held up part of the building overhang. There was no answer, and so Suzanne banged longer and harder.

Finally, the voice of Esmeralda came from the other side, promising she was on her way, a bolt was drawn back, and the door creaked open. "What . . . oh." She drew the door open further and stepped back. "Do come in, Suzanne. And your friend." She nodded to Ramsay as he followed Suzanne inside. "What might I do for you so very . . . *very* early this morning?" She had a glance outside before closing the door, then went to stir her hearth so to catch alight a twist of paper for lighting a candle. The dawn was still more of a promise than a fact, so the room was nearly as dark as if the night were still pitch-black. Once there was light to see by, Suzanne spoke.

"Esmeralda, I have another request to make of you. And here is a half crown for your trouble." She handed over a coin, which the astrologer deposited without hesitation in a tin cup that sat atop her mantel.

"Very well. What is it you require? Another reading?"

"I wish another reading. Not of my own chart, but of someone else's."

She held up her palms and shook her head. "Not the king. I won't tell you anything about the king's horoscope, for it would mean my neck. I'm the only woman in the kingdom entitled to read his chart, and that is only for his own sake. 'Tis the one confidentiality that is sacrosanct, and I absolutely will not say a word to you or anyone else on it."

Suzanne shook her head. "Not the king. We've seen what happens to those who meddle in the king's fate, and I value my neck as well as you do yours. There have been too many heads perched on the bridge belonging to men who thought they had something to say about the fate of a king for me to have any interest there. No, I need a reading for the boy we spoke of some days ago."

A skeptical eyebrow raised. "The one whose name has eluded you, and never mind his birth date?"

Suzanne smiled and drew the duchess's letter from inside her doublet. She'd not taken the time to change her clothing that morning, and still wore the man's outfit from last night. "I have not only learned the poor victim's name, thanks to your last reading and a suggestion from my friend Throckmorton, but I also have from his mother the exact time and place of his birth."

Esmeralda's face brightened and she lost the sleepiness in her eyes. "Oh! You've found him!" She began to reach for the letter.

"Lord Paul Worthington, son of the Duke of Cawthorne. I wish you to tell me his indications just before he died."

Now the astrologer's face took on the darkness of alarm and she retrieved her hand rather than touch the letter. "Oh. Yes. The victim, who is now dead. That could be troublesome."

"Why?"

She looked at Suzanne as if she'd gone mad. Or stupid. "'Tis terrible bad luck to tell the horoscope of a dead person. One takes an awful risk to meddle in such as that."

"Not even to learn the name of a murderer?"

Esmeralda, frowning deeply, gazed off into the middle distance for a moment as she thought that over. Slowly she said, "Well, you understand that there's good and evil in everything. Nothing on God's earth is pure in either. And those of us who study the stars must consider that we're entrusted by God with information that may or may not be ours to know. Or tell."

"You're telling me you're afraid of your own power?"

Now Esmeralda looked into Suzanne's face. "All who wield power should respect it, no matter what that power is or how 'tis given to them. Every king, and every sorcerer, should respect the power in them. I do no less."

"So you won't do the reading? I should have back my coin, then."

Esmeralda snorted, frowned some more, then said, "No, I never said I wouldn't do it. But we must be careful."

"Of course."

A good rummage through the papers and books on her table, and the astrologer was ready to begin, with an ephemeris in her lap and a large piece of paper on the table at her elbow. A quill stood in an inkwell next to it, barely visible amongst the stacks of books, papers, and a plate of poultry bones that appeared left from last night's supper. Suzanne told her the date and time in question, then sat to wait. Ramsay stood near the door like a statue depicting Patience. He hadn't said a word since their arrival.

It seemed to take a very long time to construct the chart of Lord Paul, and there was much frowning and grunting in it. At one point the astrologer muttered, "Oh . . . not good. Not good at all." But when Suzanne opened her mouth to ask why, she raised a finger for silence and continued on with her work. The sun rose and a sliver of light crept onto the wall opposite the small window at the front. The astrologer worked on.

Finally she sighed and looked up at Suzanne, then at Ramsay. To Suzanne she said, "That poor boy."

"What, then?"

She gestured to the paper before her, and said, "Betrayal. 'Tis all betrayal in his life. I see nothing here but evil for him, and the most profound *betrayal*. Had I read this chart before he died, I could have predicted it. The poor boy never had a chance at a long life, nor a prosperous one."

Ramsay said, "You're saying he's better off dead?"

Esmeralda shrugged. "'Better off' would be a judgment I couldn't make. But I see his death was inevitable."

"And what does the chart say about how he died? Where should we look for his killer?"

The astrologer closed her eyes to think, as if trying to picture something. "Home."

"He wasn't at home when he died. He hadn't been there for months."

A shrug, and Esmeralda's expression was apologetic. "I cannot say why, but home and betrayal are connected with strong indications of death."

Ramsay said, "That could simply mean he was abducted from his home, and that you already know."

Suzanne's heart sank. "There must be something more, for the indication to be so strong. We must be missing something."

He replied, "Perhaps what we need is to talk to someone who may know something other than where Mars is in the sky."

Esmeralda turned to frown at him. "You doubt the stars?"

"No, 'tis you I doubt. You've only told us what we already know."

"And how, then, did I know it? I've not heard a word about this since your mistress was here asking about her own chart several days ago. I never knew the name of the victim until just this morning."

Ramsay didn't seem to have a reply to that, and only pressed his lips together.

Suzanne said, "There must be something else we can learn."

Again Esmeralda shrugged. "All I might tell you is to look to the boy's home. That is where you'll find the answer to your question. But tread lightly. This chart has such strong indications of death, there might be danger to others."

Suzanne then remembered her own chart, and how it had brought Esmeralda to her in the first place. Suddenly she was uncomfortable with this, and she said to Ramsay, "Come. Let us return to the Globe."

"Surely you won't quit the chase, mistress," said the astrologer.

"I don't know for certain what I'll do at the moment. Thank you for your effort and expertise." With that, she left in a hurry, with Ramsay behind her.

Outside in the street, Ramsay said as he hurried along beside Suzanne, "Are you afraid now?"

She walked head down, her legs scissoring quickly along. "I can't tell what I am. But I've got a disquieted feeling about all this. Suddenly it's all too shadowy. Too hidden."

"Too deathly."

She stopped to examine his face. He didn't seem any more sanguine about this than she was. "Death is everywhere. It can't be avoided. *Media vita in morte sumus.* In the midst of life we are in death."

"But this was in your chart, and I cannae blame you for not liking it."

She made a humming noise of agreement, then continued on her way.

Chapter Fifteen

On returning to the Globe, Suzanne found the mummers onstage, rehearsing a short commedia dell'arte bit that included some tumbling. She gathered it would be to complement the next production, though she couldn't remember which was next up after *Twelfth Night*.

Inside the 'tiring house she found small clusters of actors occupying assorted spaces, rehearsing. Suzanne was too tired from too little sleep to care what play it was, but on her way to her quarters in the basement she paused in the stairwell when she heard the voices of Liza and Wally going over some dialogue from *Twelfth Night*. Since that play was well into its run and should not need rehearsal, Suzanne was curious what they were up to, hidden away down here like this. Unseen, she sat on a step to listen. It was Wally's voice speaking, as Olivia.

"... *I heard you were saucy at my gates, and allowed your*

approach rather to wonder at you than to hear you. If you be not mad, be gone; if you have reason—"

"Wait."

"What now?"

"It's all wrong."

"Don't start again."

Suzanne started to rise, to separate the two and prevent a shouting match, but Liza's next words made her pause.

"I'm not. I swear it. This is the part I was talking about. You're playing this as if you were a man pretending to be a woman."

"I am a man pretending to be a woman."

"But you don't want the audience to think that. You've asked me to help you pass undetected."

Suzanne sat again to listen some more. She began to see she might not want to interrupt this.

"How would you do it, then?"

Suzanne's eyebrows went up. This was new.

Liza replied, "Not so much hip. After all, you can't flaunt what you don't have, and your farthingale is no substitute."

"Well, I've no bosom, either."

"But you have padding, and the lack doesn't affect the way you move. The way we walk, it's all because of our hips. If you don't have them, you can't help but walk like a man. You either look like a man walking, or you look like a man trying to look like a woman walking. So you must bring attention to your bosom."

"Which I don't have."

"Show us your padding, then." There was a moment's pause, then she said. "That's it. Shoulders back."

"They are back."

"Stop trying to hide your lack."

"I don't want to show the edges of the padding."

"Nobody is looking there. They're looking at your neck-line. The edge of your costume is in the front, not the sides, and you've marvelous padding. I wish my bosom was as well dressed."

That brought a chuckle from Wally, and Suzanne stifled one as well.

"So," continued Liza, "let us hear that line again."

"*It is the more like to be feigned; I pray you, keep it in. I heard you were saucy at my gates, and allowed your approach rather to wonder at you than to hear you. If you be not mad, be gone; if you have reason, be brief: 'tis not that time of moon with me to make one in so skipping a dialogue.*"

"Excellent. I would never know you were a man."

"If only there were something I could do about this face of mine. I so wish my face were soft and oval, like Kynaston's."

"He's no woman. I am, and I have a square jaw like you."

"You've nothing to overcome."

"Nonsense. I would be far prettier with an oval face, but it wouldn't make me look any more like a girl."

"I would like to be pretty, truth be told. I think it would be a sweet life to be a beautiful woman and have men shower me with gifts and want to take me to bed."

"And put their hands up your dress, and tell you what to do and what not to do, and then beat you when you disobey."

"There is that, I suppose." His voice turned bright for a change of subject. "So, what was that other spot you wanted to work out?"

"Act II, Scene II. *I left no ring with her.* It feels exceedingly strange to be talking to Malvolio one moment as a boy, then the next to myself as a woman. How do I make that transition?"

"Simple enough. One moment you're putting up the façade, and then Malvolio leaves and you drop it."

"But how do I do that?"

"Here . . . stand like this."

Suzanne continued to listen as the two worked out their differences and began to cooperate. It did her heart good, and though it was a bit late for *Twelfth Night*, she thought it boded well for future productions of other plays.

EVENTUALLY the two finished their private rehearsal, and quickly Suzanne rose from her seat to make footstep noises as if she were just then descending from the floor above. Then she came down the steps to meet Liza and Wally on their way up, nodded good morning to them, then let herself into her rooms to undress and crawl into bed. Sounds of the mummers thumping against the stage boards outside her window lulled her to sleep.

Exhausted, Suzanne spent a large portion of the day sleeping. Though she would have liked to have pressed her investigation without wasting time on rest, her thoughts had all collapsed in on themselves until they were a worthless jumble. She had no choice but to lie down for a while.

But not a long while. During that afternoon's performance of *Twelfth Night* she went into the audience, sitting as she usually did in the third gallery over the entrance doors. She knew the role of Viola so well, her lips sometimes moved along with Liza's voice. Some muscles twitched with the memory of past performance, as if by her effort she might guide Liza in her movements on the stage. Suzanne would never play the role again, for she had grown too old for it, and she missed it. She watched Liza play a woman pretending to be a man, opposite a man playing a woman in love with her, thinking she was a man. And that actor was a sodomite in the bargain. It was a mishmash of gender confusion that might even have boggled the very author of that play.

As she laughed at the dialogue, she saw that, while Wally as Olivia was very polished and Liza as Viola was not, there was a subtle undercurrent between them that added an extra layer of insanity to this lively, sophisticated comedy. The joke of the play, of course, was that Olivia was in love with a woman who could never return that affection. As played by Wally, Olivia presented as terribly silly and not entirely sane. In Wally's skilled hands, the role was that of a manic, out-of-control girl. Liza, less skilled but more genuine, presented as down-to-earth and entirely ordinary. Sensible, and earnestly in love with Olivia's brother. Suzanne would not have thought it possible, but the differences in style and in the actual genders of the actors gave the play a giddiness and the characters a tension of contrast even more than what Shakespeare could have achieved with two actors who were both men. The audience could tell who was real and who was not, and they responded to those subtleties with laughter.

About the time the scenes moved on to an exchange between the clownish servants Fabian, Feste, and Maria, played by two men and a boy, the bench next to her was filled by a new arrival. She looked up to find Piers had joined the audience. He said, "I haven't seen you here much lately."

She returned her attention to the stage below. She knew

the scene by heart, and laughed appropriately at all the funny spots, though her focus wasn't truly in it anymore. "I've been busy."

"I thought you'd been asked to lay aside the job you were doing for Constable Pepper." Piers also gave the appearance of watching the actors. It wouldn't do to let anyone see he wasn't interested in the performance, though Suzanne knew he was not. It was a rare play that caught his attention. Though he'd acted as a child, it had never been his calling.

"My business is my own."

"The constable's business, you mean."

"I do what I like, and Pepper has no sway over me."

"Mother, I wish you would never mind these investigations that have you all caught up. You've no business doing Pepper's work for him. There are many other things you should be doing that are far more appropriate for a woman your age."

Surprised, she turned to look him in the face. "A woman my age? More *appropriate*? And how is it that you know so much about what I should do or not do?"

"I am your guardian."

"My legal guardian, and a figurehead without any real significance."

He sat up straighter to make himself taller and as imposing as he could. "I beg your pardon, but—"

"Very well, I mean only that I'm an adult, I'm not senile, and I am competent enough to have taken care of you by myself for nearly twenty years without the slightest help from your father, my father, or any other man. I believe I've proven myself and earned some autonomy."

"My only concern is for your safety."

A sigh of exasperation escaped her, and she rolled her eyes.

"So many, so concerned for my safety! I wonder where you all were when you and I were starving and on the streets. I find that men are ever more concerned about women when money and the control of it are involved. When I was penniless there was nobody to have a care whether I lived or died."

"I cared. I would have done anything for you." It was his injured little boy tone, and suddenly she felt terrible for what she'd said.

"I apologize, Piers. But you know those were very difficult times. I rather think I deserve to maintain my independence, at least where the small things are concerned. Where I go and to whom I speak should be my own choices, especially considering how well you have benefitted from those choices in the past. More than likely you wouldn't be here talking to me, had I not stepped outside the bounds of propriety from time to time when you were a boy."

He gave a small nod of agreement. He said, "You should know Ramsay asked me to talk to you."

She chuckled. "Dear Diarmid. Not Daniel, then?"

Piers seemed puzzled she should even bring him up. "Of course not. Old Throckmorton only ever cares what happens to you when Ramsay is involved. It's as if he can smell it, and he appears out of nowhere only to thwart your suitor."

The word "suitor" gave her a chuckle, for she felt herself so beyond such proprieties it was similar to calling her a "lady" or referring to a mule as a thoroughbred. "I haven't seen Daniel in days, though Ramsay has accompanied me everywhere."

"And that is why I think you should desist in your investigation."

"Because I'm spending too much time with Diarmid?"

"Because the activity is dangerous. Ramsay accompanies you everywhere for fear you will be harmed."

"And it is terribly sweet of him. The fact that I allow him to do it should speak to my sensibility concerning my own safety. I'm not so foolish that I would keep him from protecting me. Truth be told, I rather enjoy having a fuss made over me. 'Tis such a rare thing for me, 'tis something of a novelty. He amuses me, and I have to smile every time I see him waiting for me when I leave the theatre. I have to wonder why he doesn't have anything better to do."

"He does. A great many things, and his income is suffering for not being able to attend to his usual business."

"He's not in any of our plays at the moment."

"But you know he has business concerns, importing from and exporting to Scotland."

"Smuggling."

"He's no patents, and no right to do business of any sort, so in order to make a living that doesn't require being cast in one of our plays, which you know is not dependable money, he must occasionally slip beneath notice of the crown. We all do it when necessary, don't we?"

Suzanne realized in the past she'd broken the law enough times in various ways that she could have no argument against that. And so she said nothing.

After a long silence, Piers said, "Very well, then. If I may have your promise to never take any unnecessary risks, I'll permit you to continue with this investigation."

She turned to give him a long, stern stare, until he corrected himself. "That is, I'll stop annoying you about it if I can be certain you're safe."

"I can promise you I won't be any more careless with my life than I have to be."

Piers uttered a grunt of dry amusement, then thanked her and excused himself to leave the gallery. Suzanne's thoughts returned to the investigation, Lord Paul, and the Goat and Boar. She needed to organize in her mind the known facts.

She tried to remember exactly how she'd known the boy was not a girl. As she remembered it, he had been physically wrong. His hands were the large-knuckled ones of an adolescent boy, not the small, delicate fingers of a girl so gently brought up as he'd seemed to be. As he actually had been, it turned out. Though all tarts were forward, for it was how they were defined and how they made their living, he had seemed more relaxed in it than a real girl should have been. A girl—even an extraordinarily forward one—would have been taught some restraint that a boy would not. Again, Lord Paul had been more like a highly polished gentleman than a truly female street whore.

So far, she knew that Paul's family thought him a liability. Any family that produced a known sodomite would suffer in reputation, and it was plain the Duke of Cawthorne had established for himself a highly moral reputation particularly difficult to sustain. In Suzanne's experience, the more pristine the moral standing, the more likely the downfall in a world where social standing was maintained by vigilant self-interest. Only the poorest priest living at a distance from any seat of power and temptation could claim true purity of spirit. Only a man living outside of any society could avoid the appearance of impropriety in all things. Cawthorne, a duke living among peers who had questionable motivation in most things, had perched himself on an exceptionally high pedestal no man could hope to maintain.

So when his son showed signs of becoming a sodomite,

he had been forced to send the boy to the country and out of the way of the duke's political life. Since Lord Paul was the younger son and his older brother would inherit the title, it was possible his true nature might then have remained secret from the peerage for the duration of his life. Unluckily for them all, the coachman had seen an opportunity to make money from the family's misfortune. He abducted Paul at a moment when there was nobody to know he'd gone missing. Then, whatever had happened to him during that first week with Higgins, the boy had ended up in a dress, working as a whore servicing men who were not sodomites. The Goat and Boar was not known as a gathering place for that sort, and so she wondered what had brought Paul there. Had Higgins thought of expanding his territory? Would that have even been wise? She guessed not, since one of those clients had murdered the boy. Perhaps it was an experiment in commerce gone awry?

She considered who the murderer might have been, and how he would have discovered Lord Paul was not a girl. Many men at the Goat and Boar that night had been taken in by the ruse. She herself had been one of the few to see it, and it wasn't until she'd mentioned it to Daniel that he'd known. It was reported by Big Willie that Young Dent had put his arm around Paul, but Dent had not ever shown any awareness that the girl in the blue dress had not been a girl. He hadn't remembered the blue dress until he was asked about a girl.

Then she remembered Warren. According to Willie, Warren the flute player had also had his arm around Paul sometime during the evening. Now she wished she'd asked more detailed questions about what had happened there, and made a mental note to have a chat with Warren as soon as possible.

So now she saw her collection of facts contained a blank area between Willie's and Higgins's testimonies of Paul at the Goat and Boar, and the next morning when the body had been found floating in the river. She knew by the excessive stabbing and the severed appendage the murderer had been very angry. Out of control. It had taken an extremely powerful ire to do that to anyone, whether dead or alive, adult or child, boy or girl. The murder had not been casual, for money or for sport. The thing had certainly been done by someone offended, and the most likely reason for that offense was that Paul had sold himself as a girl. The severed willie told her that, like a big sign in dripping, red paint. In her gut Suzanne felt the dress alone would not have produced that sort of anger. It had to have been a customer—or potential customer—who had found out Paul's secret too late. Someone who may have put a hand up that dress and found himself embarrassed.

Suddenly Warren began to take on the character of a suspect. Her heart clenched, for he and Willie were both friends of hers and it horrified her to think that he could have committed such a horrible deed.

She considered other people she should interview. She needed to know whether there was someone at the Goat and Boar that night who had been a customer to Lord Paul before, and she hoped to find one, lest her friends become the most likely possibility for the murderer.

A realization formed in her mind, and when it came clear it pushed aside everything else. Her assumption was that someone had murdered the boy for being embarrassed at being approached by a sodomite. That sort of man would take pride in what he'd done, to have ridden the world of such a creature. He would have considered it God's work, and more than likely would not have thought the murder a crime. He would have been proud of his action and let his friends know what he'd done.

But so far nobody was claiming credit for the deed. Suzanne frowned as this tiny fact settled into the clump of information she was considering. Though the motive was assumed to be disgust for sodomites and moral outrage, there was no hint of rumor that anyone was bragging about it. It was a small thing, and might mean nothing at the end of the day, but it annoyed her.

The play was ending, and in her reverie she'd missed the final two acts in their entirety. She looked across at the stage gallery where the musicians sat, and saw Warren with his flute. Good. He was the very man she needed to talk to just then. She rose from her bench and made her way through the departing audience toward the 'tiring house.

She caught up to him in the green room, just before he would have left to spend the evening at the Goat and Boar. "Warren, may I have a chat with you for just a moment?"

Of course he nodded eagerly, for he depended on the money he had regularly from her, playing for performances. "At yer service, mistress."

"This way, then." He followed her through the 'tiring house and out to the first gallery, which was now empty of audience. She and Warren sat on the steps at stage right, in the open where they could talk without being overheard by anyone unseen. This wasn't a conversation for those who might lurk around corners or listen through connecting windows and doors inside the theatre structure. She said, "Warren, you may be aware I'm investigating a murder."

"Aye, mistress. It seems you're always asking around about this, that, and the other." Another man might have sounded critical of her behavior, but Warren spoke as if he thought it a very good thing that Suzanne was nosier than most.

"I'm told you were one of the last men to see the victim alive."

A shadow fell over his fat, round face and he resembled a jack-o'-lantern, with wide eyes and a turned-down mouth. "Who told you that, if I may ask?"

"Our friend, Big Willie. He says you had an arm around the tart wearing a blue dress decorated with lace that night."

"Which night?"

"Nearly a week ago. You and Willie were playing for tips at the Goat and Boar, yes? You'll remember the public house was particularly crowded that night. One could hardly move."

Warren nodded. "Right lively crowd it was, as well. Willie and me was cramped for space. I went home a good several pounds heavier than when I got there. Made me nervous to walk around with that much cash a-jingling in my purse."

"You left before Willie did. For what reason?"

Warren shrugged. "No reason. I only felt like leaving. I'd made enough money for the evening, and wanted to go home."

He had nobody to go home to, and so Suzanne doubted his story, especially in the light of what Willie had told her two nights ago. "I'm told you had occasion to have your arm around the victim before you left."

"The boy in the blue dress."

"You know he was a boy, then."

"Everyone knows the body floating in the river was a boy in a blue dress. Everyone knows that's the murder Pepper gave you to look into."

Of course. All of Southwark knew by now. But she continued her questioning. "By his account, you were one of the last to see the boy alive."

That alarmed him so he became quite agitated and his jowls quivered. "Oh no, there must have been plenty to have groped him after me. That boy went straight from me to someone else as soon as I learnt he weren't no girl."

"So you knew about that before he was killed."

"Of course, I knew. I goosed him like I does all the tarts in that place, and when I found his pocket were filled with jewels, I rigged in my arm real quick-like and left him alone. Went back to playing my own flute, and never mind his."

"What did you see after that?"

"Naught. I saw nothing at all. I swear it on my life."

"Oh, come, Warren. I know you far better than that. In fact, there are few men who wouldn't have watched him closely for the rest of the evening just for the amusement of seeing others make the same mistake you did. How many men did you see him with who did not feel under his dress? Particularly those who went outside with him?"

Warren blushed a deep red, giving him even more of a pumpkin look about him. "I swear, Suze."

"Warren . . . I'm your friend. I need you to tell me."

She let him think on that for a moment, then he sighed and said, "All right, then. There was a number of them. As a tart, that boy had a talent, he did."

"And who was the last one you saw with that talented tart?"

"Dunno his name. Never seen him before."

"What did he look like?"

Warren shrugged. "Dunno, maybe big. Big shoulders. He stood out a bit in that place, dressed all in old clothes but looking like they weren't his. Rather like he'd stole 'em off a clothesline or such. Like they didn't fit so well as they should."

"What did he do that you saw? How did he act?"

"Well, when I saw him was when the little tart went up to him and offered himself. All batting his eyelashes and tapping certain spots with his fan then hiding behind it."

"And what did the bigger man do?"

"Nothing that I saw. No reaction at all. Which I thought was a mite strange. Most of the men there liked being all made over by the pretty girl, but this here fellow, he was a block of stone, he was."

Suzanne was excited by this development. "Did he seem angry? Did he look as if he were threatening the boy?"

Warren shook his head. "It was like he'd expected it. Like he knew all along the girl was a boy and needn't have a feel of it."

"And he didn't mind?"

"I wouldn't say that. They argued some. The tart put up a good face, still trying to seduce him. Then I suppose they came to terms, for then the big man took him by the arm and escorted him from the Goat and Boar."

"They both left the public room?"

"Yes."

"And did you see the boy after that?"

"No. I left myself, soon after."

Suzanne gave him a stern, questioning look.

He held up his palms. "Honest. I left once the show was over. I could see when they left they wasn't coming back."

"How did you know that?"

Warren shrugged. "I dunno. I could just tell. This were a special customer, one who knew that tart. Besides, I was getting bored by it all. I stopped caring what sex he was, and watching everyone in the place get themselves serviced by a boy wasn't so interesting anymore. 'Twere funny once or twice, but three times, four times, five times . . . it just was boring."

"The man you saw; how did he move? Graceful? Clumsy?"

"The average, I'd say. He seemed muscular, and deft enough with his weight—graceful on his feet—but no more graceful than the average."

That didn't sound at all like Higgins, especially with the way this man was dressed. Higgins had been described as exceptionally graceful and fashionable. She guessed every stitch he owned would fit him perfectly. "And you're certain you don't know the name of the man who took the boy from the room?"

Warren shook his head. "Haven't the foggiest idea."

That was a severe disappointment. Suzanne slumped in momentary defeat.

"Is that all you wanted to know, Suze?"

She thought a moment, then nodded. There seemed nothing else he could give that would be useful. Then she remembered and laid a hand on his arm to keep him in his seat. "Warren, did you see Dent put his arm around the boy?"

Warren laughed. "Sure I did. I nearly busted out with screaming laughter, I did."

"Did he seem to guess the truth?"

"No. Not Dent. After a moment he let go and then went on about his business."

"I see. Then thank you, Warren. Do let me know if you hear anything about the boy or that customer of his."

"Will do, Suze." With that, Warren tucked his flute case under his arm and left the theatre.

Suzanne went to find Ramsay. She needed to talk to Higgins again.

Chapter Sixteen

It was still quite early in the evening when she and Ramsay arrived at the house in Haymarket. Suzanne repeated the special knock she'd heard on her first visit here, and the door was answered by the same fellow who had opened it the last time. But tonight he wore men's clothing and his head was bare of wig. He hadn't yet shaved, and so his face bore a dark shadow that covered enough of his throat to look like a creeping mold on a drain pipe. His eyes appeared somewhat the worse for wear from too much drinking, or whatever else he might have imbibed the night before. Or the weeks before. Red rimmed his lids, dark bags hung under them, and his skin was pale and waxy looking. When he saw both Suzanne and Ramsay at the door, his jaw dropped in surprise and dismay.

"What're you doing here? And who's he?" More than offended at the disrupted protocol, he appeared afraid of Ramsay. For his part, Ramsay said nothing and made no move, but remained still as stone, though watchful as a raptor.

Suzanne replied, "This is my good friend, Diarmid Ramsay, who is only an escort for a woman moving around town on her own. A personal guard, if you will." In her experience, whenever she tended to business most people addressed whatever man might be nearby, so she felt it necessary to explain Ramsay's function here. She hated being ignored, and today had neither time nor energy to tolerate it. "I'm here for another chat with Master Higgins."

"He's got nothing more to say to you about anything."

"I think he'll talk to me if he doesn't wish to answer to the local magistrate. I'm certain I can talk my other good friend, the Earl of Throckmorton, who has no love at all for sodomites, into having a chat with his good friend . . . the king." She was, perhaps, overstating Daniel's influence, as well as Charles's interest in the matter, but this man didn't know that and probably never would. "I would encourage cooperation from Higgins in my investigation."

The fellow fumed, apparently assembling something to say rude enough to make her go away, but he seemed to sense she would not be put off by mere words, and Ramsay would not react well to a verbal assault any better than to a physical one. So he stepped back and let the door swing open to admit them. "Enter," he said. "Master Higgins is still upstairs."

Suzanne and Ramsay stepped inside the house. The smells tonight were of stale wine and lingering smoke, dirty clothes, leftover food, and filthy bodies. There were fewer men in the room than the night before, and they were all asleep. Some on the floor, huddled in blankets and stinking clothing, some on sofas. One fellow had made a bed of the dining table, surrounded by plates of half-eaten food and glasses emptied of wine and spirits. Suzanne and Ramsay proceeded to the spiral stairwell and made their way up.

They found Higgins and his companion entwined on a large bed near a window that looked out over the street. Moonlight washed over them there. At the other end of the room the hearth flickered high with a newly laid fire, and several candelabras threw light. At their approach, Higgins raised his head sleepily and gave them a baleful gaze. The companion looked up, and grunted. Without speaking, he drew a bedsheet around himself, rose from the bed, and made his way out via the stairwell. Higgins watched him go, looking as if he wished he could follow, then rose and sat on the edge of the bed. Its deep, very expensive, down-filled mattress poufed around him. Suzanne found herself wondering how someone who plainly had a great deal of money would willingly live in filth like this. Had she made enough money for that sort of luxury during her days servicing men, she was certain she would have made a home far less dirty and smelly than this. Even Maddie's brothel had not been this nasty.

He leaned his elbows on his knees and his head tilted as he gazed up at her. "What is it you want this time?" He sounded more impatient than angry, and Suzanne surmised she might get what she wanted if she gave the appearance his evening wouldn't be terribly disrupted by it.

"I need more information about how Lord Paul Worthington came to be in the Goat and Boar the night he was killed."

A great, impatient sigh escaped Higgins, and his head hung from his shoulders. "I've told you all I know."

"I don't think you have. I think you know where the coachman Thomas might be found."

His back went up, hands on thighs, as offended as a

slighted countess. His willie dangling over the edge of the bed between his legs detracted somewhat from such dignity, but he showed not the least embarrassment for it. "I do not. As I said last night, I have not the slightest idea where he's gone since he left the duke's employ."

"Why do you lie to me? For what reason do you hide him from me?"

"I say again, I'm not hiding him."

"He comes here regularly; I'm certain of it. Surely he's a trusted member of your tight little circle of like-minded men. When he parted ways with the duke, surely he must have come to you for sanctuary. Or at least a hug. He couldn't have wandered entirely into the ether; he had to find somewhere on this earth to go."

"He is quite self-sufficient, I assure you. He's a man who can stand on his own two feet, and he doesn't need me to kiss him and make it all better. When the duke chased him off with his sword, Thomas ran the faster and escaped with his skin intact."

"How do you know the duke threatened him with a sword?"

Higgins sighed. "I don't. I just imagine he must have used one to chase Thomas away. Where Thomas went from there is anyone's guess, and I wouldn't hazard one myself. He isn't the sort to cry on a shoulder or expect others to carry him. As I've said, I have no idea where he is at the moment." Higgins gazed blandly at her, and looked her straight in the eye without wavering.

If Suzanne had harbored any doubt Higgins was lying, it was allayed at that moment. That straight-on, unwavering gaze was the favorite technique of every inveterate liar she had ever known. And there had been many. That look was invariably calculated to impress her with pure heart and righteous honesty, but she knew better. The longer and steadier the gaze, the more fear of discovery of the lie and the less honest the heart. More than ever before, Suzanne now knew for a dead certainty that Higgins not only knew where she could find Thomas, but he could give her an exact address from memory.

"Tell me where to find him."

"I'm telling you—"

"You're lying to me. Stop lying. If it will help you to trust me, let me explain that I don't think he killed Lord Paul."

"Of course he didn't kill Paul. I trust even you to know that. But I do not trust you to not have him in the watch house on a charge of sodomy—"

"Or abduction."

Higgins nodded vigorously and held out his hand in agreement. "Yes. Or abduction. You see my point, then. Thomas is a criminal, was justly fired from his post, and surely would rather not have a visit from anyone asking about a boy who was murdered."

"You said you cared about Lord Paul. You told me you cared about him and you miss him."

Higgins nodded, with a frown and a sideways glance as if he knew he was going to hear something he would rather not.

"But it seems to me you don't have so very much regard for his memory. You claim Paul was happier here than with his family. If you loved him so well, then why aren't you outraged that this has happened to him? Why are you not straining at the bit to find his killer? How come you aren't telling me all you know that might lead me to him?"

"How would it help you to find Thomas? What could he possibly tell you that would help?"

"I won't know that until I talk to him. I can't know what bits are missing from the story. I can only ask questions of everyone until I find enough answers to make it whole. I need you to point me to the whereabouts of that man, who we know has spoken to Paul at length, and who convinced him to come here."

"'Tisn't as if it were a Herculean task, convincing him. He came willingly."

Suzanne doubted it, but held her tongue for the moment. "Be that as it may, if Thomas has information, I should hear it. If he doesn't, then he goes on his way and no harm done."

"You would release a known sodomite and abductor without arresting him or reporting him to the authorities?"

"I came here without bringing the constable, didn't I? I could have had constable, magistrate, and a bevy of armed guards here to arrest you at this very moment, did I hate you and wish to clear the city of sodomites. But I did not. And will not, for it's not what I'm out for. I wish to find a killer, and anything less is simply not my concern."

"You think I'm not a killer?" He leaned toward her, tilted his head, and stared hard with narrowed eye.

She responded in kind, and stepped toward him as if to stare him down. "Give me proof you are, and I'll have you in chains in the blink of an eye. But until then I'll settle for having the murderer of Lord Paul dangling from a gibbet. I've no time, nor energy, to spend on the likes of a former coachman who buggers men."

"Thomas prefers to be buggered, truth be told." He looked away and thought a moment. Suzanne let him. Finally he sighed, having come to a decision. "In any case, perhaps there's some benefit to finding the killer. If Paul died because he was dressed as a girl, I would like to see one who hates us that much pay for his crime."

"Excellent choice. Tell me where to find Thomas, and help me catch the killer."

Higgins sighed again. "Very well."

THOMAS, it turned out, had recently taken rooms not far from the Haymarket, in a redbrick tenement. The building was not terribly old, and the quarters he occupied were on the first floor up from the ground floor. The building was plain but sturdy. There didn't seem to be a draft in the stairwell, and the neighbors coming and going appeared at least somewhat polite and neighborly. Rather similar to the neighbors Suzanne had once had in Horse Shoe Alley during the interregnum, who were pleasant enough to her and rarely got into fights with each other. With Ramsay at her back, Suzanne knocked on the door.

Some grumbling came from within, she heard heavy boot steps, and the door opened a crack. "What yer want?"

"I'm looking for a coachman named Thomas. Would that be you?" She spoke in her best imitation of the upper classes, based on her quantity of conversation with Daniel since his return, as well as the many dozens of men in Parliament who had hired her services over the years. Her ploy was that she would hint to Thomas that she might like to hire him.

"Yes, mistress." He drew open the door and stepped back. "What might I do for you?" He seemed puzzled, and rightly, that a gentlewoman would do this sort of errand herself.

But she ignored that puzzlement, and smiled broadly and graciously, ever so pleased to find him at home. "May we come in?" The better to not have the door slam in her face when she revealed her true interest in him. He looked beyond her to Ramsay, and she added, "Ramsay here is my escort. His only function is to protect me from bodily harm while walking through the streets. He speaks to no one, ever. Rarely, even, to me." She crinkled her eyes to indicate she was a good-humored woman making a harmless jest. Thomas obliged her with a chuckle. Then he stepped back again and indicated they should enter his quarters.

He was an ordinary man, and Suzanne found herself eyeing him to see whether his sexual quirks were evident. She found nothing to indicate he was different from any other man, not a smudge of face paint nor a whiff of perfume. His dress was plain, but clean and well mended. He'd taken care with his grooming, and it was apparent he visited the baths occasionally. He wore no jacket at the moment, but that could be forgiven since he was at home and had not been expecting visitors. Even now he went to the next room and returned donning a plain, wool jacket. As he tugged his conservatively ruffled shirt sleeves through to be visible, he said, "How may I be of service to you . . . my lady?" He addressed her without any idea of who she was, and so hesitated.

"Mistress Suzanne Thornton, good man. I am here to ask some questions, at the request of those investigating the murder of Lord Paul Worthington."

The coachman paled and glanced at the door to gauge his chances at escape, then returned his attention to her and raised his chin. "What about it? I had nothing to do with that."

"I beg to differ." She glanced over at Ramsay, who stood guard at the closed door. The coachman would be staying put.

The room, of course, was not terribly large, but it was a comfortable size. At the opposite end it boasted a single window with glazed panes and wooden shutters. One door to the right appeared to lead to a small kitchen-like area, and to the left seemed to be the inner sanctum where he slept. This room contained little more than an upholstered chair and a sofa near a modest hearth, a bookshelf containing nothing more than a half dozen or so small books, and a medium-sized trunk. She thought about settling on the sofa in order to entrench herself, but thought that with Ramsay at the door such a move might make Thomas more apprehensive than necessary. So she stood between Thomas and Ramsay, and spoke standing. "I know you worked for Jacob Worthington, and that you abducted his son, Lord Paul Worthington, about three months ago."

"I did no such thing." He attempted to sound indignant, but his voice held that false note of an inexperienced and untalented liar. He was quite transparent, and it took no skill to read him.

"I have it from Mordecai Higgins. He's the one who told me where I could find you."

The look of surprise made Thomas's face go entirely slack. For a moment he couldn't speak.

She said, "He confided in me because he thinks you can help us find the killer, though you probably don't know you can."

Thomas was able to shut his mouth then, and now he appeared curious. "How would I know who killed him?"

"You may know something that, when placed next to the things I already know, might point us in the right direction."

"Such as?"

"I'm not sure. Tell us what happened when you were asked to take Lord Paul to Kent." She looked toward the sofa. "May I sit?"

He nodded and gestured to the seat, and she went to rest

her feet. Ramsay remained at the door, preventing escape as subtly as possible. As she sat, Thomas made a couple of false starts, then said, "I was asked to drive the boy to stay with some cousins down there."

"You never arrived."

The lie Suzanne had seen forming in his eyes disappeared. He realized she knew more about what had happened than he'd thought, and he had no way of knowing what she knew and what she didn't. He said, "No. But I can tell you there was good reason not to go. Poor Paul was terrified of those people. They hated him."

"For what reason?"

"He was one of us."

"So young?"

He raised his chin again, struggling for dignity. "I knew when I was no more than ten."

"But to be taken away from his family?"

"They didn't want him. We did."

Suzanne found herself unable to reply as she began to comprehend the utter betrayal of every adult in that boy's life. The only people who wanted him did so because they had a use for him, and his parents had laid him off on relatives to have him out of their way. In addition, those relatives hadn't been enchanted to have him, either. She swallowed hard. For a long moment she couldn't speak. Finally she was able to croak, "Tell me what happened."

Slowly he settled into the chair opposite. He leaned toward her in an effort to keep his words private, away from Ramsay. For his part, Ramsay pretended to not hear. "We all knew what he was. His parents denied it, but everyone who lived or worked in that house knew what was happening to him. We all understood that Lord Paul was unlikely to ever take a wife if he could avoid it. To be sure, he might have been forced to marry, but since he was the younger son it wasn't so very important for him to produce an heir. His parents chose to keep him out of sight of society, and they thought of that as the most gentle way of dealing with their problem."

Suzanne nodded, for what he said was nothing new. "More than once a family has taken that route with a child that would put them at a social disadvantage."

"And I suppose that sometimes it's the best way. Keeping him in London and requiring him to behave in ways unnatural to him would have been torture. But sending him to Kent was not the answer for him."

"Why not?"

"They hated him there. His mother's cousins were as embarrassed by him as his parents, and so they hid him from the world. Sending him there was nothing better than if he'd been imprisoned in the Tower. Worse, in truth, for in the Tower of London there would have been fellow prisoners. In addition those cousins mocked and ridiculed him, they kept him locked up in an apartment of rooms . . . they wouldn't even let him eat with the family. There was no contact with anyone other than the maid who brought his meals."

"Why didn't he complain of this to his parents?"

"And what would they have done? Had he returned home, his parents would more than likely have done the same thing. Hidden him away, and hoped that one day he would quit his behavior. That is how that sort think. That our nature is a matter of bad behavior and nothing more. Lord Paul's family all thought that if they punished him he would eventually stop being that way." A thought came, and Thomas added sadly, "And now he is no longer being any way at all."

"So you thought you were rescuing him."

"That is exactly what I did."

"How much were you paid by Higgins for delivery of the child?"

Thomas fell silent and only gazed dully at her. She waited for a reply, but received none.

Finally she said, "I would point out that he is dead. Your rescue failed."

"We took him from a family that hated him."

"To make him a whore, working for Higgins?"

"To free him so he might make his own way in the world."

"At twelve years old."

"Better than to be imprisoned and cut off from the world. At any age. Better than being hated by his own family, who should have been the ones above all others to love him. Better than being made to feel worthless."

Suzanne remembered how it had felt to be denigrated and ridiculed for being a girl, and how the best she could ever hope for from her father was to be ignored. Again words choked her. Unlike Paul, she had thought Daniel had loved her once; the boy had nobody. The image of Paul Worthington receiving no regard from anyone but those who would use him made her chest hurt so that she could hardly breathe. The image of his bright, cheery smile, and the joy in life he'd shown that night in the Goat and Boar, brought tears to her eyes.

She blinked them back. "I'm sorry. Let us continue." Thomas waited patiently for her to ask another question. She said, "How did you engineer the abduction?"

"'Twas no abduction. He came willingly."

She answered sharply, "The law considers it an abduction." A look from Ramsay brought her back from her anger, and she continued in a gentler voice, "But to get to the point, how did you go about what you did?"

"I talked to him. I knew he was desperately unhappy. When they sent him to Kent, we talked on the way."

"You convinced him that he needed to leave his family?"

"I told him he needn't stay with people who would treat him badly. We talked about the things they did to him whenever he was with his mother's cousins. He told me how he hated it there, and how he also hated his family in London. He'd never felt welcome anywhere, at any time of his life."

"Did you tell him if he went with you he would be required to perform certain acts on strange men? And that the money he earned by it would go to another stranger?"

Thomas didn't answer that very quickly, and Suzanne knew what the truth was before his reply. But he was truthful. "No."

"Because you know it is not a good life for anyone, and least of all for a child."

"He was close to becoming a man."

"He was not one yet. And now he never will be. What you did was—"

"Mistress Suze," said Ramsay from the door. "It grows late."

Startled into focusing on her mission, she blinked and stammered for a moment. Right. The investigation. "We need to learn who killed him."

"Yes, you do," said Thomas.

She sifted through her thoughts, then asked, "So you were able to turn your carriage around before arriving in Kent, and take Lord Paul to Higgins without him raising a fuss. And Higgins took him in to train him."

"To show him another way to live."

Suzanne shrugged that off, not wanting to wander into those weeds anymore. She said, "Why was he in the Goat and Boar that night and not in the Haymarket at Higgins's house?"

"I couldn't say. I don't know. I can only surmise that Higgins thought it would be lucrative for his girl-like boy to service the far more numerous men of the ordinary world. After all, there is only so much money to be made in pederasty. There is a far greater number of randy men wanting girls, involving far less risk."

"Is that common, to send boys out disguised as girls?"

Thomas shook his head. "Lord Paul was special. He had the grace and culture to fool anyone. Higgins knew he had a treasure in Paul. He thought Paul could make him a great deal of money as a girl."

So Thomas corroborated that. Suzanne continued into another line of questioning. "Why did you quit your post in the Worthington household?"

He blinked, surprised. "You don't know?"

"What should I know?"

"I ran away. To be sure, I would have been arrested, had I lingered. And in fact I was fortunate to have not been slapped in chains immediately. As it was, I was locked in my quarters in the stable and only escaped by prying the door lock." He spoke in an *of course* tone, and seemed to think her stupid, or inattentive, for not knowing this. "I was able to pack my few belongings in a satchel, and made my way to the Haymarket and safety."

"For what were you detained?"

Again Thomas blinked, and made an odd grimace that was half smile and half frown. He shook his head, bewildered. "Why, for the very crime we've been discussing. I was charged with the task of delivering Lord Paul to his cousins in Kent, and instead I took him to Higgins in Haymarket. When the duke found out—"

"He knew? You left the household weeks ago."

Thomas nodded. "Three weeks ago. I was called into his grace's bedchamber that evening shortly after New Year's, and queried about the whereabouts of his son. It seems he'd had a note from the cousins in Kent, which let him know Lord Paul wasn't with them."

Suzanne looked over at Ramsay, who seemed as surprised as she. Cawthorne had known his son was not in Kent long before she'd brought him the news two days ago. And he'd pretended ignorance. Neither had he mentioned the situation to his wife. She asked Thomas, "How did you respond?"

"I put him off as best I could. I insisted I'd taken him to Kent, but did not claim to have seen any family member receive him. I told him that Lord Paul had been left in the hands of servants, and that I'd not stayed at the house for more than a minute. I said I'd taken a room for the night, in the nearest town, before setting off on my return trip to London the next morning."

"Did he believe you?"

"No. He insisted on the truth. In fact, he beat me for it. He was terribly angry."

"Rightly so."

"Perhaps. In any case, he cracked me over the head with a walking stick, and continued hitting me until I was on my knees before him, begging him to stop. I believe one of my ribs may have been cracked; it still hurts a mite." He absently laid a hand over his right rib cage. "Finally I told him I'd taken Paul to a friend."

"You told him where Paul was?"

"Certainly not. I would never have given away the location of Higgins's house. I told him to look in Bank Side."

"What did you tell him Paul was doing there?"

Thomas shrugged. "I said I'd left him with a friend, and

Southwark was the first place I could think of where I had no friends. It seemed the sort of place a man of the peerage would never venture."

Suzanne thought of Daniel and all the others of the nobility who frequented the Goat and Boar, and wondered where Thomas had gotten his impression of Bank Side. She said, "So you didn't know you were sending Cawthorne to the very place he could find his son?"

"I'd never known Higgins to go there; I had no idea he was selling Lord Paul as a girl."

This news rattled around in Suzanne's head like a die in a cup, and it bounced off all the other things she knew about what had happened to Paul Worthington. If the duke knew Paul was not in Kent, and instead thought he was in Southwark, then surely he would go looking for the boy there. But then why not alert the constable and enlist his help in the matter? Of course, she answered her own question by reminding herself that Cawthorne would not have wanted any sort of public scandal regarding his son. It wasn't until she'd gone to him with news of his son's death that he'd finally contacted Pepper in the matter, and that was for the express purpose of putting a stop to an investigation that would become known to the public.

She then realized that she'd never told the duke where the murder had occurred, but Cawthorne nevertheless knew what constable in all of London had sent her. "Did you tell him your fictional friend in Southwark was a harlot's attendant?"

"He may have inferred it."

So Cawthorne more than likely went to Southwark in search of his son, knowing he was likely to find him in the company of an unseemly crowd. Bank Side was not a terribly long street. It was only a matter of time before he would encounter Paul in that blue dress. The scenario that came to mind at that point made Suzanne's jaw drop, and she gasped. She remembered the tall, broad-shouldered man Warren had seen in the Goat and Boar. The one wearing clothing that didn't appear to belong to him. The one who had spoken harshly to Paul, then pulled him from the public room by his arm. Rage filled her as realization grew. She said to Ramsay, breathless, "I think I know who killed Lord Paul."

Chapter Seventeen

"We must speak to the duke," Suzanne told Ramsay as they settled into their hired carriage and left Thomas's tenement. Outrage pounded in her ears, and she could barely breathe. Her voice was choked and low, and the words were difficult to get out.

Ramsay made an effort at soothing her, but with a sense that she might lose control of herself, his apprehension put an edge on his voice. "We should leave him alone, and let this sleeping dog lie."

"He's killed his son."

"He's a duke. There's nothing you can do. You've already been warned off this case. The constable certainly won't pursue it, and 'tis unlikely the magistrate will want to stick out his neck for this. There's no hope of succeeding at anything other than putting a rope around your own neck."

"He murdered his *son*!"

"He murdered his *sodomite* son."

"Surely, Diarmid, you cannot think that justifies—"

"No, I do not. But that is how the crown will see it. And nearly everyone else in London as well."

"The magistrate won't ignore the law. He cannot. He must prosecute."

"With what? What hard proof do you have that Cawthorne killed Lord Paul? And who would think a member of the nobility would do such a messy, ugly thing to his own son? Even though the boy was not entirely a boy, what the duke did was not within the realm of normal anger. Nobody will believe it."

"So you do believe he did it?"

"Aye. I do."

"Then tell me your reasoning. Tell me your proof. Help me in my thinking."

Ramsay considered for a moment, then said, "When you told him his son was dead, he lied when he said he thought Paul was in Kent. He knew Paul was with a harlot's attendant, he believed Paul was in Bank Side, and there was a man fitting Cawthorne's description seen with Paul in the Goat and Boar on the night of the murder."

"So there's my proof. He lied about what he knew and he was the last one seen with Lord Paul before he died."

"I'm no magistrate, but will that be conclusive enough to overcome the duke's privilege?"

"Nobody is privileged to kill outside of war or execution of legal sentence."

"You know that may be truth in theory, but in practice it's entirely false. Men of his rank often get away with murder."

"It was his son, who was also a member of the nobility."

"I suppose that would make a difference. But the risk to yourself is high. Is the pursuit of a man so much more powerful than yourself worth what it will do to you if you attack his grace and fail?"

"I've no fine reputation to protect."

"You have much to lose other than your reputation, make no mistake. Your theatre. Your son. Your . . . life. The duke could make a great deal of trouble for you. He's of higher rank than Throckmorton, who is your protector in all things relating to the crown. Were Cawthorne to decide to ruin you, he could. And by his reputation I believe he would not hesitate."

"Only if I fail to convince the crown of his guilt."

"There is a high risk of failure for that. He is a peer and his testimony will be received as gospel. That's not true about anyone else involved."

She fell silent, thinking hard. She certainly would not like to lose her theatre. Nor her freedom. And in the final analysis, Lord Paul was not her personal responsibility. It was not her job to investigate crime. The authorities, whose job it was to catch criminals, had told her to quit her questioning, and she'd already carried this thing much further than was safe for her. If Cawthorne heard of her talking to anyone about Lord Paul, he would certainly retaliate, and never mind what would happen if she accused him publicly. If she failed to make her case, there would be terrible repercussions.

But when she remembered the mutilated body of Lord Paul, her rage boiled over again and she shook her head. "I can't give up. I must pursue this."

"Why?"

She gave an angry snort. "When I try to imagine myself not doing anything, not telling what I know and just sitting on my hands, knowing that Jacob Worthington murdered and mutilated his own son, I know I simply couldn't live with myself forever after. Knowing that man was at large, living his sanctimonious life in comfort, having never paid for his crime . . ." The words failed her and her throat closed with her grief and anger.

"Perhaps God will take payment in good time?"

She shook her head, swallowed hard, and said through gritted teeth, "Not good enough." Then she pounded on the carriage wall by the driver. "Driver, take us to Westminster. Orchard Street, if you please."

SUZANNE'S anger made it possible for her to screw up her courage enough to tap with the knocker on the door of the duke's house so late in the evening. Candlelight in the upstairs windows, where the shutters were still open, told her the family was still awake. When nobody answered her knock she picked up the brass tapper and knocked hard again. Still she waited.

Ramsay, behind her, said, "Perhaps we need to desist for the evening. You could send Pepper in the morning, and you'll have done your duty."

She wished he would be silent, for his words only stirred her feelings and made her angrier at the duke. "Nonsense. We both know Pepper is spineless and lazy, and would never face Cawthorne if he could avoid it. Going to Pepper is no better than simply giving up." She pounded on the door with her fist. "Besides, our best chance of convincing his magistrate of Worthington's guilt is to coerce a confession from him. Catch him by surprise, and he may give us the very thing we need to hang him."

"You seriously believe he will confess to you?"

"'Tis our only hope, my dear Ramsay."

Finally, the duke's manservant came to the door, and opened it but a crack.

Suzanne drew herself up erect, chin up, as dignified and authoritative as she could manage. "Good man. I wish to speak to his grace, immediately. 'Tis a matter of great importance."

"I'm afraid his grace has retired. Certainly he is not receiving visitors at this hour."

"This can't wait. I must talk to him."

"You may send a message in the morning." With that, the manservant closed the door.

Immediately Suzanne pounded with the knocker, and the door opened once more. Before he could tell her again that the duke was unavailable, she said quickly, "Tell the duke that I know who murdered his son. Also tell him that I have a witness who saw him at the Goat and Boar that night." Then she spun on her heel and marched away to the carriage, followed by a surprised Ramsay.

They rode in silence for a time, then he said, "Do you think that was wise?"

She stared out the window at the blackness of the world, and was too angry to reply.

IT didn't take long for her to hear from Constable Pepper. The very next morning she received him at breakfast as before. He was quite agitated, and addressed her in a loud, angry tone that carried an undercurrent of fear. Twice his voice cracked with desperation.

"You cannot continue to harass the duke this way!" His face reddened, and even seemed to swell.

She set aside her fork and knife, and drew herself up to

address him with all her dignity. "My dear constable, you should know I think the duke is our culprit. I believe he has murdered his son. Letting him get away with it would be a crime in itself as well as a sin."

"You have no proof."

"There is a witness who can identify the duke, who saw him remove Lord Paul from the Goat and Boar late that evening."

"What witness?"

"Warren. He plays the flute for our performances."

"A musician?" His amazement at her stupidity seemed to choke him. "He'll be no help. Cawthorne will of course deny, and 'twill be his word against a musician's. You'll have made an accusation for no reason. Naught will come of it, and I'll be ruined."

"Nonsense. You'll be a hero. You'll be lauded for your principles, and rewarded by the king for plucking one of the worst Puritan thorns from his side."

"The crown will never bring charges, for the backlash from Parliament that would surely result."

"His magistrate would be quite happy to charge the duke, if he thinks the king will benefit from it."

"You cannot convince him of that, I vow."

"Charles can. And Daniel has the king's ear, at least somewhat."

Something flickered in Pepper's eyes as he considered that, but then he shook the thought from his head. "It would never come about so easily, you can be sure of it. Nothing in life is ever that simple. If you don't desist immediately, you will destroy me!"

She gazed at him for a moment, imagining life without Pepper. The idea appealed to her.

Pepper appeared to grasp the meaning of her silence, and took another tack. "Where, exactly, is your witness?"

"This time of day, he's more than likely asleep."

"You'll tell him to stop disseminating lies about the duke."

"He isn't screaming these things from the rafters. And in any case, I cannot tell him to stop, for they are not lies."

"They are lies! The duke did not kill his son!" Pepper's face purpled more, and he fairly jumped up and down in his frustration.

It was time to put a stop to this. "Very well," she said. "I'll never mind the duke and put all of this out of my mind. I'll say no more about it to anyone."

Pepper sighed, and relaxed. His fists unclenched, his face began to return to its normal pasty complexion and he took some deep breaths. "Very well. Thank you."

"Good day, then, Constable."

"Good day, Mistress Thornton." And so he left. Suzanne returned to her breakfast, calmly turning over in her mind how she would go about snaring the duke for his magistrate. She decided to visit the Haymarket once more.

Unwilling to wait for Ramsay to present himself so he could accompany her, she hired a carriage on her own and ordered the driver to Westminster. She only needed to talk for a moment with Higgins, about what he would say if asked to testify regarding the night Lord Paul died. She was settling into her seat, drawing her coat around her and straightening her clothing, deep in thought about what she would tell him, when just as the driver slapped his reins against his horses' backs, a pounding came on the carriage door. It flew open unbidden, and Ramsay climbed in before the horses could make any speed. He pulled the door closed behind him, latched it, and settled into the seat opposite her.

"And where do you think you're going?" His tone was gentle but firm.

Her tone in reply was as insouciant as she could manage at the moment. "Oh, Ramsay. I didn't want to disturb you. You've spent so much time watching over me lately, I didn't think it would be necessary to bring you along on this trip. I'm only off to the Haymarket again."

"Suze, I live to accompany you. I wish to see you safe. But most of all, I wish to see you."

That made her smile. Sometimes she forgot Ramsay was pressing a suit for her hand, and that morning she had been preoccupied with her business with the constable. They rode in silence across the river and to Westminster.

But when they arrived at Higgins's house, there was no answer to her knock. She and Ramsay waited in the street, where vendors cried their wares and throngs of people passed by. There was no answer. She knocked again, the same special knock that had opened this door twice before. No answer. She stepped into the street to look up at the window above the door, and saw the shutter make a slight, furtive movement in closing. Then nothing. Nothing moved, nothing sounded.

Ramsay said, as if making a passing comment of no importance, "It could be we've worn out our welcome."

"I suppose it would be asking too much to expect him to tell the crown what he told me."

"You mean, admit in open court he'd abducted a duke's son then turned the boy out as a sodomite and a prostitute?"

Suzanne's heart fell as she realized how stupid she'd been to think she could count on Higgins for that. "We must talk to Thomas, then, and hope he will be more reliable."

"My hopes are not high."

"Perhaps I can convince him."

"Only you might succeed at that."

But Thomas proved no more reliable than Higgins had, and Suzanne never had a chance to convince him of anything. A knock at his door was met with silence. No sound or movement from within. "He's not in," she said.

"I suspect he's not coming back."

She looked at Ramsay to see if he might be joking, and found he wasn't. "Absconded?"

"Again. I think 'tis likely you've frightened him off."

"That can't be. He's nothing to be afraid of."

"Other than hanging."

Anger rose again, and she drew some deep breaths. It was her strong feelings in this matter that hurt her judgment. She needed to stop letting emotion cloud her mind and begin thinking more clearly. "See if he's here."

Ramsay hesitated, but then complied. He took the door handle, turned it as silently as its cheap mechanism would allow, and gently shoved the door ajar. There was no fire on the hearth inside; nothing lit at all. He opened the door wider, and found the coachman quite gone. By the light from the single window Suzanne could see the few books in the bookcase had been taken, and the single trunk as well. She didn't need to look in the bedchamber and kitchen to know they would be just as empty. Ramsay said, "Your proof against Cawthorne grows thin."

"Warren will help us." He must. He was all they had left.

THEY found Warren at the Goat and Boar. He sat at a table with Big Willie, the two of them filling the time before they would be required to play for that afternoon's performance. The fire in the hearth nearby burned merrily, warming them well before they would spend three or four hours in the stage left gallery where there would be no hearth or brazier. Suzanne and Ramsay sat with them. Suzanne went immediately to the point with Warren. "I need your help."

"Sure, Suze. What d'you need?" He took a long draught, and smiled at her. Warren was an agreeable sort, for the most part.

"You saw something in here the night that boy was killed."

"Oh, I caught an eyeful, I did. That boy was a handful. I told you that."

"I think you saw the murderer, and I know who it is."

Warren's face went slack with surprise. "Do tell!" He and Willie sat up straight and gawked at her.

"I think that man you saw leave with Lord Paul was the killer, and I need you to identify him for me. If you can tell me this man we suspect is the same man you saw that night, then we'll have our killer."

"God blind me! And who is he?"

Suzanne knew it would be foolhardy to tell him who the killer was, lest he back out on the spot, so she said, "I think it would be best to let you see him first, rather than tell you who he is, so it won't prejudice your identification. I wouldn't want you to think he was the man you saw only because I told you he was."

Warren nodded. "Right." He probably didn't understand what she'd just told him, but so long as he didn't persist in asking who the killer was, she let him pretend he knew why she wouldn't tell him.

"So, you'll come with me now, and have a look at him?"

He glanced over at Willie, and told her, "I can't just now. You know I can't. Willie and me, we've got to play this afternoon."

Willie gestured with his nearly empty cup and said, "Nah, Warren, we can get by without you for today. Go on and help her."

"But I need the money. I can't get paid if I don't play."

"I'll pay you," said Suzanne. "You won't miss your pay today for coming with me."

Warren looked from Suzanne to Willie, then said to Suzanne, "Very well, then. Let's go have a look at this killer of yours." He sounded morbidly eager to gawk at a murderer as he rose from the table and reached for his coat hanging on the back of his chair.

As he donned it and Suzanne and Ramsay rose from the table, Ramsay whispered into Suzanne's ear, "You haven't told him he'll need to testify against a duke in open court."

"First things first," she whispered in return. "He'll know when he needs to."

"When you need him to."

"Same thing."

THE carriage they'd hired that morning yet lurked on Bank Side for a fare, and so Suzanne flagged it down once more to take them to Westminster. But she ordered the driver to stop and let them out on King Street, nearly half a mile from the duke's house. Ramsay stayed with the carriage, and Suzanne and Warren took a stroll down Orchard Street in an attempt to glimpse the duke without having to knock on his door.

They walked as if a married couple on their way somewhere, with a purpose and destination beyond the duke's house. The cold weather had cleared the streets of pedestrians, and that made them more conspicuous than Suzanne liked in their approach. Every house in the street seemed quiet, crouched on the land and huddled among hedgerows and old trees. Gardens were bare of leaves, and brown lawns sported patches of ice. Suzanne's shoes slipped and slid on the icy road, and she raised the collar of her cloak against the cold air. Warren was so cold his teeth chattered and he stuffed his hands with fingerless gloves beneath his arms. As they walked past the duke's house on the opposite side of the street, they saw no stirring at the windows. Once past it, they paused to consider what to do next.

"Who is this fellow you want me to see?" Warren stared at the magnificent house across the street, and his voice betrayed apprehension.

"You'll see." There was some truth to what she'd said about not wanting Warren to be prejudiced in his identification. It wouldn't do for her to tell him who he was to identify. Now, gazing across the street, she could see activity near the coach house at the back. She took Warren's arm and moved toward a tall hedgerow that ran between the duke's house and the one next to it. They slipped between the bushes, barely hidden by leafless branches. From that vantage they could see a driver readying the carriage, fussing with the tack here and there. Then he climbed up and urged the team of two horses forward to the front of the house. There it halted and the driver waited.

Warren whispered, "That ain't him." He pointed with his chin to the driver. "He ain't even close to the feller I saw at the Goat."

"I know." Suzanne didn't take her eyes from the carriage.

He peered at her, more curious than ever. They continued to wait.

Within a minute or two the front door opened, and out stepped the duchess, followed by the duke. Warren had a sudden intake of breath. Not quite a gasp, for it was cold and he was shivering, and besides, he wasn't given to emotional demonstration. But it was enough to tell Suzanne she'd been right about the man Warren had seen that night the week before.

The duke glanced in their direction. Suzanne and Warren stood still as rocks and hoped the dense branches of the hedgerow would hide them enough. Then the duke went on his way and climbed into the carriage. The driver slapped reins against the horses' backs and moved off down the driveway to the street.

"That's him, then? That's the man you saw that night?"

"Who is he?"

"He's the boy's father."

Warren looked at her, as if searching her face for humor. When he found none, he whispered, "Good God." They watched the carriage roll away.

"He's the Duke of Cawthorne."

"Well, I can see he's someone of importance."

"You'll tell the crown you saw him that night, then?"

Warren nodded. "That sort shouldn't be allowed to live."

Chapter Eighteen

N ow Suzanne had to determine how to go about accus-
ing the duke. Plainly Constable Pepper would be no
help in this. She needed to talk to Daniel. He would have to
make the accusation to the magistrate for her, in order for it
to be taken seriously. She was so determined to bring Cawthorne to justice, she assumed it would be a matter of course
that Daniel would do exactly as she asked. Surely he would
want a murdering peer to be brought to justice. But once
again she found she was wrong about Daniel.

"I wish I could accommodate you, Suzanne, really, I do."
They were seated by the fire in the front room of his quarters
at Whitehall. The room was tucked into the ground floor of
one of the older Tudor-era buildings, and wasn't particularly
cozy, so they sat very close to the flame for warmth. Suzanne's
feet were quite cold, but she resisted the urge to remove her
shoes and rub some circulation into them.

Daniel's demeanor was somewhat grumpy today. She'd

ignored his wish that she refrain from visiting him at the palace, lest his wife get wind of it, and had easily slipped past the guard at the front entrance on King Street. These days she was presentable enough to be let inside the palace without much fuss. The palace guards didn't know her face, but they knew her type and let her through the front without question. It would be far more difficult to approach the king himself, and she'd never tried it. That would bring her up against a vigilant personal guard who would never let her through. Approaching Daniel, however, was little more than a matter of locating his quarters in the maze of old buildings and knocking at the door.

Now she dug her fingernails into the arms of her chair and struggled to keep her voice even. "You can accommodate me, I'm sure of it. And you must. It would be a travesty for Cawthorne to be free any longer than it would take for a warrant to be written out for his arrest."

"Your proof is terribly slender."

"Warren saw him at the Goat and Boar that night. The duke was the last man seen with Lord Paul. Furthermore, he was incognito, wearing a disguise. Plainly he was up to no good."

"You think he went there with the intention of killing his son? And you think it on the basis of his odd costume?"

Hearing it put that way made the theory sound as unlikely as Daniel's tone suggested. She told herself not to let him undermine her confidence. She must keep faith in herself.

"I believe he went there to find him, and plainly he didn't wish to be recognized by others in the tavern. Whether his original intention was murder or not might be debatable. The fact remains, however, that the boy was murdered and

Cawthorne was the last to be seen with him. Even more to the point, he lied to us the day we first went to speak to him. He told me he thought his son was in Kent, when he knew very well the boy had never arrived there. We also know that he had been told his son was in Southwark."

"Very well, let's say he did do this thing to Lord Paul. There are those who would maintain that the killing was justified. Cawthorne would be seen as a man defending the reputation of himself and his entire family. Had rumors started that Paul was a sodomite, it would have ruined not only Cawthorne, but his heir as well. Paul's brother."

"Murder is murder. Lord Paul was a child, and deserved protection from his father, not death."

Daniel drew himself up in anger. "Lord Paul was wearing a dress, for the love of God!" As his voice rose Suzanne could see the embarrassment of that night redden his cheeks. He sat back in his chair and crossed his legs away from her, and he glowered at her as if she'd suggested he put his arm around Lord Paul again.

"Murder is murder!" She was aghast she had to argue this at all.

"I think you should let it lie. There's nothing to be gained by making an accusation, never mind that the duke could destroy you. I am surprised you're even bringing it up to me."

"Of course I'm pursuing this. I can hardly stand by and do nothing. The boy's mother came to me and begged me to find her son's killer. She's heartbroken, and wants justice. I want it for her."

"But consider, Suzanne, how much more heartbroken would she be, were she to learn her husband was the guilty one? How much pain would you cause her then?"

Suzanne wanted very much to reply to that, but only

made a guttural noise in the back of her throat then shut her mouth tight. He had a point, and it was a valid one even to her. The duchess's wish for justice could no longer hold if her husband were revealed as the criminal. She couldn't possibly benefit from the duke being hanged. Or even imprisoned. The entire family would be destroyed. In fact, the duchess would not be served even by knowing the truth herself. For a moment she half believed justice might be better served if the entire matter were set aside. Let God sort it out, for it was too knotty a problem for mortals to decide.

But, no. When she thought again, she still couldn't ignore that a murder had been done and she knew who had done it. "I can't, Daniel. I simply can't sit by and allow him to get away with it."

"Consider that even if you could convince the magistrate to charge him, he might yet be acquitted. And then where would you be?"

"Newgate, more than likely."

"Exactly. He would have you arrested for something fictional inside of a day." His voice lowered and softened, and he went so far as to rest a hand on her knee. "Let it drop, Suzanne. Don't pursue this, or it will be your downfall."

She gave a wry smile. "If it were, it would be no more of a downfall than I've already had."

"But think of those you would bring down with you."

"You?"

"I was thinking of Piers. I know you care about him, far more than you ever did care for me."

Suzanne opened her mouth to reply, but two things wanting to be said stuck in her throat so neither would come as words. First, that it was her feelings as a mother that made her so horrified by the death of a child. The other was that she cared as much for Daniel as she did Piers. She always had, and even now she couldn't imagine not being entirely wrapped up in him just as she was in Piers. In the end it was the overwhelming strength of both those feelings, so much a part of her soul, that kept her from saying anything at all. Instead she looked around for her cloak, then rose as she said, "If you won't help, I must go now."

Daniel seemed disappointed she wouldn't reply to his comment about himself. Plainly he'd put it out as bait, and that made her glad she hadn't swallowed it and declared her love for him like the foolish girl she'd once been. He was married, and her feelings for him then and now were irrelevant to everything save his own pride. It had always been so. She owed him a debt of gratitude for setting her up in business with the Globe, but not at the expense of her own pride. Not anymore. He rose, to see her to the door though it was only a few feet away. "I really do wish I could accommodate you."

"I might believe you, were you to promise me something. One small thing to show me your sincerity. If I find anything more to help my case, will you reconsider?"

Daniel thought about that for a moment, then slowly nodded. "I suppose I can. If you can present evidence for a solid case that proves without doubt he is guilty, then I'll consider pressing the Southwark magistrate for an arrest."

"Well, that's something, then."

"But remember two things: that your evidence must be irrefutable and that it must not be obtained by harassing or annoying his grace in any way."

Suzanne realized how difficult that would be, but also knew that anything less would raise questions about any evidence obtained and leave them all vulnerable to retaliation by the duke. So she nodded, then bade him good-bye.

In the courtyard outside Daniel's quarters she stood a moment in the icy weather, huddled in her cloak and muff, organizing her thoughts. What to do next? She was at a loss.

A page ran up to her and, bouncing on his toes before her, said, "Mistress Thornton? Suzanne Thornton?" He was a very young boy, and his breathless energy made her feel very old indeed.

"Yes?" She peered at him, wondering how the boy knew her name and trying to remember whether she'd seen him before. He wore black livery, which announced him as a servant of one of the many Puritans in Parliament. Personally, she knew no pages belonging to Puritans.

He said, still dancing in the cold though he was bundled into a heavy wool coat, "I'm instructed to escort you to the office of his grace the Duke of Cawthorne. Immediately, if you please, missus."

"I'm ordered to go?"

"The duke wishes it." The boy was certain that was enough to make it an order and she would obey. And he was right. To disregard the request would bring repercussions, for herself and the page as well. It wasn't his fault she feared and loathed the duke, so she had no choice but to go.

"Very well. Lead on."

The duke's quarters were in an area of the palace newer than the building where Daniel stayed while at court, and were more spacious. But they weren't more richly decorated, for Puritan Cawthorne could not display his wealth in that way, even had he wanted to. As a peer he needed to show he had wealth, and therefore power, but as a Puritan he was required to show it more subtly than the more libertine members of Parliament. So his clothing and furnishings were of plain design and subtle color, but were nevertheless of the highest quality materials and workmanship.

The front room where Suzanne awaited his grace, deserted by the page who had hurried to another room, was modestly furnished with a table and some chairs that were highly polished and marvelously burled wood. Though the fire was well fed and threw a great deal of warmth and light, the hearth was unembellished and made of flawless marble. There were no paintings nor tapestries on the walls, and no curtains at the windows. Only plain, brown shutters controlled the light and heat in the room. However, beneath her feet was a carpet of brown wool thick enough to make her totter on her heels. At the moment the shutters were closed, for the day was quite cold and a heavy overcast made it nearly dark as night outside. The carpet quite defeated the cold stone floor.

This time the wait for the duke to see her was short. He entered the room wearing a smile, and a plain black suit of clothes relieved only by a simple silver collar draped over his shoulders, and white shirtsleeves that gathered at the wrist. No rings on his fingers, and no other adornment. But every stitch was of silk and fine linen, and so perfectly tailored as to seem he'd been born in them.

Knowing what she now did about him, the cold, flinty light in his eyes now struck her as devilish. Evil in the most profound way. On first meeting him she'd wondered whether he owned a soul, and now she was certain he did not. Though overtly religious—and he literally wore his religion on his sleeve—she knew in her heart he'd never known God in any meaningful way. It curdled her blood to stand in this room with him, breathing the same air. It made her feel poisoned.

She thought back to her first meeting with him, and wondered why she hadn't known on sight that he'd killed his son. There was nothing subtle about him; the way he addressed the world was as black and white as his wardrobe. How had she not seen immediately that he was a killer?

"Mistress Thornton."

"Your grace." She curtsied for the sake of form, and begrudged it.

He sat in a nearby chair, and gestured to one on the other side of the small table nearest the hearth. "Do have a seat. Make yourself comfortable." A welcoming smile curled the corners of his mouth, but it never reached those eyes. He narrowed them at her, as if trying to see inside of her. As she sat she found herself avoiding his gaze, lest the abyss look back were she to stare too long. She perched on the edge of the chair, unable to make herself comfortable.

"Mistress Thornton, I think you and I may have wandered into a misunderstanding."

"Have we?" She tried to keep the sarcastic edge from her voice, difficult though it was. Ramsay, she now realized, had been right about the inadvisability of unnecessarily antagonizing the duke. Even talking to him at this point was probably a bad idea. She would want to excuse herself from this chat at the earliest opportunity.

"When you brought us the news of my son's death, I'm afraid the duchess and I both reacted badly."

"Perfectly understandable. I know how I would feel, were I to have heard the same news about my son." She blinked as that horrifying image tried to rise, and fought it down. Her greatest fear on this earth was that she might outlive Piers.

Then she realized why she hadn't seen the truth in this man when he'd lied to her about not knowing his son was not in Kent. She'd never asked herself the right question. The idea that a man could murder his own son was so unthinkable to her, and the lies he told were so many and so obvious, she'd never thought he could be successful in hiding something so very heinous. Now she looked at him—the fire of evil in his eyes—and thought herself stupid for not seeing his crime written on his face.

He was saying, "The next day I ordered Constable Pepper to remove you from his investigation. I told him I didn't wish to have you stirring up an enormous fuss over something so upsetting to the duchess. I'm afraid I was inconsiderate in ignoring the compensation you would lose—have lost—by being dropped from the constable's employ."

"He wasn't—"

"So, in perfect fairness, I would like to make up for your loss of income." He reached into a pocket of his jacket and drew out several large silver coins. He counted out five in his hand and set them on the table before her. "Five pounds. Will that suffice?"

"Constable Pepper wasn't paying me, your grace."

Real surprise crossed the duke's face. "Indeed? You were doing the work gratis? Is poking about in other people's business a hobby for you, then?"

"The constable sometimes asks me to assist him. I've a talent for analyzing the stories people tell, and finding holes in a narrative. I'm an actress, you see, and have read and memorized many plays. I know fiction when I hear it, and can tell a liar when I see one." Now the edge of hostility was creeping into her voice, though she struggled to keep it out. She needed to flee, and quickly, lest this turn into an ugly confrontation that would do her no good. "So, in a way, you might say the assistance I provide the constable is a pastime." She didn't see any point in telling the duke the details of her arrangement with Pepper. It was enough for him to know she wasn't being paid. "I gain nothing more than the satisfaction of having taken a criminal from among the population of London and putting him where he belongs." That was also true.

The stern tone he'd had on their first meeting returned, and it was an effort not to flinch. "I must insist that your investigation come to a halt. 'Tis far too upsetting for the duchess. The both of us are apprehensive there may be talk of it at court."

"Surely not. The king must sympathize with your grief. Surely your friends at court must be considerate of the tender feelings you have for your son."

"The duchess is terribly overwrought. I would have the matter entirely ignored. There is nothing to be gained by pursuing the robber who killed my son."

"It was no robber."

Cawthorne's eyes narrowed. "I believe it was."

"With all due respect, your grace, a robber would not have bothered to cut the body as this murderer did after Lord Paul was dead. A robber might have stabbed his victim once or twice, in order to get hold of a purse, then he would have fled as quickly as possible. He never would have loitered about, continuing to stab after the victim had died, severing an appendage and stuffing it into the mouth." The duke did not blink when she revealed this, and anger rose in spite of herself. Her voice thickened and her brow knotted as she spoke.

His reply was angry. "Be that as it may, the duchess and I do not wish the crown to pursue this matter further. Since you are not employed by the constable's office, and have no authority as an investigator, you needn't bother yourself further. In fact, you are constrained from it." Cawthorne pushed the stack of pound coins toward her across the table. "Take these, and consider yourself released from all obligation to Pepper. Go on with your life. You might consider quitting the pursuit of criminals altogether. I suspect you aren't as talented at it as you think."

"I think I am." She ignored the money, and looked straight at the duke. "I know I am. I believe I perform a vital function, tracking down murderers so they don't commit further crimes."

"Take the coins, Mistress Thornton."

She stood. "Thank you, no." A strong, perverse urge to pick them up and do what she was told filled her heart, and she clenched her fists against it. It would have been so easy to simply give in and take this bribe. She thought of the security this money would bring to the troupe, the things it would buy, the ease it would bring her daily existence. And by letting the duke go on with his life, ignoring that he'd committed the most heinous deed she'd ever heard of, though she'd lived her entire life in a town known throughout the kingdom for terrible deeds, she would go her own way and their paths might never cross again. The idea of it was mighty appealing. But she steeled herself against those selfish thoughts. "I wouldn't feel right taking your money, your grace. If it's all the same to you, I'll go home now." She turned toward the door.

"Woman!" The duke rose, and so did his voice.

She stopped, but didn't turn to face him. Her heart thudded in her chest, and she could feel heat on her face.

He said, "You will not speak to another soul about my son and what happened to him. If I hear anything further of your investigation, I promise you I will make you regret it."

"And how will you do that?" Her voice tightened, and the words came with difficulty.

"If you believe I stabbed and mutilated my son, then think hard on what I might do to someone who is not a member of my family."

Terror skittered through her and made her bones feel cold. Now more than ever she was convinced the duke had done the murder, and even more than that she believed he would carry out this threat. She turned, and with every bit of grace she could muster she made a slight curtsey, then turned and left the room without asking to be excused.

Outside the door, she picked up her skirts and broke into a run. Palace residents and servants gawked as she passed, but she couldn't stop until she was out of the palace and on King Street, hurrying along the cobbles at a skipping half run. When finally she stopped, she found herself trembling and not entirely certain how far she'd gone. She looked around to gather her composure and gain her bearings.

Carriages passed and throngs of people walked along the street. Slowly her heart calmed until it stopped thudding in her ears. She looked back the way she'd come, half afraid she was followed by the duke and his dagger.

Then her blood ran cold and she gasped for breath. A man behind her was staring at her. Openly, and not even caring that she might see him do it. He stood at the corner of the building on the closest corner, next to a downspout that drained out at his feet. He wore no wig, and his narrowed eyes and grim mouth told her he wasn't interested in hiring her for sexual services. He must be following her.

When she looked straight on, however, the lurker had melted into street traffic. As if he'd magically disappeared. She looked around for him, but saw nothing and nobody untoward. Certainly nobody she'd recognized. But she'd have sworn there had been a man staring straight at her. She continued walking, hoping to find a carriage to flag down and hire, but there didn't seem to be any without passengers. She walked onward.

The walk all the way around and across the bridge to Southwark would be monstrous. And dangerous. In the depths of winter it would surely be dark by the time she arrived at the Globe, and if there were someone following her he would surely take advantage of that darkness. However, there was nothing for it but to keep on.

She walked north in Whitehall Street, past the Scotland yards toward Charing Cross. She thought briefly of making for one of the river stairs in hopes of finding a barge to take her directly across the Thames, but she hated to wait alone on the bank for a boat that might never come. Anyone following her would find her easily taken, were he to find her there. So she walked onward.

In an area where the crowds were a bit thinner, she hazarded a glance backward and thought she saw that same man duck into an alley off to the side. She stood and watched that spot, but he never reappeared. Perhaps she'd imagined him.

At Charing Cross were thick crowds, and when she looked back she couldn't tell whether that man was following her again. Once more she thought she might have been imagining him. After all, she'd been told in the past her imagination was active and vivid. Nevertheless, she hurried onward, at a walk she hoped was quick but not so quick that others thought she was running from authorities.

Now she was on the Strand and veering east, still a long way from the bridge and looking for a coach to hire. Or even a sedan chair that would be carried by strong men who might prove protection. If only her favorites, Thomas and Samuel, might happen by! But she saw none available today.

Where had they all gone? Any other day the chairmen would be swarming in hopes of a fare. She glanced behind and hoped not to see the man following her. Then she thought she should hope to see him, for then she would know where he was. She looked ahead now, fearing he might leap out at her. Her heart pounded, and she walked faster.

Finally she found a carriage and flagged it down. Without waiting for the coachman to leap down and help her in, she threw open the door and climbed in on her own. Her skirt caught on her shoe, and she had to yank it clear before settling into the seat. The coachman came to secure the door.

"Maid Lane in Southwark. The Globe Theatre, if you please."

"Aye, mistress."

"Posthaste, if you please, good man. There will be an extra shilling for you."

"Aye, mistress." The coachman hurried to his seat, and the carriage lurched into motion. Suzanne put her head out the window to look behind, and there she saw that same man, in the street and staring after her.

She settled back into her seat, and drew several deep breaths.

What to do now?

Chapter Nineteen

That afternoon at the Globe, Suzanne watched the final performance of *Twelfth Night*, thinking hard about how to encourage Daniel to press his magistrate to charge Cawthorne with his son's murder. The duke's anger had quite frightened her, and filled her with dread for the future. Having lived on the street in the past, she knew well how horribly things could change, and how quickly, when one had little influence in the world.

Earlier, she'd been quite frightened at having been followed. Now, as she watched the play without really seeing it, her pulse skipped just a little too quickly for comfort, and her thoughts kept turning to the duke and his threat. She calmed herself by telling herself it had been done only to frighten her. It was coercion and nothing more. After all, there had been plenty of opportunity for that man to attack her, had he wished. But he'd let her go and she hadn't seen him since. Surely it was only a tactic to frighten her.

So she needed to work out what next to do about the duke. If she wasn't going to give in to the duke's demand, then she needed to take decisive action of some sort. Only Daniel could convince the magistrate to initiate proceedings. Daniel would not help unless she had more proof of the duke's guilt, and so that was what she needed to find. There was nothing else for it.

After the performance, Suzanne decided to cast about the neighborhood for more eyewitnesses. There had been many more men and women there that night than she'd talked to, and though seeking witnesses was a shot in the dark, she might stumble across something useful. Now that she could describe the duke and the outfit he wore that night, perhaps she could jog some memories and someone in addition to Warren might remember seeing him with Lord Paul. Perhaps if she had enough people to say they'd seen the duke at the Goat and Boar, talking to Lord Paul and leaving with him, then the crown would see fit to bring a case against him. There was always safety in numbers, and she believed there could be a chance the law would frown upon this murder in spite of the duke's power if there were enough people to speak against it.

She wouldn't take Ramsay with her on this foray, for he would only intimidate her prospective witnesses, and would press her to cease her efforts while he was at it. His heart might be in the right place, and he made her feel safe, but tonight she needed a light and persuasive hand rather than the bludgeon of a large, loud protector.

As she left her quarters she peeked out the door to see whether Ramsay was waiting for her. She didn't find him sitting on the stairs, so she ventured forth at speed. At the upstage doors she peeked once again and looked out over the stage to the galleries and the front entrance. The house was empty of audience, they having all gone home. Only some boys were at work, picking up orange peels and chestnut shells from the pit and gallery floors. She caught the attention of Christian, who climbed to the stage and hurried over.

"What can I do for you, mistress?"

"Christian, would you be so good as to have a look out the back and see whether Master Ramsay is there in the alley?"

"Right. You want to talk to him, then?" He started off, but paused when she stopped him.

"No. I wish to avoid him. If he's there, say nothing to him and come tell me."

A puzzled look furrowed Christian's forehead, but he went to look without saying anything more than "Yes, mistress."

In a moment he returned to inform her that Ramsay was loitering against the wall in the alley across from the theatre's rear door. Suzanne nodded and thanked him, then headed for the front entrance doors. She slipped out onto Maid Lane, and blended into the traffic away from the side alley, then headed for the Goat and Boar.

To avoid the possibility of being seen by Ramsay she wended through some empty alleys and closes. Though the days were somewhat longer now than at the solstice, they weren't nearly long enough yet for the sun to still be up by the end of the afternoon performances. The darkness of early winter nightfall hid her well. She knew these streets thoroughly, and made her way in full confidence of getting where she was going. The Goat and Boar was not far. She turned up the collar of her cloak and buried her hands in her muff, put her head down against the cold, and hurried on.

As she passed through the pool of light surrounding a torch outside a coffeehouse, she noticed a shadow from behind stretch before her. It continued to follow her until the darkness swallowed her again. Just beyond the limit of the light, she turned to glance behind, for it must be Ramsay having discovered her attempt to avoid him.

But it wasn't. Though the silhouette was tall and broad shouldered, the gait was absolutely not Ramsay's. The man following her did not have the swagger that was his habit. This man walked plainly and ˚gracefully. And when she looked toward him he slowed to a stop. And waited.

Fear fluttered to her breast. She couldn't see who was following her, but she could only conclude that the man was up to no good. Otherwise he would approach her and speak to her. It was plain he was waiting for her to move away from the light. She realized that because the only light in the alley was behind him, she could see only a silhouette. But he, on the other hand, could see her quite well.

She looked around the alley. Beyond that light was utter darkness. Back the way she'd come there was the torch and a circle of safety. Inside the coffeehouse this time of the evening would be people who might protect her. Or at least would make an attacker hesitate. She took a step toward the door, hoping to slip past the figure and join whatever men she might find inside, but the silhouette took a step toward her. She stopped.

The figure also stopped. He stood like a statue, not moving or even seeming to breathe. His stance was casual. Not tense, but ready to move whichever direction was necessary to keep her from the light. It was the attitude of someone accustomed to physical superiority.

She took a step to the side in order to go around him, but he also stepped to the side, blocking her way. Suzanne halted, tensed for what he would do. He reached to his belt and withdrew a dagger. He held it to the side, point upward, so she could see it well.

Panic tried to steal her wits. She fought it down, but could hardly think of what to do. All she could think was how she wished she'd brought Ramsay along with her.

She looked behind her at the alley farther into the darkness, and couldn't see what or who might be there. She knew this alley well. She knew where it led, and she knew there were empty barrels stacked a few yards beyond her vision. There was a hole in the cobbles a little beyond the barrels. The alley at that end came out on Bank Side, not far from the Goat and Boar, and if she made a run for it she might make it to another place with a number of people. Now she had to decide whether to take the chance of getting past that knife and into the coffeehouse, or turning the other direction and hoping to disappear into the darkness.

Her hesitation robbed her of whatever advantage she might have had if she'd been able to decide. The figure rushed at her.

With a rabbit's terrified reflex she spun and fled the opposite direction, into the darkness. The barrels were just ahead. She held out a hand to find them, and dodged to the side as she touched them. Her footing wobbled on the cobbles, but behind her she heard a satisfying crash as her pursuer stumbled into the barrels. They came tumbling to the ground, and there were more bumps and crashes as the assailant stumbled among them, rolling in the street. Suzanne ran on, and leapt over the hole. A few more steps, and behind her came a thud and a cry.

"Come back here, you whore!" The voice belonged to the Duke of Cawthorne, shouting orders at her as if she would blindly obey for the sake of form.

Again, she ran on.

But he was large, and fast. He regained his feet in a trice and surged onward. From the darkness behind her came gasping of pain and angry grunting. Suzanne navigated by dim outlines here and there of reflected light from distant sources, but couldn't see within the deep shadows all around. She held out her palms to feel the brick wall she knew was ahead, and there she would make a turn to the left, where she might possibly come upon another torch so that at least she would be able to see her way to Bank Side. But not wanting to smack headlong into the wall slowed her down. Running footsteps approached from behind. Before she could reach the end of the alley she was grabbed from behind, jerked backward by her hair.

She twisted, but he held her in a solid, painful grip. To her horror, he was able to detain her with only one hand, which gripped her throat. It pressed her against his chest, and his voice reverberated through her and shuddered down her spine. "Hold still, you stupid whore."

She tried to scream, but the large hand cut off her air. She grabbed at it, and dug in with her fingernails. He cried out, a feral, angry roar. His other hand slammed into her flailing arm. The dagger went into her arm. Oddly, it didn't hurt much. Only a slight, metallic pain. She continued to struggle, and again caught the blade with another part of her arm. The hand holding her throat loosened in the fray as he cursed his bad luck, and she drew a deep, ragged breath. She screamed again, this time at full throat and the sound echoed from the surrounding buildings.

"Shut up!"

"Let me go!"

He struggled to throttle her again, but she twisted to

deny him sufficient purchase. The dagger tried for her throat, but missed her entirely as she grappled.

"Hold still!"

"No!"

There came a thud, and Cawthorne grunted once. Suddenly his grip released, and Suzanne staggered to keep her feet as the duke fell to the ground. Another figure had come behind, and now she watched that shadow draw a small dagger from his shirt and face off against the duke, who felt of the back of his head and said, "Who are you?"

"The archangel Michael." Angel he might have been, but Suzanne recognized Ramsay's voice. He continued, "You murdered your own son, and you'll pay for it."

"That's hardly your business. He was my son." He scrambled to his feet, and squared off against Ramsay, his dagger at ready.

There was a black moment of rage from Ramsay, who then muttered, "I believe you're a man who just needs killing." Then he attacked with his *sgian dubh*.

Cawthorne parried and backed toward Suzanne. She wished she had a knife of her own, and would gladly have cut his throat from behind. Instead she balled her fist and whacked the side of his head. He staggered and Ramsay attacked again, but the duke was close enough to parry and he backed around, away from Suzanne, to recover. Now Ramsay was between Suzanne and Cawthorne and she was no longer in a position to help.

Suzanne's screams had attracted others, who called out alarm and came running with shouts of "Murder!" Men with some candles and a torch swarmed from the coffeehouse up the alley, and others in the surrounding tenements poked their heads from windows and held candles to see what was all the ruckus, shouting "You leave her alone!" Ramsay ignored the chatter of onlookers wanting to know what was going on and warning each other of the big man with a knife.

Ramsay made another foray, and this time was able to open a long cut in Cawthorne's arm. Though the *sgian dubh* had a very short blade, the thing was uncommon-sharp. The duke gave a yelp, and jerked back that arm, but again recovered his en garde.

"Hold still so I can cut yer throat," Ramsay mocked, his brogue thickening in disgust.

"You'll hang for this."

"Then I've nothing to lose by making certain you're dead first."

"You're mad."

"You're soon to meet your maker." Then Ramsay shouted, "Och! leave him alone, he's mine!"

The duke took a glance behind to see who was there, and found nobody near. Ramsay took that brief slip, and drove a stab at Cawthorne's throat. The small knife went in to the hilt. A spray of blood covered them both.

The next two stabs were probably unnecessary, and definitely the three after that were in excess. The duke collapsed to the pavement, dead without a doubt. He lay on the street, in the midst of an expanding pool of glistening blood. Ramsay watched him, alert to know whether he might still be alive, and ready to make sure he was not.

Cawthorne's dagger lay on the cobbles, and Ramsay picked it up.

"Are you all right?" he asked Suzanne.

She shook her head. In a fit of unleashed rage, she hauled back and kicked the dead duke. She staggered back, then did it again. Then again, her ragged breaths feeling sharp in the cold air. There were no words for her anger, only the need to damage the evil at her feet.

Finally Ramsay took an arm and restrained her. "Where are you hurt?"

She pulled open her cloak, and held out her forearm for him to see the two stab wounds, and blood spreading along the white fabric of the shirt she wore. Along with the surrounding crowd she and Ramsay stared at the dead duke. Her terror hardened into anger. A knot formed in her heart and grew so large it choked her. Her fist clenched, and at that moment she wished with all her heart to hold that dagger in it and do to him the horrible thing he'd done to his son.

Then she shook the thought away, for she didn't want to be that sort of person.

Chapter Twenty

Ramsay's action in killing the duke was determined on the face of it to be self-defense and defense of another. There could be no question of it, for dozens of witnesses—all neighbors of Suzanne and the Globe—stated exactly what had happened, and the stories were consistent. Ramsay spent only one night in the neighborhood lockup, and was released the following morning with a gracious "good day" from the turnkey, who had won more than a pound from him at poker in those few hours.

Suzanne went to his rooms when she learned he had been released. Like most single men who were neither indigent nor wealthy, and neither servants nor apprentices, he lived in a flat of rooms that were more or less clean, and free of vermin. They were on the third floor, just below the servants' garret and just above a noisy couple enjoying a late-afternoon rendezvous. As Suzanne knocked on Diarmid's door, a bed-stead banged and thudded against a wall downstairs, and a male voice was taking the Lord's name in vain loudly and in imaginative fashion.

Ramsay's door opened, and she found him caught by surprise with no shirt. Then a wide grin crossed his face. "Och, I thought you were the boy to deliver my dinner!" He ducked back inside for his shirt. "Come in! Come in and have a seat!"

"I hope you're not disappointed."

"I hardly could be. Come, sit." He indicated a carved wooden chair that would accommodate her skirts, and she sat. He drew on a linen shirt with slightly foppish ruffles at the wrists, and tucked the tail into his breeches without fastening its ties. Most of it hung out in any case, and he let that go while he hunted down a jacket to put over it. He wore no stockings, but did find a pair of shoes to make himself barely presentable.

"I'm sorry," she said. "I should have sent Christian before me to announce my impending visit."

"Nonsense. I'm happy to see you at any time of day or night." He leaned forward for a closer look at her. "How is your arm? Were the cuts deep?"

She held out the bandaged arm and rucked back her sleeve to show him the linen strips wrapped about it. It had taken a very long time for the bleeding to stop, and even now some pink seeped through the dressing in little spots. But she said, "No. They hardly bled at all. His was a long knife, but the blade went to the side too much for it to even hit the bone. It doesn't hurt much."

"That's excellent." Then he sat back in his chair and his expression darkened. "But I must tell you it was extraordinarily stupid to walk about the streets like that without an escort. He would have killed you."

"I couldn't take you with me for the interviews I sought."

He leaned forward once more to speak directly into her face. *"He would have killed you."*

"He didn't."

"Only because I was there. Had I been escorting you and not had to go searching for you once I discovered you'd gone without me, he never would have approached you. So tell me you'll never do anything so foolish again."

She wanted to tell him that, and it was her first impulse to obey. But she stopped herself and thought over her reply. Slowly she said, "I very much appreciate what you did for me."

"I saved your life."

"Yes, you did. And I can never repay that."

"I don't expect payment. I did it for your sake only."

She gazed into his face, and saw there was no irony or mischief in it. He was sincere in what he said. But she knew it was nevertheless untrue. "Diarmid, I know in your heart you think that, but I still cannot believe it."

"Why not?" His expression darkened with puzzlement.

"I think you wish to control me."

"I wish you to be safe."

"And you think the only place I can be safe is under your control. Under your direction. I'm to do what I'm told, because I'm incompetent to decide for myself what is best for me. To you, I'm a danger to myself."

Anger gathered, and Ramsay shifted in his seat. "You certainly showed no sense in deciding to go wandering off through Southwark alone and after dark."

"I had a need."

"He nearly killed you."

"And now I carry a very sharp dagger with me." She reached into her muff and produced the small knife she'd installed in it that morning. The knife grinder on Maid Lane had sold it to her, with a plain scabbard to protect her hands, and had sharpened it well so it resembled the *sgian dubh* Ramsay carried.

In a flash Ramsay reached out and grabbed the knife. She made a swipe for it, but he held it up and away from her. When she rose to chase it, he avoided her, moving it from hand to hand as she attempted to grab it back. "See? Now you've armed your assailant. You're a woman, and do not have the strength or agility to use this."

"I can learn."

"You can get yourself killed."

She finally gave up pursuing the knife, and returned to her chair, flushed, exerted, and angry. "I need to be able to move freely in the world. There are things I must do by myself."

"Give me an example."

"How would it be for you if you were required to wait for someone to be available to escort you everywhere you went? Would you want your entire life to revolve around the schedule and willingness of another person?"

"I have spent more than a week arranging my life to suit your needs."

"One week. A generous thing, but you can hardly continue that way. You have business to attend to, and cannot follow me about every day."

"I wouldn't need to, were you to marry me."

Exasperation made her roll her eyes, though she knew it would only irritate him. "That is exactly what I'm talking about. If I married you, I would be nothing but a prisoner. I would be under your control at all times and you would tell me when and where to go. I could not live my life as I pleased."

"But I would please you. You would have everything you

needed and would never need to go traipsing off in the night to question suspected criminals."

"Or spend time with my friends, or shop at the exchanges, or anything else that might interest me. For that, I might as well be in the lockup for the rest of my life. How can I possibly continue this life, which I enjoy very much, if I'm limited to these walls?" She held up her palms and looked about the room to indicate the living space she expected would be hers if she accepted his proposal. Then she returned them to her lap, leaned toward him, and in a lowered voice said, "Tell me, Diarmid, when you first put forth your suit, did you care a fig about me?"

At first he looked as if he might not answer. He glowered at her from beneath his eyebrows, appearing to sulk. But apparently he was thinking. He said, "I was attracted to you. Anymore, I'm not so very certain."

That stabbed at her heart, for she had become very fond of him and wanted him to like her. But she said, "You cannot say your attraction was based on love. You could not love me, because you did not know me."

"Nor you me, but I could have accepted that."

She sighed, exasperated again. "But I could not. I could never marry someone I didn't love. Not after twenty years of struggling on my own. Not after having raised Piers by myself and having earned my place in the world by myself."

"Are you saying you don't care about me?"

"Of course not." The words came out without thought, and she caught herself, but then she continued, "I do care about you. I find you entertaining and exciting. I admire your intelligence and the protection you have provided me." His scowl smoothed out some. "But I don't want to tie myself to anyone. Especially I don't wish to imprison myself with someone who wants to shield me from the world."

"Why wouldn't you want to be shielded from the world? I find it little charming, myself. My greatest wish is to become wealthy enough for my money to shield me from the worst of it."

"But you would never wish to be required to stay within these rooms every day for the rest of your life."

"I would allow you to accompany me to the Goat and Boar."

She closed her eyes and took a long pause to avoid a cry of frustration at his lack of understanding. Then she opened them and said in a calm, level voice, "I do not care to ask permission. I am currently quite able to decide for myself whether to go to the Goat and Boar, or across the river, or to bloody Whitehall Palace if I please. You offer me nothing more than a modicum of safety, which I have never before had and therefore cannot miss or appreciate."

He apparently had no reply for that, for he sat and gazed at her for what seemed minutes. Finally he said, "Very well. I withdraw my suit. I no longer wish to marry you. But I do not withdraw my offer to keep you safe within my abilities to do so."

She nodded. "That suits me. May I have my dagger back?"

He looked at the knife in his hand, then handed it to her handle first. "'Tis a good weapon. Learn to use it against an opponent, and perhaps I'll become a mite more sanguine about your wanderings through London."

She accepted the weapon and returned it to its scabbard in her muff. "I think I can agree to that without misgiving." She rose to leave, and he stood also. "I must go now."

His expression said he wondered why, and she couldn't reply with the truth. The truth was that she didn't trust herself to stay longer, lest she succumb to the urge to let him seduce her. He said, "I have food coming." A glance at the door indicated how late the boy was in delivering it. "There should be enough to share, if you would like to stay for a while."

"Thank you most kindly, but I have things to attend to and must leave."

He nodded, clearly unhappy she was running away. He followed her to the door more than escorted. For her it was an escape. But he caught up with her when she reached it, and held it closed for a moment. He stood close. She felt the warmth of his body at her back, and liked it very much. It was difficult to refrain from leaning her head against his chest, but she didn't do it. She only turned her head a little to hear him speak in a low voice.

"I wish you all good luck in your dealings with the world. And I hope it treats you better than it does most souls." Then he leaned down to kiss her, and she raised her face to let him. The kiss was warm and soft, and in that moment she wondered what it might be like to be married to a man like that. She wondered what it might really be like to be married at all, the way she'd wished for it when she'd been young.

Before releasing the door and opening it for her, he said, "I'll come to the theatre tomorrow, to see how your arm is healing."

She smiled. "I'd like that."

OVER the next week the death of Cawthorne felt to Suzanne as if a canker had been removed from the city of London by the wave of a healing hand. A murderer had been eliminated, and the lives of everyone who knew Jacob Worthington had been freed of palpable evil. The Duchess of Cawthorne had justice for the death of her beloved son, and without damage to her own reputation. The truth of Lord Paul's proclivities was quashed well enough for it to never become rumor among the upper classes, even though it was rampant among the workers, beggars, and thieves of Bank Side. Nobody of importance ever attended to that sort of scurrilous, unfounded talk among the lower classes. Since the duke had died without trial and the crown was not interested in trying him posthumously, the duchess's other beloved son succeeded to his father's title and their lives proceeded without the ruination that would have resulted from a conviction.

Suzanne no longer feared repercussion. Daniel no longer was pressured to influence the magistrate. Constable Pepper had credit for solving the murder of a son of nobility, regardless that the murderer had been nobility himself, and in spite of the fact he'd done nothing at all in aid of learning that fact. Even the duke's memory suffered little, for nobody at court wanted to admit in any public way that one of their own had the capacity for the sort of brutality Cawthorne had owned.

It was as if the entire existence of Jacob Worthington had gone up in smoke, and the hole he left in the surrounding society closed over instantly without a scar. The privileged were exceptionally deft at smoothing over problems in public, and so the plastering was expected and accepted.

A week after the case was settled, Suzanne thought about that as she walked to the rooms of the astrologer who had set her on the course of finding Lord Paul's killer. She'd thought of the duke as an encompassing evil, so large and influential that to let him go without punishment would have brought sickness upon everyone and everything in his vicinity. It was heartening to see the world around him heal itself so quickly and so well. Life went on, and there seemed little damage to those still living.

But then when she thought of the little boy who had died, her heart clenched and tears rose to her eyes. She shoved her hands deeper into her muff, hugged it to her belly, and lowered her chin into the collar of her cloak as she made her way across the bridge. She remembered Paul's bright, joyful eyes. His wide smile and outgoing ways. She'd only seen him once, and that for only a few minutes, but for that brief time she'd seen a bright, graceful soul that should not have been taken from the earth so soon.

When she arrived at the astrologer's shop, she handed Esmeralda a silver half crown and thanked her for her help in the investigation.

"But you've already paid me for it." The woman held the coin in her palm, as if it might bite her if she closed her fingers around it.

"I only paid you for a reading. You did far more than that. Your visit to me moved me to an effort I might not have made otherwise. Together, we removed a blackened soul from the earth, and for that you should be rewarded."

Esmeralda thrust her hand out to give back the coin. "With all due respect, mistress, it seems to me that what we did should be something we do without expecting reward. We all should remove blackened souls from the earth at every opportunity, even when there be no money in it. And I daresay you had no reward for yourself beyond the satisfaction of knowing evil had been vanquished."

It was true. Pepper would keep his promise to not harass her Players, but expecting him to offer cash would be absurd. Even if he had it in excess, he was far too close with his money to give any of it to her, even as an investment in his reputation for successfully pursuing criminals. Suzanne, on the other hand, knew that cash was an excellent way to show appreciation for a job well done and to encourage such work in future. She wanted Esmeralda to have the money. "Then," she said, "if you want to feel you've earned this, let me have another reading."

In an instant the coin disappeared into the astrologer's pocket. "Why, yes, of course I'll be happy to give another reading! Have a seat!" She gestured to the usual chair and hurried to gather her ephemeris and other tools. "What would you like? Future, or personality?"

"Near future. The next year or so, I think." It would be nice to know whether the theatre would be successful enough to not fold before the next season.

Esmeralda searched down the chart she'd drawn up on Suzanne's first visit, and spread it out on her table. This time the reading took very little time, and she quickly was able to crow with glee.

"Oh! I see grand things for you in coming months! I do love when it's good news!"

Suzanne sat at the edge of her seat, eager to hear. "Do tell." This was rather fun, to hear that good things were to come.

"I see love. Much love, from a Taurus. Do you know any who are Tauruses?"

"I'm afraid I don't know what a Taurus is."

"Someone born in May. Strictly speaking, anyone whose birthday falls between April twenty-second and May twenty-first."

Daniel leapt to mind. His birthday was on May eighth. He would be thirty-nine in the spring. Her heart fluttered a bit, and for a moment she didn't know how to feel about this.

Then she remembered a comment Ramsay had made about his age. Not long ago he'd mentioned he would be thirty-three sometime in May. Her mouth fell open. "Both of them are Taurus."

"Both of whom?"

Suzanne shifted in her seat, not entirely comfortable speaking of this to a near stranger. Her history with Daniel was long and troubled. She had almost no history with Ramsay, and did not want the same sort of trouble with him. She said, "I like my life. I don't think I want love from any Tauruses."

"'Tis a terribly strong indication. Strong enough to suggest marriage one day."

Suzanne frowned. "Marriage?" She'd spent many long years regretting her refusal to marry. Raising Piers with no family for herself and no father for him had been singularly difficult. Now she was independent in ways she'd never before imagined possible. The theatre supported her in a modicum of comfort, and there was promise of even better. To her, a master was someone who beat and ridiculed. She'd been bullied half her life, and these days she looked upon marriage as an institution suited for weak women who needed a master to tell them what to do. As she'd told Ramsay last week, she abhorred the thought of being under the control of any man, though she'd not told him it was because she couldn't imagine any man having her best interests at heart. None ever had, not even him. She asked, "Are you certain?"

"Naught is ever certain, other than death, and that comes when it will. I can only see what I'm shown."

"Do you see any violence?" A small voice in the back of her mind wanted to know whether she'd made the right choice in rejecting Ramsay.

A puzzled look crossed Esmeralda's face. "Violence? I told you, what I see is love. Much of it."

"How do I know which one loves me?"

The astrologer frowned down at the chart, still puzzled. "There's no telling, by this. It would be one, or both. Did I know the exact time of each birth, I might be able to see the stronger indication. But from this I can only say that at least one of them would give up his life for you."

Ramsay. His bravery in her defense showed her that, though his inability to see her as a competent adult also showed he didn't have her best interests at heart because he didn't know what they were. As for Daniel, Suzanne would wish for him to love her that much, but she knew there was very little he would give up for her. Certainly not his life. Surely Ramsay was the one indicated by the chart. She stood. "Is that all you can see?"

"I would say this is a wealth of information. You have the sort of friend most women would pray to know. I suggest you treasure him."

"Thank you." Suzanne fell into deep thought, and barely noticed her surroundings as she bade Esmeralda good day and left the astrologer's shop.

Love was something she'd thought had passed her by a very long time ago. Her parents had certainly never loved her, and her brothers and sisters had largely ignored her as well. If Daniel had ever loved her, he'd stopped doing so long ago. Of course Piers loved her, and his regard was what had always sustained her. The idea that Ramsay could come from nowhere and be the man she'd always longed for but had learned could never exist seemed to her a fantasy as wild as the faerie tales that ended with a kiss from a prince. Impossible. Absurd.

So deep in thought, her feet took her to Dunning's Alley and her father's former house. She finally came to herself as she stood before it, next to the gnarled oak tree. That old tree had changed a great deal since the days it had both shaded her and taunted her. "You can't climb me," it seemed to say. "You will never climb me." She tried to imagine herself removing her pattens and shoes and finding a toehold and finger hold to pull herself up and make her way to the upper branches. If she tried she would fall, she was certain. Or else she would find herself stuck there, unable to descend. Then she would look like a fool. A silly old woman trying to be a girl again. Who had never really been a girl to begin with. She wondered who she had ever been. What had her father thought she was? What about her had made him dislike her so? What had she done—or not done—to deserve the treatment she'd received?

And now, what about her caused Ramsay to love her? Or even notice she existed? What quality had attracted him? What had she done—or not done—to deserve his regard? She didn't know. All she knew was that she was at a loss to understand what he could see in her, for he plainly did not know her.

From the corner of her eye she saw a figure standing at the entrance to the alley. For a brief, panicky moment she thought she saw her father. Standing hipshot, one hand leaned against the corner of the brick to his right.

But when she looked she found Daniel. He gazed at her with a look of puzzlement. The cold winter wind blowing through the alley into the close tossed the feather in his hat so that it switched like a horse's tail, but he ignored it. He peered at her as if trying to see into her.

She said, "What brings you here?"

"I was leaving the Exchange, and saw you were headed here. So I followed."

"Why follow? Why didn't you speak to me there?"

"I knew you were coming here. I didn't want to distract you."

It struck her that of all the people she knew anymore, Daniel was the only one who would have known what this place had been to her. "Again, then, why follow?"

"I wanted to make certain you were well. You've been through a harrowing experience, and I worry that it might have a lasting effect."

She drew her hand from her muff and held out her bandaged arm. "It's healing. It will continue."

"I don't mean that. I mean here." He touched his breast over his heart. "Sometimes the heart takes more effort to repair than the body."

"Indeed." For a brief, fantastical moment, she felt the same warmth she'd once felt when she'd believed Daniel loved her. The depth of his gaze was as it had been when they were both so very young and the ugliness of the world had appeared as something that could be vanquished. When she could dream of a time when evil did not reign and a place where she could be safe from harm. In that moment, she wanted to believe that the man indicated in her chart could be Daniel.

He gestured to the alley behind him and said, "May I offer to carry you to the theatre? My carriage awaits. The new production opens tonight, and you don't want to miss it. Little Wally, I'm told, is beyond fabulous as the mother of Coriolanus."

The spell was broken, and Suzanne took a deep breath. "Of course he is. We should hope the king's men never hire him away from us." She went to him, and he hugged her shoulders as they entered the alley together.

"Oh, you shouldn't wish such terrible things for his career. He deserves better than the likes of us."

Suzanne laughed, and was glad to be free.